Just Another Mzungu
Passing Through

Jim Bowen worked as a coach for the Nairobi Provincial Cricket Association from 1996-98. He now runs holidays for disabled people on his family's farm in west Wales and is working on his next story.

Just Another Mzungu Passing Through

Jim Bowen

PARTHIAN

Parthian
The Old Surgery
Napier Street
Cardigan
SA43 1ED

www.parthianbooks.co.uk

First published in 2008
© Jim Bowen 2008
All Rights Reserved

ISBN 978-1-905762-33-0

Editor: Norman Schwenk

Cover design by Marc Jennings
Inner design by books@lloydrobson.com
Typeset by Lucy Llewellyn and books@lloydrobson.com
Printed and bound by Gomer, Llandysul

Published with the financial support of the Welsh
Books Council

British Library Cataloguing in Publication Data

A cataloguing record for this book is available from
the British Library

*For Kenya and the Kenyan peoples, whose kindness
and hospitality gave me two unforgettable years.*

1

I wish I could remember the way I first saw it – through the fresh and innocent eyes I had then and not the cynical ones that I have now.

I wish I could remember how it first felt to stand at the top of the aeroplane steps in the early morning January brightness and to look out across Jomo Kenyatta Airport towards the dust-blown Kenyan wilderness beyond the wire. To wonder about the wildness there, and not just to see the cracked tarmac beneath my feet. To see the acacia trees and scrub and to hear one million cicadas playing violins in the distance.

I am sure I must have been thrilled by the colonial façade of the decaying buildings, the superb starlings that must have been there, and the black kites hanging in the clear sky, when I still thought black kites were rare like the red kites back home and not as common as the crows which peck their carrion feasts from the rubbish dumps and slums that surround the city. And the heat on the back of my neck, even though it was only eight in the morning – that must have surprised me, and the dryness of the red sandy dust blown in from the Sahara.

I can remember the missing steps on the non-moving moving-staircase as if I stood above them now. And the dangling strip lights above the juddering baggage carousel and the piece of stained and fraying rope which acted as the flush on the toilet cistern that had no lid.

The sullen man behind the immigration desk waving me away for not completing a form correctly but not telling me which part of it I had filled out wrong. That must have made me smile at the time, I am sure, before I came to know the way Kenya works, that if I had offered him *chai* he might have been more helpful. He couldn't have been less welcoming if he had tried.

And then through the unattended customs desk, past the big black cleaning ladies in shiny blue acrylic overalls and multi-coloured headscarves pushing battered tin buckets with broken-ended mops, and sliding them across the stained concrete floors. And on out into the mad scrum of the arrivals lounge and the first battle to keep hold of my possessions as a dozen Kikuyu taxi drivers fought for my attention.

Then Donald Otieno appeared holding a cigarette in one hand and a board with my name on it in the other. '*Karibu Kenya* Mr Griffiths,' he said holding his arms wide and welcoming. 'Welcome to Kenya,' he said gently and his face crumpled into a smile. He guided me through the crowd and out to his vehicle and bounced me up the Nairobi-Mombasa Highway towards the city.

I will never forget Donald Otieno.

2

2

I remember driving up the highway, past the people walking along the roadside. Men, neat in dark nylon suits and polished shoes, and women with babies on their backs in shawls and bundles on their heads like in the travel programmes on television. The smells of the market-stalls set out inches from the tarmac and the small *duka* kiosks selling fruit, soft drinks, chocolates and Rooster cigarettes one cigarette at a time.

The smell of the fruit and the diesel fumes and the sweet magnolia trees and flowers. The tiny, skinny children with huge white smiles and shiny black skin running along dirt tracks parallel to the highway, running to school, dressed up smart in bright red and blue uniforms, boys in short trousers, girls in longer skirts, some wearing shoes with socks pulled up to the knee, others barefoot but oblivious to the thorns and sharp stones in their path.

The sight of the city ahead of us, growing nearer and larger with the tall glass-fronted hotels and Kenyatta Conference Centre that, from a distance, make the Nairobi city skyline look like any modern city in the Western world.

The posters for Coca-Cola and Fanta on huge billboards also could have been from anywhere in the world, but all the faces on them were black, which seems obvious now, and I am amazed I had ever imagined they would be anything else. Other billboards advertised Toss and Omo washing powders, Tusker Beer, Uchumi and Nakumat supermarkets and other brand names which became so familiar to me over the next two years.

'There are as many accidents on Kenya's roads each year as there are in England,' said Donald as we passed an overturned lorry on the central reservation. 'Kenya has only 50,000 vehicles while there are over 30 million cars on the roads in England,' and he smiled toothily at the equation.

The highway was pock-marked with cavernous potholes, and huge piles of garbage lined the gutters and pavement. Shiny shoes walked round them and skipped from one side of the road to the other ahead of the rushing vehicles, while street-children danced between the traffic and competed with the street-corner cripples in their pleading for charitable help.

We came to rest at a packed roundabout, and I peered up at the luxury hotel to our right, but then a lorry pulled up beside us and gunned its engine, filling the car with putrid black smoke through Donald's open window. The lorry edged forward, forcing its way into the traffic on the roundabout. There was a screech of tyres, and a packed minibus-taxi, known in Kenya as a *matatu*, ploughed into its

4

side, spilling people into the street through its open side door and front window.

Donald seemed barely to notice as he took advantage of the break in the traffic and turned quickly left along Ngong Road.

With one hand on the clasp ready to release my seat belt I looked back at the wreckage. 'Shouldn't we stop and help?' I asked.

Donald changed gear and shot past an ancient Mercedes on the inside lane before swinging in front of it and charging up the hill; he found the road blocked by another *matatu* waiting at a junction and cramming in still more people. 'If you stopped at every accident you saw in this country,' he said grinning again, 'you would never get anywhere.'

3

I handed in my notice at the school I had been teaching at in Cardiff when the father of a pupil threatened me outside the school gates one afternoon. It was the same day my divorce papers came through.

The previous day a fifteen-year-old boy had been excluded for pulling a knife on me in class. It was during the first lesson of a new year, September term, and we were doing a dictation. I came to a comma midway through a sentence.

'Oi! How do you spell comma, Mr Griffiths?' the boy shouted. A few children laughed, and I told him not to be stupid and to concentrate on his work. He got up from his desk, walked up the aisle with an exaggerated swagger, pulled a small Swiss Army knife from his pocket and held it up, pointing at my throat.

He was half my size, and his hand was shaking with fear, and I could see tears in his eyes as I reached up slowly and twisted his wrist until he dropped the knife at our feet. Then I let go, and he stumbled back against a desk and began to cry with shock.

The school's headmaster listened to what happened and shook his head. 'You should never man-handle a child, Griff,' he told me. 'You have been teaching long enough to know that.'

The headmaster called the boy's parents and excluded him until the end of the week, but the next day there were reporters waiting outside the school when I came in to work.

The school trustees met at lunchtime and formally cautioned me for my behaviour; and at the end of the day the boy's shaven-headed father and three of his buddies met me at the gate.

The next day I handed in my notice and bought a copy of the *Times Educational Supplement*. I applied for four jobs, was interviewed for three, offered two, and picked Greenfields School in Nairobi, Kenya.

I stayed in Cardiff until the end of that term, got my injections, had a party and, four months to the day after the knife incident, Donald Otieno dropped me in Greenfields School housing compound, saying I should make myself at home and that the headmaster, Mr Rivers, would be along sometime to check I was OK.

So I found my rooms, scattered some clothes around and went to bed.

I slept most of the afternoon and was woken by Donald tapping on my door to tell me that Mr Rivers was in his office waiting to take me out for supper.

The tall, grey-haired Mr Rivers looked me up and down as we shook hands and walked towards his 4x4, my jeans,

8

sweatshirt and trainers just about tidy enough for an evening out at the Nairobi Club. 'It's your first evening in-country, and it's not right for you to be alone here, Griff,' he said and winked kindly. 'You are one of our Greenfield's family, and I hope you will feel a part of it in no time at all.'

He pointed out the Yaya Centre as we bounced along Argwings Kodhek Road heading in towards the city. 'It has a good supermarket, bookshop and post office,' he said. 'It's owned by Nicholas Biwott and has the best imported food. Even Marmite,' and I smiled at his delight. 'We have only been able to get Marmite for the last five years!'

'Glen Stevens' family live down there.' He pointed up the potholed Tigoni Road. 'They are missionaries from New Zealand and good members of the club. He hopes you might help out with some coaching in his mission school during the holidays. He is trying to teach some of them cricket, but see how you feel.' He pointed to a large complex of wide, low buildings as we edged around a roundabout with much more caution than Donald had shown earlier in the day. 'That's the city crematorium.' Behind it a series of tower blocks spread down the hill, and, further on, the plains of Nairobi National Park which opened up below us. 'Beyond it is the Nyayo Estate,' he said, 'with the Kabira Highrise and Madaraka further down again. They are a couple of Nairobi's concrete slums as opposed to the tin ones like Kawangwaire and Mukuru where Glen Stevens' work is based.' He spoke quickly and I tried to take it all in.

'Nairobi Hospital is up on the left. It's a private hospital with some of the best doctors in East Africa. All Greenfields' ex-pat staff members have health insurance as part of their contracts, and it is there you will be going if you do get ill.

It's much better than Kenyatta Hospital.' We passed the sign to another vast grey building on our right as we turned left into the Nairobi Club. 'That is Kenyatta Hospital,' he frowned. 'Patients steal each other's blankets in there. It's certainly one to be avoided.'

In the Nairobi Club's cricket pavilion Mr Rivers hung his club jacket on a rack by the bar, and we sunk into two low leather armchairs and looked out across the scorched brown grass towards the whitewashed walls of the squash clubs and leylandii hedge on the far side of the cricket field. Sacred ibis, with their round, white bodies and long, black, curved beaks walked in the outfield, and more black kites circled high overhead.

A dozen middle-aged Asians walked round and round the boundary rope, some in small groups and some in couples, with the woman walking a few steps behind. The evening light accentuated the magnificent colour of the women's saris, and the acacia trees on a bank beyond the boundary glowed in the low evening sun.

'This is my favourite time of the day,' said Mr Rivers gently, leaning towards me as he gestured for the drinks waiter. '*Mbili Tusker baridi tafadali*,' he called with authority. 'We are so close to the equator that dusk lasts for such a short time.' The red-waistcoated waiter hurried over with our two cold Tusker beers. He opened the bottles and left them frothing on a table in front of us. '*Asante sana*, Jacob. Thanks,' he said to the waiter, glancing up and smiling at him. 'It is an amazing light.'

We sipped the bitter hoppy beer and ate *samaki wa kupaka* – grilled white fish and coconut cream – with chips and *bajias* and a hot sweet and sour sauce. The fish was tilapia, freshly caught and delivered from Lake Victoria in western Kenya. It tasted like British perch, but without the bones.

'I have been here nearly twenty-five years,' Mr Rivers said, as he sat back and sipped slowly on his beer. 'I started on a two-year contract like you, but I was up-county near Limuru. It was a very different time then.'

'Pre-Marmite,' I ventured.

'Exactly,' and he smiled thoughtfully. 'It takes an age to be accepted by the families of the earliest white settlers who are still here, and I am only just starting to be considered a permanent fixture here.' He lowered his voice and leant towards me as a couple of other club members joined us around our low table. Mr Rivers introduced us and we shook hands formally before he continued. 'The KC's – the Kenyan Cowboys – are white Kenyans whose families have been here for generations, since Colonial times. They have survived the struggle through *Mau Mau*, independence, the change from Kenyatta to Moi and everything since then. It takes a long time for them to really consider you part of the permanent Kenya scene.'

'It is understandable that they don't have much time for transitory workers on short-term contracts though,' said David Brown, a junior from the High Commission. He wore a Nairobi Club tie like Mr Rivers', but he had his tucked into his trousers which were pulled high up his belly. With his light-coloured linen jacket and dark brown brogues he looked like he was auditioning for the role of a lowly overseas diplomat in the film version of a Graham Greene novel. '"What's the point of making friends," they ask, "when you will be moving on before long?"'

'Just another white bloke passing through,' Mr Rivers nodded.

'It's a waste of effort,' David Brown continued. 'And they think of us "contracted workers" as Gypsies. A lot of the time it's as if there are two white tribes here.'

'You will find my Greenfields staff support each other though,' said Mr Rivers. 'I am sure they will help you adjust to life here. My niece, Sally, teaches Games to the girls, and I'm sure she'll help you settle in. They are a good team, and they form invaluable backup.' He crossed his legs and took another drink of beer. 'I am very fortunate to have most of them.'

'People at the club here give me good backup,' said Yuri Ceffyl, a Russian-born South African who worked as a pilot for AMREF, the flying doctors. 'Especially when Anya, my girlfriend, is working away.' He was the star opening fast bowler of the Nairobi Club team. 'Yah, it is a good place to be,' he nodded. 'Good people, yah.'

'They are,' agreed David Brown. 'It is good to come here for practice on a Friday evening and then sit in the clubhouse with the lads, have a few beers and swap stories, talk about cricket and forget about other things going on out there.'

'You will see,' Yuri said with a grin. 'There is an unfunny joke that is often made about this place. "What is the difference between a tourist and a racist in Kenya?"'

I shrugged and said I had no idea.

'Two weeks,' the three men chimed in together. 'The answer is two weeks,' and they shook their heads sadly.

4

My rooms were in the small staff accommodation compound on the edge of the school playing-fields. It was owned by the school, but managed by a fierce Luo lady who called me *mzungu*, a term used for all white people. She told me to call her Madam as she laughed off my comments about cockroaches the size of mice living behind my bread bin.

There were a few staff houses around the school, but this sixteen-unit compound was where all new staff started out. There were six rooms on the ground floor and ten smaller ones up a flight of concrete steps on the floor above. My rooms were on the first floor, and I was able to sit in my doorway and peer over the high, spiked wall that surrounded the compound.

Security guards, known as *askaris*, dozed at the locked gate, a large, deaf Dobermann padlocked to their chair with a short chain. I learnt quickly to make a lot of noise as I approached the *askaris*, to be sure they were awake, so they could hold back the snarling beast when I left the compound. As they got to know me the guards and the dog became friendlier, but from the start I realised the sign reading '*Mbwa Kali*' – 'Angry Dog' – on the wall outside was no exaggeration. The dog was hit and killed by a *matatu* a few weeks later, but the sign stayed, and the *askaris* protected the housing compound alone.

Our *askaris* were Somalis from up near the northern Kenyan border. The school's priest, Father Marcus, found them work at Greenfields, and they took turns to go back north to their home-places with him during school vacation. Madam brought them a bowl of maize-flour dough called *ugali* at the start of their shifts, and we in the apartments took weekly turns to fill their battered Thermoses with sweet tea each evening.

Being on good terms with your *askaris* was vital, Donald told me, and ours, being Somalis, were harder to become close to than many. Donald was from the lighter-skinned Kikuyu tribe, who considered themselves the chosen ones – the Children of God. They, and the much darker Luo people, were the largest tribes in Kenya, and they looked down on each other and everyone else, but particularly the Somali, and Donald was very wary of the *askaris*.

Outside the compound a row of *duka* stalls sold newspapers, bananas, bread, pints of milk in thin, plastic bags, single hard-boiled eggs and chocolate bars that for some reason didn't melt in the heat.

I spent my first morning sitting on a towel on the concrete step outside my door flicking through the *Daily Nation* newspaper, trying to make out what I could about the country.

Pretty much all the paper told me was what President Moi did yesterday, what he was due to do today and how many people died in accidents on the Nairobi-Mombasa Highway.

I looked over the compound wall and watched a man sitting in a faded deck-chair next to the *dukas*, beneath a sign which said, '*Onyango son of Suji Expat Bamba*,' with painted pictures of heads below. He bought cigarettes one by one from the *duka* kiosk, and called out to passers-by. A little while later I saw him hacking away at someone's hair and realised what an '*Expat Bamba*' was. Sometimes he hung a large piece of card from a tree reading '*Back in five minuets*' and he and his deck-chair would be gone for days.

All the Greenfields overseas staff started off living in Madam's compound, but most moved away very quickly and found places of their own around the city. Madam was bitter about this, but it was understandable because she wasn't the most amenable person. Each flat had a flush toilet, warm water, a fridge and a mosquito net over the bed, so they were not bad places to live, but she was a cold and domineering woman who would poke around your room when you were out and steal biscuits if you left any in view.

There were many single-roomed servants' quarters across the far side of the compound which were occupied by members of the Greenfields domestic staff. Donald Otieno had been living in one for years, and I watched him through my bathroom window washing at the servants' cold-water tap near their communal pit-latrine. He made Nyambura laugh as she washed her bright plastic bucket and carried fresh water back to her room which was next door to his. Nyambura worked in the school kitchen, and was taking care of her sister who was slowly dying of Aids in her room. She gathered

15

flowers each day from the trees and bushes surrounding the compound, filling the room with their sweet blossom and forcing away the atmosphere of illness.

Donald was always clean, tidy and dignified, with shiny leather shoes and spotless trousers. In height, he was barely up to my shoulder, but he stood so straight and with such poise that I felt ashamed slouching next to him in my dusty trainers and faded sports gear.

Early in the morning the *muezzin* at the Mosque boomed out the call to prayer, and I turned over and burrowed my head in my pillow. It was so hot at night that getting to sleep was a struggle, and until I got used to it, I dreaded this early morning wake-up call.

In the middle of my first full day I walked down into Nairobi to do some shopping. Mr Rivers told me I would find all the food I would need in the Yaya Centre, but I wanted some fresh air and to see Kenya's capital for real.

Greenfields School stood in a fifteen-acre plot in the Kilimani East District between Ngong Road and Adrwing Kodhek. After watching a queue of people waiting for a *matatu* minibus on the corner of Ngong Road and then cramming themselves in with two-dozen others, all sweating from the heat and close confines, I decided to walk.

The school was a couple of miles from the city centre and the walk followed a dusty path running along the side of the aged tarmac road. As I dropped down Valley Road I passed a few barefoot street-boys in rags shouting at cars and banging on windows when they stopped at the traffic lights.

'*Mzungu*,' they yelled at me as I approached. '*Mzungu! Howareyoufine!*' and they left the cars and surrounded me with grins and giggles. '*Nipe shilingi*' – 'Give me shillings' –

they called and pawed at me with sticky dirty hands and arms.

'OK, guys,' I laughed. 'OK, get off and I'll give you *shilingi*,' forgetting what I had heard about street-boys and figuring they needed the few pennies more than I did, and anyway, I thought, what harm could possibly come of it?

I gave them five shillings each and walked on with them following me in a wave as I crossed Uhuru Park and headed into the city. At first I politely told them to go back and then tried to get rid of them by ignoring them, but one boy in a filthy Newcastle United football shirt wouldn't leave me alone and kept jabbering away '*Howareyoufine, Howareyoufine,*' and clinging to my hand. He called me '*rafiki*', meaning 'friend' and asked me for more money. Every few minutes he'd drop back and I'd breathe a sigh of relief, but then he'd appear again, pulling at my sleeve and calling me friend.

At each set of traffic lights we passed people selling newspapers – *Time Magazine, Cosmopolitan, House and Garden* – and yet more street-kids calling '*Shillingi tano*' at every car that stopped. Many of the kids were high on glue and sucked away at small plastic beakers. It was a tragic miracle they stayed alive for even one day on these crazy roads. They danced around the cars, while older beggars sat forlornly on the roadside. Many of the older ones had a limb missing, or were blind, but some were seriously deformed with elephantiasis and cerebral palsy, and their families pushed them around in battered wheelchairs and low-wheeled boards, their deformity being a major asset when it came to begging.

Shoeshine-boys, leaning against office-block walls, offered to clean my trainers for a few shillings, while hawkers sat on low stools selling single boiled sweets and peanuts wrapped in small newspaper pouches. Some sold roast maize from small barbecues they fanned with dusty cardboard strips. Other men sat by large potholes in the middle of the roads chipping away at boulders with small tin signs in front of them that said they were 'volunteers'. They said 'Hello Sir' to each passing car and held out their hands for donations, but with so many cars going by they spent so long with their hands out that very little chipping got done, and it was usually weeks before the potholes were filled and drivers got used to swerving round the boulders in the roads along with the potholes they were intended for. With the power of the rains, flash floods washed the chippings away, and it wasn't long before the volunteers appeared again, hands out and hopeful.

Shop *askaris* stared at passers-by and flicked flies away with horsetail swats as they chatted together quietly from their chairs in shop doorways. These *askaris* were paid one hundred shillings for a twelve-hour shift, and at night they sat inside the shops behind boarded-up and grilled windows, hoping nothing would happen, while street-children slept in groups on the doorsteps outside beneath newspapers and filthy blankets. For the equivalent of one pound a night I am not sure how much of a fight I would put up to protect a shop full of trinkets.

I stepped into a souvenir shop on Mama Ngina Street and spent time talking to the Indian shopkeeper about Masai shields and Samburu blankets. I asked him about a chess set made of soapstone. I had promised to send one home to my father.

When I told the shopkeeper I was not a tourist but the new Games teacher at Greenfields School, he was all smiles and shook my hand. He said his son, Rikesh, was in his third year at Greenfields and that he was a fine leg-spinner. He hurried his wife to pour me a cup of spicy tea which was brewing up in an ornamental urn at the back of the shop.

The shop was full of amazingly patterned batiks from Somalia and Ethiopia which he said could be risky things to sell. There were many warlords in northern Kenya and Ethiopia, and one had to be careful not to get caught up in any tribal troubles buying from one warlord rather than from another. Big Men up north have bigger friends in government who could revoke his work permit in an instant. Being a white man, he said, I was lucky and he knew he could talk to me without getting into trouble. The colour of your skin carries a lot of weight in Kenya, the shopkeeper said.

Idi Amin had expelled his parents from Uganda when he was a child, he said. They had settled there after working on the Antebbe-Mombasa Railway, and he didn't want to be kicked out of Kenya in his turn. His brothers were living in Blackburn, in England, but his parents were too old now to start again somewhere new. They lived in a high-walled compound near the Aga Khan Hospital and very rarely went out.

He showed me pictures of some northern pastoralist women with huge loops in their ears, necklaces and earrings that dingle-dangled from the tops of their ears. They sat weaving some of the blankets he had for sale in the shop. I spent the equivalent of an *askari*'s daily pay on a few postcards and promised I'd be back to look at some chess sets he was expecting.

I drank a Tusker beer in the New Stanley Hotel's Thorn Tree Bar on Moi Avenue, wrote the postcards and watched people trying to use the phone boxes on the pavement edge outside. I went to post my cards at the Central Post Office on Haile Selassie Avenue, a huge barn of a building with customer windows on each side of the great hall. The concrete stairway in the middle of the hall didn't go anywhere but blocked the flow of people, and there were hundreds of people, all milling around and queuing up at one window after another as each window was for something different – some for stamps, some for packages, others for overseas items and more again for drivers' licences and official documentation.

The walls were covered with flaking, yellowed, white gloss paint, done at a time when there was a budget for maintenance, and flies and mosquitoes gathered around the strip lights planning their next drive on the swarm of sweet-smelling, sweaty people below.

I stood in the doorway and looked out across the sea of heads and made my way to the Overseas Mail section. As I approached, I saw just one other white face amongst the mass and recognised Yuri, the big South African pilot I'd met at the Nairobi Club. We greeted each other with handshakes, and he stomped off to another office to try to pick up a registered package. 'It will cost me hundreds of shillings in *chai*,' he told me, rubbing his fingers together and shaking his head in resignation at the battle ahead. 'I will see you. We will go for beer, yah? Go well.' I smiled and nodded and turned back to the window, determined to try out my few words of Kiswahili.

Outside again, I bought some bananas from a *duka* and watched people fighting to get on and off *matatus* parked near the railway station. There were huge women wearing polyester tents that you'd expect to burst into flames in the

20

heat, and many skinny men in dark suits with drainpipe trousers who skipped across the road with complete confidence in their survival. Many drivers seemed unsure what direction they should be going as they sped up and down the two-lane highway.

I chewed a banana and turned to look as a rush of people flooded towards me shouting '*Mwizi! Mwizi!*' – 'Thief! Thief!' – and I saw the street-boy in the Newcastle United football shirt who had called me friend running ahead of them. He had terror in his wide eyes and a mango in his hand. He saw me and a look of relief crossed his face. He changed direction and headed towards me, thinking perhaps that my white skin might save him, but then he tripped on a pothole and fell, sprawling at my feet, and I lost sight of him beneath the mass of kicking feet and swinging arms. My body froze, and in the yelling I became momentarily deaf; all I could feel was the frantic excitement of the people round me – like being caught up with runaway foxhounds, delirious with blood lust at the thrill of the kill.

The flow of people drew me forwards, but then I felt someone grab my arm and tug me free, and I turned to see Yuri by my side. He dragged me away through the crowd. 'Come on, big guy,' he said. 'Let's go for that drink, yah.' He opened the passenger door of his Trooper and pushed me in. 'You don't want to get involved in that.' I turned to look back, but he took my head in his hands. 'Leave it, man,' he said looking directly into my eyes. 'It is over. You do not want to see what is left.'

Yuri nudged his way across Haile Selassie Avenue and parked again barely a minute away on Kimathi Street. He climbed out, smiled reassuringly at me, and I trailed along

21

behind as he waved at a man yelling '*Mzungu*, I watch your car.' He led me round the corner to the 4Ex Tower block and into the La Scala restaurant. I stared blindly at the waitress while he ordered tea and cakes and sat talking about cricket and flying a plane and anything he could think of to take my mind off the lynching.

He told me about a Tom Petty and the Heartbreakers concert he had been to in 1991 in Paris, when he was working there for a short while and they were promoting their *Into the Great Wide Open* album. He saw Metallica play in Canada the following year, when a riot broke out and the band's singer, James Hatfield, was injured by some fireworks thrown. Guns N' Roses were part of the bill that night, and he had never been more excited about any concert. He saw Johnny Clegg and Savuka play in Johannesburg many times. They always played a pretty fine gig.

I asked where the toilet was and ran up the metal spiral staircase, getting there just in time to throw up in the toilet pan. I splashed water on my face and stared for a long time into the mirror. 'Why didn't you help him?' my hollow eyes and grey face asked me back.

Downstairs again, Yuri had ordered more tea. He looked at me sympathetically as I sat down, watching my face and, no doubt, asking himself how I would cope with what I had seen. 'Dropped your lunch, huh?' he said eventually, and he smiled. 'You look better, big guy. Yah, you do. It's a natural reaction. Don't worry about it. Now you have just got to forget about what happened. It will become something you saw on television soon, OK? It will fade, I promise you.'

I shook my head and told him it was my fault the boy had left the safety of the lights up at the Panafric Hotel. 'I gave him money,' I said in a whisper holding his gaze. 'I know I shouldn't have, but I did, and he followed me all the way down into town. He called me friend, and I didn't even try to stop them killing him. I should have done something,' I said, and my voice trailed away. 'I mean, how could anyone do that? How could anyone stand back and do nothing?'

Yuri called to the waitress and asked for our bill in Kiswahili. 'Street justice is one of the joys of Africa,' he said quietly once she had gone. 'Nothing you or I do or say will stop that. People on the street are the penal judges here, and they pass sentence with speed and volume. Once the call goes out, there is no stopping it. If others get involved, well, I have seen what happens to them. In Pretoria I saw three people necklaced with burning tyres, two of whom were Christians from my church. They were trying to save the sinning thief, but the mob saw them as accomplices who deserved the same punishment. The best thing you can do is to forget about it now. You must forget, OK,' and he rested his hand on my shoulder as he stood up. 'The boy will know you could do nothing. His suffering is over now.'

We left the restaurant and walked back to Kimathi Street. He waved again to the man who promised to look after his car, and we crossed the road to the Uchumi supermarket on the far side of Moi Avenue.

'I have a favour to ask you, Griff,' he said flashing me a grin. 'If you are not too busy this evening?' And my mind filled with the image of me sitting alone in my bedsit, staring at the walls and seeing flashes of a black-and-white-striped football shirt getting trampled beneath a mass of feet.

'No,' I said holding my hands wide and shaking my head. 'I don't have any plans.'

He led me through a mass of people in the supermarket and up to the second floor where the gardening and building section stored *pangas*, poles and knives, and we chose the three axe-handles that felt most comfortable in our hands. I felt like a little boy choosing my first cricket bat with my father in Bill Edwards' sports shop on St Helen's Road in Swansea, picking up pieces of wood, feeling the balance, the evenness of back lift and the imagined power of the follow through, except here we were swinging axe handles baseball-style like Babe Ruth, not practising the sweet straight drives of Alan Jones, David Gower and Sunil Gavaskar.

We bought one each and a smaller, lighter, one and laughed in the street as we walked back to the car. 'Where in UK could you buy lethal weapons like those blades without a licence and walk down the street with them uncovered?' said Yuri. 'Here, it is the Masais' tribal right to be armed, and you can buy anything you want at a price. I was offered an AK-47 assault rifle in Turkana District not long ago. Guess how much for?' I shook my head. 'Just twenty US dollars. Incredible!'

Yuri gave ten shillings to the man who had promised to watch the Trooper. 'It's a protection racket,' he smiled. 'If you don't pay, the next time you are down here you find you have no aerial or that you are missing a wing mirror. Funny coincidence that.' And we pulled out onto Moi Avenue heading north towards Westlands.

Yuri spoke in short, clipped sentences typical of South Africans, but he had very little of the usual South African abrasiveness. What he said appeared considered, rather than bravado and words for the sake of it, and when he asked me to help because he believed his house was going to be raided that evening, I couldn't for a moment think he was joking.

'I am meant to be away in northern Kenya for the next few days,' he said, 'and Anya got back early this morning after three weeks in Rwanda. Our house-girl, Monica, came to Anya as soon as she saw her, crying, and saying that she heard our *askaris* plotting to raid the house tonight.' They would never have had the courage to do anything if the *mzee*, the master, was home, but with Yuri away and Anya there alone, they were rubbing their hands at the easy pickings.

When Yuri and I drove though the compound gate, bounced up the drive and climbed out of the Trooper, the *askaris* came out to greet us. Their faces fell as we unloaded our kit and Yuri's rucksack and walked towards the house, and we watched them from the kitchen talking in hushed frustrated voices and gesturing toward the house.

Anya smiled and made some tea. She was a short pretty woman in her early thirties with very black hair and a determined stare, and she looked gritty enough to take care of herself. She carried a pistol in a waistcoat pocket, but to a Kenyan criminal, one, or even better, two big white men in the house would be more of a deterrent than a woman, even if she did have a gun.

'Yesterday,' said Anya, 'they were acting strangely. Standing up at the hedge along the back fence, throwing things over to the path behind. I asked one what he was doing, and he smiled and pretended he didn't understand me, that he didn't understand my Kiswahili. Today they asked Monica when exactly Yuri was due home and she was so upset when she told me, and so keen to run away from here, that I knew it was time to call for help.'

25

'It's a pleasure to be here,' I said as Yuri laid our weapons out on the kitchen table. The three axe-handles looked good, and Anya smiled as she tried the weight of hers. Then Yuri opened his rucksack and took out his pistol – a Beretta – and a box of bullets. He saw me staring at the pistol, and he smiled as he said, 'With some of the places I have to go, man, I would be mad not to have a little friend close at hand. I am not going to carry it all evening, but it will be here if needs be.' He loaded the gun and put it, and the bullets, in a drawer. 'You have yours with you all the time,' he said to Anya, 'and mine up here, and we will carry our clubs wherever we go, yah?'

Anya led me round the house, pointing to the doors and the windows, all of which were barred and locked from the inside. We carried our axe-handles, Yuri twirling his through his fingers like a pool cue and Anya holding hers ahead of her like a Jedi Knight. I felt like a vampire slayer with my sturdy piece of wood and found myself grinning. We must have looked ludicrous.

'I don't know how many copies of the keys to the doors and windows there are,' Anya said. 'For all I know the *askaris* each have a set already.'

The *askaris* were still gathered together outside their hut near the garage. They had stopped talking and were just glaring towards the house, and we smiled at their obvious disappointment.

'On our first night here there were noises on the roof, and Yuri called the security agency that provided these guys,' Anya said wearily. 'It turned out that one of the *askaris* had climbed a tree and was stealing avocados from it. He kept trying to hold too many, and he kept dropping them; and they bounced on the corrugated tin over the lounge-room and rolled off onto the lawn.'

'When we found out what the noise was, we thought it was really funny and wanted to let him off, but the agency wouldn't hear of it, and they sacked him on the spot. They wouldn't even let him finish his shift.' She turned from the window and shook her head. 'This is the last straw. We are moving, yah?' and Yuri nodded his agreement.

'No point in having a base that is not secure. No point,' he said.

'Good. A retired police officer now manages the security agency,' she continued, 'and a lot of ex-policemen work for him.' She tried to smile but brought her hand to her eyes to hold back tears. 'That should make me feel safer, but it doesn't.' Her voice became a squeak, and Yuri put his arm round her shoulder and rubbed her back while I stood by the door feeling useless. He had a gentle way for such a big man. 'I'm sorry,' she said. 'I know I'm being stupid. I am sorry.'

We closed curtains in rooms with lights on and left the curtains open in rooms with lights off, so that we could see out and not be seen looking. We jammed chairs up against door handles so they wouldn't open, and hung wind chimes on them so they would jangle if anyone tried them, and we opened all the internal doors so we could hear and see more easily throughout the building.

It was a beautiful house, light and airy with almost more windows than walls. The tiles in the kitchen were sand coloured, and flooring throughout the rest of the house was tanned parquet block. Even the magnificent mats in the lounge-room were the same sandy colour. The walls were all white with mosaic hangings and batiks and many large photographs.

The house smelled of the flowers in the garden. Frangipani, bougainvillaea and rose bushes of many colours. The lawn was immaculate and the avocado, peach and passion fruit trees were full of fruit. I watched a cat stalk along a path and sit looking up at some superb starlings splashing in the shallow water of a soapstone bird-bath.

On the lounge room wall was a photograph of a child carrying a baby on her back. They stood in a rubbish tip, searching for discarded food, and there was a fly perched on the baby's nostril. You could almost smell the stench, but the child had an amazing smile and it was this that drew me in. So unlike the junky-smiles of the street-boys or our self-satisfied Western smiles back home. This was a truly angelic smile.

Anya said Yuri took the picture in a refugee camp in Rwanda. Like Steve McCurry's famous portrait of the Afghan girl in 1984, there was real humanity in the picture. The baby was the child's uncle and both had lost their parents in the genocide. Many parents died under *panga* blows and thumps from a rifle on the back of the neck as they hid their children beneath them. Why waste a bullet when you can use the butt of an AK-47 to meet the same ends?

Yuri poured some wine and passed me a glass. 'May as well have as much fun as we can,' he said grinning.

'You don't think it's going to annoy them,' I said, raising my glass as a toast and nodding in the direction of the *askaris*' hut.

'If they are coming, they are coming, but, even if they do, a couple of glasses aren't going to hurt.'

'Plus,' said Anya, walking into the kitchen with a cat in her arms, 'I would much rather throw empty bottles at an invader than full ones. That would be such a waste.'

Over supper we rested our weapons against the fridge and talked about other things, and by the end of the meal my eyes were streaming. 'I used to have an allergic thing about cats,' I said, 'but I thought I'd grown out of it. I'm fine with dogs, but not with cats.' I tried to smile and wiped my eyes with a damp paper towel. 'Cats are bastards,' I sneezed.

We moved through to the lounge-room, holding a glass of wine in one hand and an axe-handle in the other. It already felt the most natural thing to carry. I looked at the bookshelves, which were full of Kenya-related histories and political writings, along with novels and travelogues by Dervla Murphy, Graham Greene, Alan Paton and Elspeth Huxley.

'I know nothing about Kenya,' I admitted, pulling out a paperback copy of *The Flame Trees of Thika*. 'It's not that I'm not interested, I just never thought of finding anything out.'

Yuri came over, scanned the shelves and took out two books. 'These are the best books about modern Africa,' he said and handed me Blaine Harden's *Africa: Dispatches from a Fragile Continent*. 'That will get you started,' he said flicking through the pages. 'It will help you start to understand this beautifully fucked-up continent.' I opened the book at a chapter called 'The Good, the Bad and the Greedy' and Yuri smiled. 'You will shake your head sadly and bleed for the country, but the damn place gets under your skin.' He put the other book, Rian Malan's *My Traitor's Heart*, back on the shelf. 'That's more about South Africa than here, and it's very tough stuff,' he said. 'I think you should read Blaine Harden now and Rian Malan when you are more aware.'

29

'This guy is in exile living in the US,' Anya said, taking out another book and handing it to me. 'You should definitely read Ngugi wa Thiong'o too.'

'Certainly,' nodded Yuri. 'He's up there with Chinua Achebe and Gabriel García Márquez.'

'He is a Kikuyu who writes primarily in his tribal tongue,' Anya went on. 'But he has translated some of his novels into English. *Weep Not, Child*, and this one, *A Grain of Wheat*, are classics.' She held a slim volume out to me. 'Jomo Kenyatta locked him up for years and Moi forced him to flee. Hopefully there will be a time that he can come back and live safely in Kenya. Grow old in his home country.'

'You should always grow old with the air of your homeland in your lungs,' said Yuri dolefully.

Over another bottle of wine, Anya and Yuri took an hour to run through the last century of Kenya's history, from the British farming settlers up in Happy Valley, the Asian influx at the time of the construction of the Mombasa-Entebbe railway, then *Mau Mau* and Jomo Kenyatta's leadership and independence from British rule in 1964. Then the slow move to democracy when the former primary-school Calligraphy teacher Daniel arap Moi became Kenya's second President in 1978. Moi was from the tiny Turgen tribe and was a master of political manipulation and of tribal games, which secured him the backing of potential rivals when he needed it. Many people, however, thought of him as a puppet to other Big Men from within the Kikuyu tribe. Right from the start his leadership was brutal and corrupt.

Even the semblance of democracy faded in Moi's first decade of rule, as dissidents were imprisoned, universities closed and many tribal societies banned. Corruption blossomed and Moi became one of the richest men in the world, apparently owning top hotels in Florida and large farms in England's Home Counties.

The IMF and World Bank tried to force democracy on him by threatening to withhold financial backing for projects, and aid was suspended briefly when Foreign Minister Robert Ouko was murdered just before giving evidence to a World Bank Commission about ministerial corruption. The only kind of democracy Moi was interested in was that of a one-party state, and he fought against change for as long as he could. Eventually he had no choice, and he agreed to a partial dismantling of his KANU party's political stranglehold, and to remove the laws that outlawed opposition political parties.

There were dozens of chaotic opposition parties in the 1994 elections, and it was never in doubt that KANU would win. Together, the opposition won easily more than half the vote but individually they were pointless.

'And here we are,' said Yuri, slumped deep into a sofa. 'Kenya's next election is due next year. There is still little sign of a cohesive opposition.'

'But that is another story,' said Anya, seeing me stifle a yawn, 'and now it is time for bed.'

'Yah,' said Yuri getting up and picking up an axe-handle. 'It's been a hell of a first day here for you, Griff, and with the altitude and heat, you must be bushed. It takes some getting used to, yah?'

5

I used to lie in bed at college and think about travel. I always went home during the holidays and helped my father on the farm, while my mates went to Thailand, Morocco and the USA and came back with six-week tans and tales of exotic and erotic adventures.

The walls of their rooms in our halls of residence were covered with photo collages of young, tanned bodies in bars and on beaches, and grinning in the foreground of magnificent sunsets and scenery. I used to wonder at the things they had missed by staring into the camera lens rather than looking outwards at what was going on around them.

A gap-year seeing the world was one thing, but 'doing East Africa' in six weeks seemed a bit of a rush. I wondered what I would do with my time during my two-year contract if they really were able to see the whole region in just 42 days.

Those of my friends who had been to Kenya shared stories

of the 'Nairobi Handshake' in the Florida 2000 nightclub; where the prostitutes greet you with a smile and a hand down your trousers. Then there were the bars on Tiwi Beach where the dope is never-ending, and the stories of amazing safari tours and hotels recommended in the *Lonely Planet* guide.

They had all heard about mob-justice but no one had ever actually seen it themselves, only slept with a girl who sat next to a guy on the plane who claimed to have had. And the girl was always a beauty too.

No one had mentioned barricading themselves up in a house to protect a vulnerable woman from her own security guards.

'You are no longer an ordinary man,' Yuri said as he turned out the light to my room and shooed out the cat for the umpteenth time. 'None of us here are. You have already seen too much to have that privilege any more. You have joined a group of people who will always share that indefinable sympathy.' And he was right. In the same way that you change when you lose a parent or your virginity, you are no longer the same. Terms of reference had changed, and there was no going back.

I thought of myself at home, sitting in the pub just below our farm, and how I used to talk with our neighbours, knowing what they were talking about with the certain understanding that they understood me. We came from the same place after all. Breathed the same air and drank the same clear, fresh water. Things started to change when I left and went to college in Eastbourne, got married to an English girl and moved to London, but it was still my home I thought of when I needed direction. It filled my heart and my head, and everything I saw and said related to it in some way.

That hillside was all I had ever truly known.

After a couple of years I found a better job in Cardiff – the head of the PE department of a large school in St Fagans – and we prepared to move back nearer to my family home. London is no place for children, and we even began talking of trying for some. Laura applied for jobs in the Heath and other hospitals around Cardiff, but then she decided she liked London more than she liked me, and I decided I didn't like her enough to stay in London, so I moved back to my homeland alone.

This gave us more to talk about in the pub. Relationship strife leads to a bonding between men that develops through empathy and shared understanding. And then there is the unifying fact that the English simply don't understand the *Hiraeth* – the longing that we Welsh feel for home.

But now here in Kenya, by the light of the full moon through the barred windows, I watched a gecko crawl out from behind a picture and begin its nightly hunt for mosquitoes and tropical flies, and I wondered how I could ever explain any of this to anyone back home and make them truly understand.

Midnight in Nairobi is eight in the evening in the UK. My father would be cleaning the parlour after milking as my mother mixed powder for the calves, talking to them quietly, while Noodle, my parents' dog, chased rats around the cereal store.

I saw them in my mind's eye walk up the lane to our house, lingering in a gateway to watch the recently weaned heifers grazing from a bale of silage in a round feeder. Listening to the cattle chewing and the wind through the trees behind them and looking at the same moon that kept me awake. Maybe they'd be thinking of me.

When I woke I tried to open my eyes, but my feline allergy had gummed them together so I lay blind and confused on my mattress, wondering where I was.

I heard quiet voices from the kitchen and felt for the axe-handle on the floor by my side and smiled. We had survived the night without as much as a peep from outside. Maybe nothing would have happened anyway, even if Yuri and I hadn't been there, but who's to say? 'Better caution than regret,' is as good a motto as any.

I rolled off the mattress and stumbled into the kitchen where Yuri and Anya sat by the table eating pancakes and drinking filtered coffee. Monica was back, smiling and bustling round the kitchen, singing Christian hymns softly in Kiswahili. She greeted me with a gentle '*Jambo*, Mr Griff.'

'I have no eyes,' I said feeling my way to the sink. 'I'm sure I had some when I went to bed, but when I woke up this morning,' I wiped my eyelids with a damp paper towel, 'they were gone.'

'I've seen more awake dormice,' Anya said, and she laughed.

6

Life quietened down a little after that. I settled in at Greenfields School, got to know the teachers and students and fell into something resembling a routine.

At the staff meeting the next afternoon, on the day before term started, I found myself sitting in my new staff common-room, which was exactly like all the other staff common-rooms I had ever seen, with tired sofas, bent chairs and grumpy, chain-smoking teachers slumped in them.

Not all the European staff were back in the city after the holiday break, and all the Kenyan staff were still up country, so I was pleased the meeting only lasted ten minutes after the never-ending ones back home.

'Times are hard in Kenya at the moment,' Mr Rivers reminded us after introducing me round. He rubbed his nervous hands together as he spoke. 'Student numbers were down,' he said, 'and some of the parents were finding it hard to pay full fees.' Even the head girl's attendance looked in doubt for the remainder of the year.

'I will be honest with you,' butted in Mrs Benson, Mr Rivers' deputy head. Her tenor was far less appeasing than the one Mr Rivers found so natural. 'We have no funds left in the budget to give her a scholarship and her academic record could never justify one anyway.' She spoke very quickly with the same jarring tone of voice she used to lecture the children. 'There is no doubt she is a tremendous asset to the school, and the school board suggested that you teachers might like to commit to a sponsorship program they have started for her and a couple of others, as a sign of goodwill and commitment to the school. Nothing much is expected, just a few hundred shillings each a week. Just think how it would look to the parents of our other students, let alone those whose children have only just enrolled for next year, if our head girl left mid-year.'

'Have some time to think about it,' Mr Rivers said gently. He had his arms folded across his chest and couldn't look any of us in the eye. 'I know some of you have only just got back from the coast and are still in a holiday mood. We wanted to talk to you now and give you a chance to think and discuss this idea before the start of term tomorrow.'

'What you are saying...' said a young blonde woman who was squatting on the floor by the door. She spoke with a strong Yorkshire accent, had a cigarette in one hand and a mug of coffee in the other, and wore a baseball cap, loose T-shirt and tracksuit trousers. 'If I get this right... what you are telling us is the school board doesn't want to pay for Kajida and a couple of others to be here, but they are keen for us teachers to help carry the cost of these students' education instead?'

'That's right, Sally,' clipped Mrs Benson as Mr Rivers nodded.

'So in effect, we end up with less money in our pockets at the end of the month, which really means we end up with a pay cut.'

'Now, Sally, I wouldn't put it as brutally as that,' said Mr Rivers at barely more than a whisper. He rubbed his hands uncomfortably on his corduroy trousers. 'I can completely see your point of view, but the school board hoped you might feel able to back the idea of supporting these students' education. Without it, well,' he shrugged and breathed out a long sigh, 'without the support of the teachers, the students have no hope.'

'Do think about it,' Mrs Benson said, as she hurried Mr Rivers out of the door. 'Times are getting harder in Kenya and without an education a child stands no chance.'

Geraldine, sitting on the arm of the sofa to my left, turned to me with a frown. 'Well, you picked a good time to arrive at Greenfields didn't you, Griff?' She stood up. 'Right then, Ron my love. It's time to get back to the flat, unload our car and get back into Nairobi mood. No point in putting it off any longer.' The big, bearded Scotsman sitting on her other side rose gingerly to his feet.

'Aren't we going to talk about this?' said Erica, the Art teacher who sat on the far side of the room from Sally. 'I mean, it's just crazy,' she giggled girlishly.

'So it is,' said Ron, rubbing his trim beard thoughtfully. 'So it is. Sally is right about what they are asking. But it is so ridiculous that we are not going to talk about it.'

'I think we should discuss it and form a united stand,' said Sally. 'This country is so weird that whatever we do might come back on us later on.'

But Ron wasn't listening. 'We have just got back from the coast,' he said, holding up his hand emphatically, 'and theoretically we are still on holiday so we should leave all this negativity for a later time when we can't avoid it. I want to think happy thoughts for as long as I can.' He clapped his hands, and then held his arms wide and beckoned us to him. 'I think we should all share a group hug before we go.' One by one my colleagues climbed to their feet and joined the hug. I was last up and leant against Sally uncomfortably. 'Better?' asked Ron looking at her, and she nodded. 'Good. Now let's go. Nice to meet you Griff,' he said and patted my shoulder as he passed me on the way to the door. 'See you at school. Ta-ra!'

7

Eventually I got used to the *muezzin's* call from the mosque and used it as an alarm call to get up and go for a run around the playing-fields before the day got too hot. There were lessons all day, and then I sat on the balcony outside my room in the evenings, listening to music tapes from home and chatting with Donald and Sally over bottles of cold Tusker. They both smoked cigarettes, the smoke keeping the mosquitoes away, and discussed the difference in taste between a Marlboro Light and a Rooster cigarette.

The sunset above the game reserve to the south was quicker and more startling than sunsets back home, and the birdlife in the acacia and frangipani bushes around the school compound kept me reaching for a bird identification book. Their colours and shapes seemed so unlikely, and we watched the butcher-birds catching flies and bugs which they impaled on thorns to be eaten later. With the size and ominous menace of the pied crow and the gaudy extravagance of the superb starlings, Kenya's birdlife was something completely different, I had never seen such natural splendour so close at hand before.

Donald taught us basic Kiswahili, and Sally and I taught him our home languages.

'Good morning' in English, is '*Bore da*' in Welsh, '*Hibari za asubuhi*' in Kiswahili, and '*Eh up*' in Yorkshire.

'How are you?' is '*Sut wyt ti?*' '*Hibari?*' and '*A'right?*' The reply – 'Fine' – is '*Iawn*', '*Salama*', and '*Can't grumble.*'

Donald tried the accents too, and greeted Sally with an '*Eh up lass. A'right?*' in a bad Yorkshire accent each morning.

Donald talked about his home and growing up in the bush, and how Kenya and the Kenyan have changed during his lifetime. Three hundred years of Western social evolution has happened in seventy years here, he said, and it is only natural that any society developing this fast will have problems of one sort or another. He gave me a copy of *How to be a Kenyan* by Wahome Mutahi and promised to take me back to his home-place one weekend.

'Wahome Mutahi writes in the *Daily Nation* newspaper,' Sally said, as she peeled the paper labels off her bottle of beer. 'It's a good read. He says stuff no white person could ever get away with. It's funny, but a lot of it is tragic really.'

Sally was a sturdy, blonde, straight-talking Yorkshire lass. She always wore a baseball cap, drank coffee where others drank water and was most comfortable with a cigarette between her fingers. She used her baseball cap as an indication of her mood. If the peak was up, then she was in a good mood, but when it was down over her eyes, if you were wise, you gave her a wide berth.

She and Andrew Greeley were the only other white teachers living in the compound at the time I arrived – Sally on the ground floor near the stairs and Andrew further along the first-floor balcony from me. They came to Kenya as an engaged couple, for a new challenge and to test their relationship. If they could survive here they could survive anywhere, they reckoned, but after only six weeks, when Sally lay in bed with severe vomiting and diarrhoea and Andrew went out to buy her some rehydration salts, he met up with Erica the Art teacher, went drinking and ended up spending the night with her. 'It meant nothing,' he said to Sally the next day. 'We were drunk, and anyway you weren't the best of company.' That might have been the case, said Sally, with her leaning over, and sitting on, the toilet with equal regularity, but she didn't feel very forgiving, and she had hardly spoken to either Andrew or Erica since.

Although Mr Rivers was Sally's uncle, their relationship was a distant one. He and her mother were not all that close because she felt he had deserted their family when he moved to Kenya, and she became even colder as his northern accent started to fade. Still, Sally didn't mind how he spoke. She took people as she found them, but if you did her wrong there was no going back.

The other compound residents were members of the African teaching staff, who kept very much to themselves, and others who worked in offices in Nairobi and at the state-run Kilimani School nearby. They looked at Sally and me with suspicion as we sat there in the evenings, and they looked at Donald with open disgust. 'Whites should stay with whites and Africans with Africans' their glares said, and making friends with them was a slow process.

Sally told me that teaching in Kenya was much easier than in the UK. The children were obedient and enthusiastic and, although the kit was old, the PE Department was pretty well equipped. Greenfields didn't have a good record in matches against the other English-system schools. Most of their students were Asian and struggled to compete with the physical size of the Whites and Africans. We did well at girls' hockey though. Our little Hindus were able to make a laughing stock of many of the big, bumbling, chubby white girls.

The boys had been without a dedicated teacher for six months since my predecessor picked up malaria on a trip to Kakamega Forest in western Kenya. Kakamega is the last piece of rain forest in East Africa and the school had taken a group there every year up until then.

Malaria is the biggest killer in Africa, Geraldine told me. She was the school's nurse and, in her mid-forties, played a mothering role to the younger European staff. She and Ron shared a flat behind the Milimani Hotel near State House Road, and they often invited Sally and me there for evening meals, to watch their television and catch up on television back home by reading the TV guide that Ron had on subscription. He was addicted to *Coronation Street*, and if he couldn't watch it, the next best thing was to read about it in the guide. They had a carved sign on their door saying '*Karibuni*' and their 'welcome' was always good and honest.

Geraldine and Ron were both Scots, and a lot older than the rest of Greenfields' European staff. Theirs was a platonic relationship and they were at ease with each other like a long married couple. She was dark and *petite*, and immediately warm, but Ron was a big, extroverted ginger-headed man who

44

was always a bit guarded with me, and I never really got to know him well.

Geraldine came to Kenya after learning her husband was having an affair with her sister. She and Ron met each other a few weeks after Ron's partner, Rupert, had died of HIV. Ron, still overwhelmed with grief, was standing on Glasgow's Broomielaw Quay preparing to drown himself in the River Clyde. He had stood there all night, too scared to jump and too sorrowful to go home. Geraldine, who used to walk along the Quay early in the morning, found him clinging to the rails crying. She helped him down, brought him home for a cup of tea in her flat above a café off Robertson Street, and they became friends. They hatched a plan to get away from Scotland, and within six months they were working together in Kenya.

'Genocide and Aids play their part these days,' Ron told me as I helped him clean up his science lab at the end of a day, 'but malaria is still number one killer on the continent. There are side-effects to taking Larium. Paludrin and Cloroquin have fewer. Malaria stays in your system for life once you have it. Prevention is better than cure, and the sickness is too serious to take the risk.'

My predecessor, Phillip Pauls, didn't take his anti-malarial pills because they gave him ulcers and bad dreams. He lost two stone in a weeklong fever, and was in and out of Nairobi Hospital for a month. Then he went home.

Sally's ex, Andrew, taught English and spent most of his time on his own, reading and practising the cello. He dated Erica briefly after breaking up with Sally, but when they split up he retreated into his shell and rarely went anywhere. He played his cello in a group that performed at the French

Cultural Centre, but I had very little to do with him. He shaved once a month and switched from being bearded to having a very white, un-sunburnt, clean-shaven look which the children laughed at. But he didn't care. He started wearing black and read James Joyce, Ngugi wa Thiong'o and Mark Twain to the children, looking at the comparisons between Kenya today and the West in the past.

Erica taught Art. She was a small, flowery, West Country girl with an easy smile and a big heart. She was very tactile, and her friendly touch confused many men. She wore light, floating skirts, sandals and plenty of beads, and she hummed constantly as she skipped around the school. She could be difficult, especially if she thought you weren't taking her art seriously. Unlike Sally, who ignored people if she didn't like them, Erica was devious, and you never really knew where you stood with her.

In her abrupt way, Sally told me that Erica was a tart, who never thought about the consequences of sleeping around, nor learnt from the damage she caused. They had arrived in Kenya at the same time and started with next-door bedsits. Erica moved out a little before Christmas, once she had got bored of Andrew and told him to go back to Sally. They had been dancing at the Carnivore nightclub, Erica and Andrew, when some Zimbabwean cricketers came in, and one smiled at her and offered to buy her a drink, and that was all it took. Erica ditched Andrew on the spot, and became the Zimbabwean's night-time companion until his team's tour of Kenya ended. She couldn't understand why Andrew, who was the designated driver that evening, was upset and refused to drive them back to school, making them get a taxi on their own instead. Erica moved into a shared flat with some teachers who worked at another English-system school called Peponi. Donald told me the atmosphere in the Greenfields compound improved as soon as she had gone.

Greenfields was an old style English-system school, opened shortly after the war and still run with 1950s Catholic values. Mr Rivers had owned it for twelve years and had changed very little on this front. We had assembly each morning and prayers before meals. The boys learnt Carpentry and the girls learnt to cook. No pandering to the modern age of equality. Boys played rugby, cricket and football, while girls played badminton, learned to dance and do gymnastics. We had mixed tennis and hockey lessons, and Donald ran swimming sessions each day after school in his quiet, delightful way. He had recently qualified as a swimming-coach. 'Five years ago I couldn't even swim,' he smiled, 'And now!' He was so proud of what he had achieved, that he was now more than just a menial driver. Mr Rivers encouraged him to learn to swim and later paid for him to travel to Uganda for his Exam. 'Phillip Pauls started teaching me when he was here. It was he who gave me the confidence to try,' he said, acknowledging his friend's support. 'We have our first competition in a month. Perhaps someone will win a race,' he added, doubtful lines furrowing his forehead.

Mr Rivers taught Maths to the top-year children, most of whom were preparing for their common entrance to boarding schools in England. As well as being the deputy head, Mrs Benson taught Domestic Studies with the girls while the boys learnt Carpentry with Kennedy Ochomo, one of the four Kenyan Nationals on the full-time teaching staff. Of the other three, Mary Odinga taught Kiswahili and Music, Thomas Ngutu took Maths, and Peter Ochieng's students spoke French with extraordinary western Kenyan accents. Peter also worked as a tutor in Nairobi University and was pretty vocal on how he felt about President Moi.

Father Marcus Abdi came in to run Religious Instruction three days a week, and he had the role of school counsellor, although I never heard of anyone seeking his advice over anything. He was a big Somali from northern Kenya who talked loud and laughed long and hard at his own humour. He had a parish fifty miles west of Moyale, which he visited during the school vacations.

We all covered a second subject, mine being Religious Education, and during the April rains, when serious outdoor PE was impossible, Sally and I put together a stage play, which we hated doing, but which Mrs Benson said the students looked forward to for weeks.

'Benny says it's great PR and all the parents come dressed in their best,' Sally told me, shaking her head, 'It should be easier now Ron's promised to take over the stage design and costume, and Andrew helps Mary on the music side. But the whole thing's pretty awful.' I hadn't taught dance since my teaching practice at college, so was not overjoyed by this addition.

But, in general, teaching was easier than at home, and the children were a delight. There was less paperwork and much more freedom over teaching styles, and it was a joy to be at Greenfields after the long dark years of teaching in grey, under-funded, British schools.

Technically, the children were good at sports, and some had potential, but because of their size, and as most had never been on a winning side, morale was low when it came to inter-school competitions. I tried to encourage them, saying taking part was more important than success, but this drove Sally mad saying they'd enjoy it more if they won the occasional game. It wasn't easy to think of novel ways to have fun with a rugby ball on rock-hard earth pitches with four-inch wide, sun-dried cracks criss-crossing them.

It was difficult to encourage the children to emulate heroes when they didn't have any. A few of the children had satellite television, so were able watch international sport and British football, but apart from runners, Kenya has very few homegrown sporting stars worth following. The national football side did reasonably well in the African Nations Cup, especially under coach Reinhard Fabisch in the mid-1990s, but games in the Kenyan Football League often ended in brawls, and I read reports in the *Daily Nation* of referees running for their lives. The children at Greenfields School preferred to watch Manchester United and Arsenal on their satellite televisions than go to a game between two local sides. Even most of the cricketers, who beat the West Indies in the 1996 World Cup a couple of weeks after I arrived in the country, were completely uninterested in supporting youth development or establishing a fan base.

For a while, Erica went out with one of the senior Kenyan cricketers, but she couldn't get him to come to school to meet the children. He promised he would, and Sally and I spent a lot of time building him up in the children's eyes, arranging an exhibition game for him to watch, but then he didn't turn up, and the kids went home dispirited.

A few days later he arrived at Erica's flat with pieces of goat meat as an apology. He would come for sure the next week, he said, but he felt that he should be paid by the school to do so. He was captain of the national team after all, which made him a very important and famous person.

A few years later the International Cricket Council banned him for match fixing after he developed an 'inappropriate relationship' with an Indian bookmaker. 'I am shocked and surprised by the outcome,' he said in his press statement to the world's media, 'but it was not altogether unexpected.' I came to love phrases like this from Kenya's top sportsmen.

Erica dumped him when he stood her up once too often and she saw him through the window of the Buffalo Bill's nightclub. He had a thing for white girls, and later married and divorced a white South African, but even back then he just couldn't stay true to one woman.

Slowly, as I became more of a resident than a visitor, I learnt how Nairobi worked, and found it wasn't all bloodshed and tears, and I came to like many parts of it.

Sally and I often sat in the Thorn Tree Café outside the New Stanley Hotel and watched the tourists trying to look unobtrusive, but with forty thousand whites in a population of eighty thousand Asians and twenty-six million Africans, blending in wasn't easy. With men it was slightly different. Most whites dressed the same, with loose cotton shirts and trousers, but female tourists were much more obvious. Resident women wore loose, plain cotton shirts and skirts or long cotton trousers, and they walked around briskly with a determined stride. They avoided eye contact and their chins were firmly set. Female tourists wandered around wearing brightly-coloured shorts and flamboyant T-shirts with cameras on straps and jewellery at their necks and on their wrists. Their mouths hung open, wowing at 'Africa', and their heads turned to calls from every hawker or shout from the street-boys.

You saw them bartering in the Blue Market, the shanty of *duka*-style souvenir shops in the middle of town, trying to knock ten shillings off an ornate thousand-shilling Masai necklace and smiling when they got a bargain. Others sat grinning as the shoe-shiners shined up their walking boots and shoes, and then frowned worriedly when they were charged eight hundred shillings for the service. They knew this price couldn't be right, but how can you argue when you are sitting on a low box with a wall of black faces surrounding you? If someone did have the courage to argue, the shoe-shiner backed off with smiles at the error of communication, 'No, no my friend eighty shillings that is all. That is all.' Donald told me no Kenyan would ever pay more than twenty.

African women rarely wore trousers, as they felt they did not flatter the African build, and the Asian women, in saris, scarves and henna tattoos looked magnificent to me no matter how hot the day, nor how heavy the rain.

Apart from labourers, who were known as *jua kali* because they worked beneath the 'angry sun', most African men wore black suits, white shirts and shiny shoes, which were imported from the West via Mombasa in enormous containers and were sold as '*mitumba*'. It is the 'imported' bit that mattered, even if the styles were ten years out of date. They were sold as the latest Western fashions on low tables and stalls near the railway station and the bus depot and around Eastleigh and Muthurwa.

Asian men wore loud shirts and gold chains and grew very weak moustaches. The Sikhs were dignified with beards and turbans, but Hindu and Muslim Kenyans seemed strangely uncomfortable with their Western look.

Most of the Africans made an effort to be clean and smart,

which was amazing considering over eighty percent of Nairobi's African population lived in the slums and shanties that surround the city, in temporary houses and tin shacks which had no electricity, toilets or running water. With little else, their pride in their appearance and the dignity with which they held themselves was of utmost importance.

Watching people trying to use Nairobi's telephones was an entertainment in itself.

With only one out of every twenty telephones around the city being undamaged, there were always queues of people lined up outside each of these waiting to make a call. Most had smashed glass and cables hanging loose. If they worked it was a miracle. You could hear people shouting 'Hello, hello?' into an empty buzzing void as their coins dropped in and disappeared. They came out swearing that the damn thing was broken as the next person went in and tried the same thing. '*Jambo, jambo?*' but it was no good. A third person tried, and then a fourth before the queue gave up and moved to find another phone.

A few minutes later someone else would pass by, a smile covering their face as they found a phone with a handset and no queue! And they rushed into the phone-box before anyone else could. Then a queue formed, with people hoping they had found a phone that worked and the whole thing started up again.

When someone did get through they were so delighted, and the connection was so feeble, that they shouted their conversation down the line in Kiswahili, Kikuyu, Kiluya or whatever their tribal tongue. Young Kenyans spoke in *Sheng*, a slang language made up from many of the other languages, and the queue of people strained to follow the news of the *harambee* fund-raising event in Migwani, the tribal uprising in Isiolo, or the second cousin passing away in Kisii.

They would smile, and frown, and their patience would be amazing even when the user hung up but didn't leave the booth. 'He is calling me back,' he would tell them, as they waited in the dusty heat with cars pumping carbons from one side and street-boys staggering around on the other. Then when the phone eventually rang he would answer with delight, '*Jambo*, my brother. *Jambo*? Hello? Hello?' But then he might find that the line was dead, and in his disappointment hurl the handset at the window and storm out of the box.

With a grin and a worried brow, the next person in the queue would try his luck with the phone, and then the second and the third, each gently replacing the now cracked and broken handset on top of the telephone. Then the crowd dispersed.

And a little while later the whole thing started up again.

8

The Friends of Nairobi Arboretum met every few weeks for bird-watching days and special themed events. On Saturdays they held a series of 'Green Energy Days' with the aim of encouraging businesses and the government to take alternative energy seriously. Only a few people came, but the organisers were amazingly resilient, saying 'changes take time' and 'all we can do is try'.

With Mr Rivers' encouragement, I volunteered to help on a Solar Awareness Day, but there were more organisers than visitors, so I spent a couple of hours sitting under a tree with a woman of 102, called Mrs Jones, who, with her uncle and husband, helped establish the Arboretum early in the century.

I first met her at a bird-watching morning on the edge of Wilson Airport, on an area of rough land near the main entrance to the Nairobi National Park. She lent me her binoculars and pointed out a shrike, some bullet-bees and many other species of birds and bugs, her eyesight far better than mine despite her age. We were the only two whites out of the thirty or so people there.

Each day the *Nation* and *Standard* newspapers told stories of land-grabbing and natural habitats being destroyed by developments, and I had come to think that the majority of Kenyans were only interested in their country and natural cultural heritage if they could make a quick shilling out of it. The number of Africans birding surprised me, having thought it would be all middle-aged Europeans and tourists. There were more young African men than anyone else.

At the Arboretum we sat beneath the gum trees, Mrs Jones and I, and she told me stories about her husband's life and their travels together. Her mind, she said, was as clear as the day she left England over eighty years before, and I could visualise it when she told me about the boat trip to Australia, meeting and falling in love with Randolph, and then the journey on to Kenya where they married and she became Mrs Carla Jones.

'Randolph left for Australia in 1899,' she said. He was born in England but emigrated early in his life. 'We married in 1915 and moved to Kenya where my uncle was helping to set up this arboretum.' They ran a coffee plantation near Meru on the slopes of Mount Kenya, had two sons and lived their colonial lives to the full.

They sent their boys to boarding school in England at the age of six like everyone else did, but the boys died in July 1921 when the Imperial British East Africa Company steamer, *The Massachusetts*, sank in a tropical storm off the Cape as it brought them home for their first summer vacation. There were no survivors.

In her grief, Mrs Jones took long walks alone in the foothills of the great mountain, crying out loud to the open skies. Every night she cried herself to sleep, curled up in bed waiting for her husband to join her. Randolph shared his grief with the bottle and drank himself to sleep on the veranda. Then the houseboys would help Carla put him to bed.

Randolph drank solidly for three years, and then one day he never came back from a lone safari into the mountains. He died an accidental death, she said, with his 350 double barrel Express in his mouth.

Mrs Jones stayed on in Meru until the start of the next decade when the coffee market collapsed, and she sold the farm and moved to Nairobi. There, her ailing uncle asked her to escort him back to England. He had been in Africa for forty years and wanted to go home to die and be buried with the rest of his family in the grounds of the little village church in Puckington, Somerset. At the end of December, 1931, the two of them re-trod the path they had taken many years before.

On her final walk in the Nairobi Arboretum, the afternoon before their night train down to Mombasa and their voyage home, Carla dug up a young eucalyptus sapling of the same type that Randolph and she had brought with them from Australia. *Eucalyptus Citrioda*, the lemon scented gum. She tucked it under her arm and walked down to the Norfolk Hotel.

Back in Britain much had changed. Mrs Jones' father was dead, and with her brothers killed on the Somme and at Paschendale, she had only her uncle and mother left to call family.

She took care of her mother at their family home in

Hatfield until September, 1939, when Nazi Germany invaded Poland. Her mother looked up tearfully from where she sat in a deck-chair beside the now eight-feet-high eucalyptus tree, listening to the news on the wireless. 'I'm sorry, my dear,' she said, 'but I can't go through all that again,' and the following morning, when she went to wake her, Mrs Jones found that her mother had died in her sleep.

Now, in her forties, in a country still strange to her, she threw herself into the war effort. She had a little money set aside from the sale of the farm in Africa, and her needs were small, so she was able to devote all her time to the cause. She taught land-girls how to drive tractors and, when there were enough drivers, she joined the Auxiliary Territorial Service, manning the listening equipment on many nights, always on the lookout for enemy planes.

In the warm summer evenings a group of young women gathered in her garden beside the eucalyptus to talk and help each other through the hardship and doubt of having their men away overseas.

Mrs Jones told stories about elephants, hippos and lions, creatures that the other women had only heard about on the wireless and read about in books. To them Africa was a distant place 'somewhere sort of south-ish' and her stories about kangaroos and koalas, which she had seen hanging in trees exactly like the one they sat beside, had them sitting open-mouthed and wide-eyed. When the swallows began to gather towards the end of summer she told them how Randolph and she would wait for the first sign of their return to the tropics, knowing that the seasons were still changing 'back home', no matter how endlessly hot it seemed in the Central Highlands of Kenya.

And when she thought of Randolph, Mrs Jones cried. It was the young man she saw, not the drunk he became. She saw him in the dawn's first light, flicking back their mosquito net, his tanned, muscular back catching the sun's first rays through the curtain-less windows. Then he would stretch and wander out onto the veranda. At other times she could see his figure in the distance, rifle butt to shoulder, and then watch him raise his arms in jubilation as another kill was added to his list.

And she saw him in the night. In his sleep he looked like a child, so calm and trusting, and again she wept.

Mrs Jones leant against her eucalyptus long into the night after the other women had gone. In the distance she could see the flickering flashes as the blitz went on, often so very close, and she longed for clear nights of star-gazing. It was a different hemisphere and celestial collection that she looked at now, but she always thought of Randolph and her boys. They would be old enough to go to war, and she imagined them in their uniforms, turning girls' heads and making their mother proud.

After the war she packed up again and moved back to Nairobi and founded Greenfields School within walking distance of the Arboretum.

Behind high walls she taught Nairobi's youth the best she could as Kenya tore itself to pieces with *Mau Mau* and the move towards independence. Thirty years later, aged eighty-eight, when she finally retired from teaching, she received an official letter from President Moi thanking her for all she had done for the country.

Mrs Jones sat with me on a blanket beneath some of the huge gum trees that she planted with her uncle and young husband seventy years before. She smiled at the number of Africans who walked hand in hand though the trees and read, knees up, on the benches while young Asians played cricket on the grass. At night, the place was full of thugs, junkies and prostitutes, but on a sunny weekend afternoon it was bliss.

'This is what we hoped it would become,' she said. 'It is truly a place for the whole community. Uncle Battiscombe would be so pleased.' She smiled and rested her tiny hand on my arm. 'I do so wish Randolph was here to see it.'

9

Yuri and Anya moved into a house on Ralph Bunche Avenue, halfway between Nairobi Hospital and the Nairobi Club. It was in an adobe-style estate surrounded by a high stone wall with razor wire and a ten-foot metal gate with a spyhole, through which their *askaris* peered before opening the gate. Each house on the estate had a private garden at the back and a tiny yard at the front which itself was surrounded by another ten-foot wall.

The *askaris* smiled and waved and several became friends of mine. 'Welcome, Mr Cricket,' they grinned, and they'd pretend to bowl at me as I walked past them on the way to Yuri and Anya's house. 'You will teach this cricket, yes?' Benjamin asked often, and I smiled and promised I would.

Yuri's house girl, Monica, had a room off their yard, and above her room was a balcony you reached through Yuri and Anya's bedroom. Their bedroom was always full of suitcases half-full or half-empty, depending on whether Yuri and Anya were on the way to, or back from, a trip.

Anya worked for *Pravda*, the Soviet news agency, as their Correspondent for East African Affairs. Nairobi was her base, but she was banned from reporting on Kenyan stories after a run-in with Nicholas Biwott, who was said by many to be the puppeteer behind Moi's presidency.

In 1987 Biwott was Kenya's Minister for Energy when the disastrous $43million Turkwel Gorge Multipurpose Project took place in the Lake Turkana Region of north-western Kenya. This included a dam being built along an earthquake fault on a river that was silting up, and the construction of a fish-freezing plant on the edge of a lake that grew and shrank so much with the rains that the plant was often many miles from the water.

It was a crazy scheme, particularly because the Turkana people, whom this project was meant to benefit, are a pastoral people and look down on those who fish, thinking of them as failed cattle farmers. A Big Man amongst the Turkana people is a man who travels far with many cattle, not someone who settles in one place fishing.

Newly in-country and keen to make an impression, Anya asked some questions during a press conference with the Norwegian aid agency, NORAD, and Biwott's Ministry for Energy that were felt ill-fitting and accusatory. Naïvely, she even hinted at government kickbacks, and at the end of the conference she was called aside by one of the ministers and asked her name and agency. The minister spoke to her gently, said he was interested in her point of view and then, with a chilling smile, he assured her he wouldn't forget her.

Back with the other, more experienced, correspondents she

was asked what he had said, and then they frowned. 'That is Biwott,' one told her with a hushed voice. 'Nicholas Biwott. His words were a warning. You should get out of Kenya now.'

Pravda took the threat seriously, and their 'Head of Africa' flew up from Johannesburg to apologise to Mr Biwott personally.

'We have invested a lot in you, Anya,' he said, as she drove him back to the airport, 'and I don't want to hear of you in any suspicious car accidents.' And he was serious.

So Anya lived in Nairobi and flew to Rwanda, Burundi and the Sudan to cover the genocide in each country, to Uganda to write about Museveni's struggles with the Lord's Resistance Army, to Ethiopia and Somalia covering famine, and she spent weeks in Asmara, writing about how a succession of Conservative British governments supplied arms to both sides in the Eritrea and Ethiopian war. But she never wrote stories about Kenya.

In 1990 she met Yuri playing blackjack in the casino on Nairobi's Museum Hill, and they had been together ever since.

After cricket practice on Fridays, Yuri and I picked up pizzas from an Italian pizza-joint off Kerinyaga Road, and the three of us sat drinking beer on their balcony, watching bad American movies on the African satellite television network MNET and keeping mosquitoes away by burning frankincense that one of them had scraped off an oozing gum tree in Ethiopia.

Other times Yuri cooked barbecue on a small *giko* charcoal burner, complaining about the smoke and telling me about the *brais* they had back home. We British know nothing about barbecuing, he told me. Watching the cuts of meat go on, the garlic-salmon and sun-dried tomatoes in salads of many colours, I had to agree. A floppy burger and a dollop of coleslaw at a damp parish fête can't really compare.

They were away a great deal and didn't talk much about their trips. To them, their Nairobi home was the place where they could forget what they had seen and, for Yuri, cricket was a way to unwind. A Welsh farm-boy made good company, and my tales of home and inane stories from school brought a sense of normality to what was an extraordinary existence.

Anya had a pair of roller-blades and sped her way to and from Nairobi Club to watch Yuri play cricket, dodging potholes, *matatus*, rubbish and the street-boys who jumped out at her with a yell and a now specially tailored '*howareyoufuckoff*', which was what she had been yelling at street-boys for years.

She was short and pretty with very black hair and a determined stance that could be intimidating. After a few glasses of wine she mellowed, but more than once I saw her rip into a con man who tried to scam her when we were shopping in the Yaya Centre. Watching the confidence of an arrogant man collapse in front of this *petite* woman gave me courage not to be pushed about myself. Like in sport, a psychological edge is vital in Nairobi, and learning from her I felt myself walk taller and shrug off the bad days more easily.

South Africa in the mid-1990s was no place for well-educated white men, Yuri told me. Jobs went to the less-qualified Africans to balance the quotas in an effort to pull the country through after the end of apartheid. The Reconciliation Commission wanted to clear out the past in the hope of a bloodless transition to a better future.

In terms of history, Yuri reasoned, this would be seen as a balancing of the tables and as a growing-up time for the South

African black man, but in terms of personal frustration, it sucked. He was not even considered for many jobs for which he was well qualified, and which would have taken him and Anya back home. This trend didn't look like changing. Until it did, his plan was to stay in Kenya and save enough to buy his own light aircraft – a Cessna 150 would be ideal – and set up his own business in Cape Town teaching the new black middle-classes and tourists how to fly.

Once they were settled, they hoped to have children, and when they talked of children Anya smiled and gazed vacantly into the distance. But that was a long time off, and for now they travelled and worked and saved and cursed at the frustration of the place.

'Yuri had his sunglasses stolen today,' said Anya one evening as she put some pieces of chicken on the *giko*. We were sitting on their balcony after cricket practice.

'Yah, stolen off my nose at the Pumwani ring road roundabout. Bastard!' He ripped the cap off a Tusker and slammed the bottle down on the table beside me. The beer frothed and dribbled down the outside of the bottle and onto the low mahogany table. Anya threw me a cloth, smiled and winked.

'I saw the guy in the wing mirror coming up the side of the vehicle, but he'd got them and was gone before I could do anything. Shit man! What a country? What are we doing here?'

'Did you hear about the bus on Valley Road?' I said. 'It hit a pothole so hard the chassis ripped right off the undercarriage and slid ninety feet along the road?' I demonstrated what had happened with my hands. 'It was in the newspaper today. Nobody hurt. They all got out and walked the rest of the way into town. The remains of the bus are still there.' Anya laughed.

But Nairobi was the safest, most Westernised city in East Africa. With the best international air links, hospital service and shops. The electricity worked most of the time, there was water in the taps that was almost drinkable, and we really didn't have much to complain about. Other African cities had malaria, brown rancid running water, food shortages, civil war, flooding... the list went on.

I often slept over on the sofa in their front room, but other times, when Yuri dropped me back at Greenfields, we looked at the *askaris'* small fires glowing outside the large houses as we drove along Ngong Road, and we talked of the roulette wheel of birth.

The *askaris* huddled in great, thick army coats and woolly hats, paid one dollar a day to protect the homes from bandits. And these were among the luckier African Kenyans. In the estates to the south of the city millions more lived beneath corrugated tin and plastic sheets, living on nothing and with little hope of a future of any sort, least of all a better one.

In a situation like this it's worth stealing a pair of sunglasses off a white man's nose. The two-hundred-dollar Ray-Bans might get five dollars in the Blue Market. There is the risk of being caught of course, but when you have nothing to lose, it's a risk worth taking. Five dollars can feed your family for a week.

But what do I know? As I climbed the concrete steps to my room, with pizza-full stomach and light, beer-fuzzed head, I looked back down on my own *askaris* shutting the gate behind Yuri's vehicle. I shook my head in shame at my good fortune.

'It is all about luck, where you are born,' Yuri had said as I climbed out of the Trooper. 'And those born with a white skin always have the best cards in their hands. It's up to each one of us to play the game the best we can and to be sure we don't get caught cheating the dealer. There, but for the grace of God.... Go well.'

10

The smell of the damp earth after the rains was so refreshing, with clean breathable air, followed by the sun which became sharper and hotter once the smog had been stripped by the rain. We were baked from above and steamed from below as the rain evaporated and the puddles disappeared.

The African rains were like nothing I had ever seen before. When it rained it *really* rained, and when school classes were disrupted I sat with the children under the pavilion over-hang and talked about local cricket.

The players in the National League have great equipment and really look the part, but their temperament often lets them down. The Asians exploded at the smallest perceived slight, and most of the Africans expected defeat before they had even started, which didn't help anyone. Later, when I started coaching with Glen Stevens, the missionary from New Zealand who Mr Rivers mentioned on my first evening in

Kenya, I met African children desperate to learn to play cricket, wearing ripped tracksuits, someone else's shoes and carrying broken, homemade bats wherever they went.

We found kids smashing corncobs miles with a stick and complete confidence on the rutted mud tracks in their estates, but in formal games, with a wider bat and a round ball with regular bounce, their nerves took over and they often embarrassed themselves. Then they sat in an uncommunicative, dark funk on the boundary side. It was like this even with those who had made it to the Kenyan national team. Their insecurity came out as arrogance, and their desperation to use cricket to get out of the shanties took away the fun.

Sport is supposed to be fun, but it so often wasn't. I played in the first grade National League with Kenyan internationals and Indian ex-test cricketers, and sometimes we had riots breaking out on the boundary. Other times players incited the crowd when things were going against them. More than once I found myself standing between two red-faced and furious fathers during a youth game, trying to calm them and saying, 'It's just a game of cricket,' again and again.

I was called a 'fucking cheat' when I umpired a second division game between a Hindu and a Sikh club. It became so unpleasant I packed up midway through the innings and went home. 'Finish the damn thing yourself,' I told the chairman of the club. 'I'm not putting up with this shit.' I saw adult players cry from the pressure during a 'friendly' game. Crowd abuse and sledging are one thing, but it is usually aimed at the opposing team, not at the next person due out to bat on their own side. I saw people being bribed and felt sure that others, including those on my own team, were throwing

70

matches. But when it came down to it, I couldn't blame them. Not when they were their extended family's sole breadwinner, and cricket was their only talent. How can you be critical of someone dropping the occasional catch for money if it helps feed their hungry family, especially when everyone, from the President at the top to the policeman on the corner, are up to their own scams?

It is hard to teach children to play hard and fair when their elders are not doing so. Games seldom finished with a smile and a shake of the hand.

'Things take time,' said Mr Rivers when I talked to him about it. 'I sat on a disciplinary committee a couple of years ago where the captain of a club had chased the umpire from the ground when he was given out, waving his bat above his head and yelling, "I'll kill you, you bastard." It was right in the middle of a game.' Mr Rivers shook his head sadly. 'I asked him if, in the cold light of day, he though his actions at that time really were the right ones, and he said, "Yes, of course they were, because the umpire was wrong." I asked if he agreed with the rule that "the umpire's decision is final" and he said he didn't. Not when it is wrong.'

'But things take time.' He smiled. 'It was much worse when I got here. I felt every match might explode, and some days I thought of wearing a helmet even when I was fielding on the boundary because of all the fruit coming my way. As the only white man in the league you don't have a lot of natural allies. But you know that for yourself now.'

So I taught my sport the best I could and switched off from the politics and the silliness. I knew I would never have an experience like these years in East Africa again in my life, and it would have been mad not to make the best of it.

11

It was a four-hour bumpy bus journey to Donald's home-place, a small village outside Kitui, a couple of inches to the east of Nairobi on my map.

We arrived late on a Friday night after school, as he did most weekends, only to leave again for the city each Sunday afternoon.

Donald's home was a single-roomed brick building with mud-splattered, whitewashed walls. It had a corrugated-tin roof with a small *shamba* surrounding it in which his wife and mother grew maize and beans with mango, papaya, coconut and banana trees. There was a long-drop pit latrine out the back. The kitchen was in a separate, hexagonal, mud-walled building with no windows and a stable-door, the top half of which hung loose from broken hinges.

There was no electricity, and Mary, Donald's wife, collected water early each morning from the village borehole and carried it the half-mile home on her head in a five-gallon flagon. She boiled the water for hours to ensure its purity.

They shared their house with Donald's mother who shuffled around with a twig-broom, brushing the dust back and forth across the concrete floor. The two women spent their days in the *shamba*, where they grew almost all they needed to eat, maize and beans being the staple diet for most Kenyans. They sold what they had to spare on the roadside, buying sacks of flour to make *ugali*, sugar and salt on trips to the village market during the weekend when Donald came home.

Donald's mother was so bent over by the years of labour, she walked with her shoulders level with her hips. Still, she carried the lighter shopping on their way home, and Mary carried the twenty-five kilo sack of flour on her back. Donald walked ahead, standing tall and proud and empty-handed, back from the big city for the weekend.

On Saturday we walked miles, Donald showing off his white colleague from school to his friends and family around the village. Many of the men had more than one wife, so almost everyone was related, and we ran through the 'How are you?' 'Fine,' routine dozens of times. We were followed by hoards of children breathlessly yelling '*mzungu*' and '*howareyoufine*' between giggling fits.

We discussed school business as we walked, with the sea of barefoot children trailing in our wake. Many had babies on their backs, and all had huge grins and runny noses. Tiny, filthy hands sought mine, and when I bent down the bravest of the children touched my face and stroked my hair tentatively. Its fair colouring and straightness seemed amazing to them, and Donald told me that, except for the albino

74

African who lived in the next village, I was the first white man many of them had ever seen.

The country was magnificent, the colours so bright and fresh. Scraggy cattle and goats, tethered along the track, grazed uncomplaining circles in the overpowering heat.

One of the children hit a hornet's nest with a stone fired from a catapult at thirty paces, so Donald and I took cover in a bar with mosquito netting over the windows. We watched the children laughing and running from the hornets, dipping in and out of the sisal and tobacco plants in the fields. We sipped bottles of saccharine Fanta Orange while Donald's cousin, Bernadette, just back from Rusinga Island, told us about her experience there.

Two months before, Donald had organised a *harambee* to raise money to pay for her to travel and settle on the island in Lake Victoria, in Nyanza Province of Kenya's south-west corner. They knew life would be tough for her, being a Kikuyu in a predominantly Luo region, but with some money behind her and a contracted job to go to, she left as confident as she could be.

Bernadette had set up one of the first Aids clinics in East Africa nearby in Migwani, and was very well known around the Kitui district. President Moi officially claimed there was no Aids problem in Kenya, but despite this, Bernadette's clinics were very busy. She was soon head-hunted by the Nyanza Province Health Board to run a series of disease awareness workshops and to train nurses for mobile surgeries throughout the region. She was due to be there for a year.

There was a lot of disease around Rusinga, Bernadette said. All sorts of illnesses. There were no toilets and people defecated in the lake and in rivers, which led to their drinking water becoming contaminated. Illness swept through villages unchecked. With HIV rife, people's natural immunities were already weakened, and they died of things that they would normally survive. The number of Aids-orphans was as high on Rusinga as anywhere in Kenya, East Africa or the sub-Saharan part of the continent as a whole.

So, as soon as she arrived and settled in, she began a programme of building pit latrines in each village in an effort to keep the water supplies clean. Rusinga is a very sandy island with few trees, and her first three attempts caved in. Her Project Manager then ran off 'up-country' with the remains of the project's funds, and the women she was due to train as nurses lost interest and went back to their *shambas* complaining about her Kikuyu ways and blaming her for wasting their time.

Bernadette spent the rest of her savings on buying materials for another pit latrine, but when these were stolen as they were being delivered, she packed her bags, climbed on a Stagecoach bus and came home.

'Such is Kenya,' Donald shrugged and smiled. 'Such is Kenya.'

'I say he is my uncle,' said Bernadette as we got up to leave, 'but he is not really. He took me in when my parents died, and he sponsored me to do better. I was in Nairobi alone.' She smiled. 'There are too few good men like Donald.'

On the way back to Donald's house we stopped off at the village school, which was full of students revising for exams. The school was a mixed one with boys and girls aged from four to eighteen who slept in cramped dormitory buildings, younger children at one end and older ones at the other.

We sat in on a Christianity class and learnt about the

Ugandan saints, and then their History class, concentrating on the progress of democracy in their country. The teacher dictated for forty minutes as the children took it down word for word in silence, every one of them writing with better handwriting than mine.

Most of the rural Kenyan schools are residential, Donald told me. Wake up time is at quarter to six in the morning, with lessons running from seven to four in the afternoon. Then there is washing, clubs and activities until supper at seven. There is free time after supper until lights out at ten. Weekends have extra classes and, with the teachers living on site, teaching in the bush really is a full time vocation.

The classrooms had mud walls and chicken-wire in the glassless windows, and the smell of charcoal burning and *ugali* and beans on the boil wafted in from the kitchen block, filling the whole school compound. Sunday lunchtime the kitchen served roast meat. The rest of the time it was chapattis for breakfast and then maize and beans twice a day, every day.

Sitting in on the silent classroom I found myself ashamed of the UK and of my role as a Games teacher. Here the teachers were truly dedicated, and students tried so hard to do well. After graduation, most of them make their way to the cities, full of optimism and pride, to join the battle for the jobs they have heard of, but which in reality aren't there.

It is the same anywhere else in the developing world. Without a job, people have no income, and no secure place to live. The majority sink towards the ghetto slums, and spend their days filling holes in the roads with rock chippings, labouring for a pittance. The alternative is to return, quiet and humble, to their home village and follow their parents into the fields to grow tobacco and sisal. They work under the frown of the mother, who put up with such poverty to assure her offspring would get a good education, and the sympathetic sigh of the father who tried and failed in the same way a generation before. And at night, father and son choke together on home grown tobacco and drink themselves silly on homebrewed beer and try to forget all they learnt in school, and all the dreams they carried.

In the evening Mary polished Donald's shoes, and he sat smoking in front of the house while his mother swept it out and made horrible herbal remedies from the *mwarubaini* growing wild in the bush. She claimed it cured over forty illnesses.

Donald and I sat chatting. Mary followed every word, and Donald's mother glowered at me as she pottered. She remembered white people before *Mau Mau* and hadn't forgiven us for leaving, Mary said. Things were so much better then. There was order then, and at least you knew where you stood.

Donald was a *Jua Kali* worker when he first came to Nairobi. Aged twenty and newly married, he lived alone in the Kabira Estate, getting up at five in the morning to walk four miles to work in the tanning plant at the Athi River Junction. He'd move canisters for ten hours through rain or sun, with just a twenty-minute lunch break of *ugali*, and then he'd walk his four miles home again. A five-shilling *matatu* ride would have given him an extra hour in bed, but he was saving for his family, so every shilling counted, and he sent most of his pay packet back to them.

His father had died of bilharzia through drinking dirty water when Donald was fourteen, and it was up to him to support his wife and mother, two sets of grandparents and six siblings. They could never have managed if he'd stayed in Kitui, and Nairobi was the only hope.

After three years at the tannery, he found work with a Sikh shopkeeper, working in one of his storerooms. He was there six years when a gang beat him up when he tried to defend the store from a burglary. As a sign of his thanks Mr Singh taught him to drive, and Donald became his driver and eventually his friend.

In 1984 Mr Singh died, and his sons closed the shop to move to the UK. Before they went they arranged for Donald to become a driver at Greenfields where they had studied themselves, and where they knew he would be taken care of.

Life became easier once he was settled at Greenfields. As a teacher in Nairobi he became a Big Man in his village, and it was a role he took seriously. A decade on and he was still doing his best to save and share his money wisely.

The next morning I scrubbed my trainers, and we marched off to church – the First Church of Kenya, which preached charity, compassion and consideration above all else.

'*Dini lako ni nini?*' asked Reverend Charles Mironko when we met him outside the little church. He shook my hand solidly.

'*Yeye ni Mkatoliki,*' said Donald quickly.

'*Ndio. Karibu sana ndugu.*' The short fat cleric reached up and patted my shoulder as he took Donald aside. 'You are most welcome here, brother,' he said to me.

I smiled at the people cramming into the doorway. They were all dressed proudly. The men wore gleaming shoes and spotless shirts, and the women bright polyester dresses and wide hats. As the only white man in the village, I again felt I had let down my colour, but different rules apply to whites

79

in Kenya, and nobody seemed to notice my scruffiness.

'I told him you are a Catholic,' said Donald, reappearing quietly at my shoulder. 'Come, Griff, we should take a seat. It gets very full in here.' We passed Mary and her mother-in-law sitting at the back with the women, and we made our way up to the front where the men sat. 'He asks if you could say a prayer before the blessing,' Donald beamed as we squeezed into a pew. 'You are a guest here, and it is a great honour.'

'Donald, I can't do that,' I hissed. 'I mean, I'd have no idea what to say.' He frowned, disappointed and worried that I would let him down after he had told Reverend Mironko that he was sure I would be delighted.

'But it is an honour,' he said doubtfully.

'OK,' I sighed and spent the next two and a half hours sweating about what I could say and when I would have to say it. I'd look an idiot if I repeated a prayer we had already said. And so would Donald. It didn't help that I didn't know what prayers were being said anyway, so I prayed for inspiration and hoped that God had a sense of humour. When the time came, Donald nudged me to stand, and I pulled myself to my feet.

'When I find myself in times of trouble,' I began, 'Mother Mary comes to me, speaking words of wisdom, let it be. And in my hour of darkness she is standing right in front of me, speaking words of wisdom, let it be.' I glanced at Donald who was grinning an even wider grin than he usually did. 'And when the night is cloudy there is still a light that shines on me, shine on 'til tomorrow, let it be. When I wake up to the sound of music, mother Mary comes to me. Speaking words of wisdom, let it be.'

I sat down, and Reverend Mironko nodded thoughtfully. '*Asante ndugu*,' he said and carried on with the service.

'*Da Iawn*,' Donald whispered, and then he giggled.

On the way out everyone wanted to shake my hand.

'A beautiful prayer,' said a grey-haired old man, 'but I cannot place it?' He held out his well-thumbed bible.

'Paul,' I said and moved away. 'One of his later prayers.'

'Of course, of course. *Asante sana*.'

'You will come again, yes?' said Reverend Mironko. 'Next time we will hold a *harambee* fund-raiser in your honour. Donald, you must see that it is so. Why did you not tell us he was coming before?'

'It was an oversight, Reverend Mironko. Next time, I promise,' and he hurried me on.

'A *harambee* would cost you thousands of shillings,' said Donald, as we walked back to his house. Mary and his mother walked a few yards behind us, both smiling wide, toothless smiles at me. 'This is why I did not tell them you were coming. You spoke well. The village will remember your visit for a long time to come.' He took my hand, and we walked back to the house hand in hand like two true Kenyan brothers.

12

Something over the weekend at Donald's home-place didn't agree with me, and I spent the next three days in bed or leaning over the toilet bowl. Perhaps it was the water or the children's dirty hands on my face. Maybe the maize Donald's mother roasted over the coals needed a few more minutes, but whatever it was I was sicker than I have ever been, and I developed an irritable bowel which haunts me still.

'Western women put on weight here,' Geraldine said, when I ask for some Diralite during one bad bout of sickness. She and Ron had come to visit me in my stinky sickroom. 'And men seem to lose it. Something about us having less exercise than back home, and you lot not eating properly.'

'I'm putting on weight,' said Ron dejectedly.

'Yes, dear, but you are not your average man, are you?' she said with a lovely smile. She sat on the end of my bed, while Ron sat at my desk, and Sally leant against the door smoking a cigarette.

Sally said she was putting on a terrifying amount of weight and losing fitness. 'Early on I ate *ugali* and tried to live the Kenyan way, but lately I've been really trying, and it still keeps coming.' She flicked the ash from her cigarette outside and watched the breeze blow it back into my room. 'I don't think I've ever been so unfit.'

'You can have my vomiting any day,' I told her, as I peered suspiciously into the potion Geraldine had mixed up for me.

'And you know you should stop smoking,' said Geraldine. 'You'd feel fitter then for sure.'

'I'll stop when I get pregnant,' Sally said, 'and that isn't ever going to happen.'

The following Friday night Yuri took me to the Nairobi Club for cricket practice, but I was too weak to bowl and sat at the bar sipping a Stoney Tangawizi ginger-beer in a pathetic state. That night I was sick again, and I still can't drink alcohol without a reaction.

I lost ten pounds in weight and felt feeble, even though I had got used to Nairobi's altitude and lack of oxygen. I spent another night staring into the toilet bowl, and I seriously contemplated packing up and heading home. I was still feeling unwell at the end of a week when Mrs Benson called the staff together.

'The school board has decided that changes are needed in Greenfields,' she said. 'Pupil numbers are still dropping, and it is felt that a change of leadership at the top will help.'

Mr Rivers bought Greenfields as a struggling school in the early 1980s and had turned it around to become one of the most successful English-system preparatory schools in Kenya, but he did not have complete control over it. The government dictated that all ex-pat-owned businesses had to have a resident Kenyan partner, and all schools needed a Board of Governors to oversee their management.

'It seems,' Mrs Benson continued, 'that the Board feel that, as Mr Rivers does not have the full support of the staff, they have decided to bring in a new head teacher starting from the beginning of the next academic year in September.'

'Of course he has our support,' said Geraldine, looking round and finding a room full of nodding heads.

'He is a very good boss. A fair man,' Ron added.

'And he owns the damn place,' Sally scoffed.

'That's all very well, but the school board have overall control, and it seems they feel that, as neither he, nor I, could persuade you to support their Sponsorship Program at the start of the year, then he is no longer someone you look up to and respond to, and they feel this is clearly not a good situation for a school.'

'But we do look up to him,' said Erica wide-eyed at the injustice. 'And the children love him.'

'There can't be complaints about the exam results we are getting?' said Andrew. 'Our common entrance results are among the best in the country.'

Mrs Benson shook her head. 'He will still be involved in the school, just more as a figurehead than policy leader, that's all.' She said this slowly, as if she was unsure of the truth in her words. 'He will still be involved,' she said quietly.

'A new head might bring new ideas with him?' said Thomas Ngutu the Maths teacher. 'Who knows, maybe the school numbers will pick up again?'

13

The whole school ate lunch together in a great barn of a dining-hall, sitting on benches at long, low, yellow Formica tables. Year groups sat together, with teachers sitting at the head of tables to serve the meals and keep order. Not that there was ever much need to keep order.

We spent most of the meals talking cricket at my table, and how much better India were than anyone else. When South Africa, Pakistan and Sri Lanka toured in October 1996, and then New Zealand and England 'A' the following year, the boys' voices rose a whole octave in delight. But no one was as good as India, they said, and Sachin Tendulkar was like a god to them.

Watching the Pakistani Shahid Afridi take only 37 balls to score the fastest hundred in one-day cricket against Sri Lanka at the Gymkhana Club was a great spectacle. Chatting with South African players like Brian McMillan, Fanie de Villiers and the great Allan Donald after their game against Kenya meant more to me than it did to the Greenfields boys. India were the best team in the world as far as they were concerned, even when they were losing, and Sachin was the best of the best, and everyone else was fairly irrelevant.

The lunchtime menu was the same from week to week, with mutton stew and chapattis on a Monday, right through to tilapia on a Friday. This only changed when some fishermen on Lake Victoria thought that poisoning the lake might be a good way of fishing. They poured great vats of poison into the water and then paddled their boats around and collected the fish by hand as they floated to the surface upside down. A dozen people died in Kisumu and many more became ill around the county before the story got out, and our Friday meat-free Catholic obligation changed to cheese quiche.

Father Marcus ate with us on days when meat was on the menu.

'There is nothing so good for a man's soul as a plate of *nyama choma*,' he would say as he forked more than his fair share of the meat onto his plate. Sometimes some of the children on his table ended up with just a smear of gravy or some gristle, and when they complained his voice boomed around the dining-hall, 'Blessed are the hungry, for in heaven they shall feast,' and then he'd laugh and tuck into his earthly bounty.

Trying to run Games classes in the heat of the afternoon sun with children who hadn't eaten anything was a nightmare, and they'd wobble around and collapse with fatigue in the middle of a hockey match. I mentioned Father Marcus's eating habits to Mr Rivers, who shook his head sympathetically and decided that Father Marcus should always sit by me in the future. 'You can discuss theology or something,' he ordered with a smile. 'Anything to stop him eating all their food.'

So Father Marcus did sit by me, and he spent most of the meals talking about his life as he braced himself with hands on the table, head pointing heavenwards and stomach reverberating with his laughter.

'Many years ago now a street-boy approached me when I was waiting at the traffic lights up in the Westlands area of town and asked for money,' he said. 'I usually dismiss them politely, but for a change I thought, why not ask *him* for money? Just to see what would happen. So I put out my hand and I said, "You give me money" before he had a chance to ask me for any. "Come on, it is your turn to give," I told him.'

'I was very surprised when the street-boy said, "OK, how much do you want?" and I said, "Give me what you have." and he held out twenty-five shillings. I took the money from him and pretended to drive away and the child turned and stepped back from the road with no complaint.'

'I was amazed by this and called the boy back so I could return his money and added one hundred shillings more of my own, making him promise to buy clothes and food.'

'The very next day, when we were filling up the vehicle at the Sarit Centre petrol station, the same boy approached the car. I didn't recognise him until he said, "Look at the clothes I have bought with the money you gave to me." He was very smart and was smiling because he was so proud of how good he knew he looked.'

'I thought about it and made an appointment to meet him the next day at my church to talk, and by the end of the week I had decided to help him. He is now enrolled at the Kyamtwoii Youth Polytechnic back in his home-place, living in the church compound and studying Carpentry. It costs me five thousand shillings a year to keep him there.' He shrugged expansively. 'But it is nothing,' he said.

On Wednesdays Father Marcus always claimed a meeting in town, so missing out on the pasta salad lunch, and he sloped off down to Buffalo Bill's on Milimani Road, where the barbecue was always cooking and *nyama choma* was nearly always ready. He thought no one knew. Nyambura told Donald she saw him one day walking up the steps to the restaurant dressed in street clothes and no longer with a dog collar, but he denied it.

Donald said he'd told my predecessor, Phillip Pauls, and Phillip had tried to make a joke about it with Father Marcus, but he grew angry. 'You mistake me for someone else, *mzungu*,' he said with real bitterness. 'Of course, we all look the same to you.' So it was never mentioned again and the children relaxed in his absence knowing at least on Wednesdays they were going to get a decent-sized meal.

14

The last six weeks of the post-Easter term were spent in chaos as the rains came down outside, and inside the children rehearsed for the school pantomime, learning lines, simple dance moves, and helping Ron turn huge hardboard sheets and blankets into scenery.

Mrs Benson decided we should write our own show, which we called *Hot Diggerdy*. It was appalling, with the absolute minimum of a plot. We had the older girls dressed as fairies on a quest to find the secret of the power of flight, which their leader had lost because she felt she had no friends and was lonely. If you are lonely, life is hard and your heart refuses to fly, and that was it.

Along the way, the fairies met some candles who helped them through the scary 'River-Road Land', and the boys turned up dressed as soldiers to fend off the evil powers of Loneliness. Their friendship song warded off a few random monsters, played by some of the teachers, who leapt out to scare them.

The girls loved dressing up as fairies and candles and covering themselves in make-up, but the boys hated it and made every effort not to be there. When the production was staged everything that could go wrong did.

Nairobi's electricity depends on the hydro-plants in Uganda. Since Kenya hasn't paid its complete bill since 1993, electricity is restricted in different areas of the city on different days. Our electricity-free day coincided with the pantomime, so Mary's electric keyboard didn't work and the singers had to sing unaccompanied. The lead fairy's harness got caught on a curtain, and she was left dangling upside down for the second half of the show. Half a troupe of soldiers got stage fright and stayed at home. Donald's 'Alexi – the King of the Fish-People' was fast but scary, and Peter Ochieng's giant, French-speaking 'Frog Monster' was so drunk he couldn't walk and slumped against a cardboard tree, which collapsed under his weight, and he had to be rolled away. Father Marcus's efforts at dancing bounced several of the candles right off the stage.

In the end the only thing that saved us was the six-year-old candles' dance as they sang, 'Where does the light of a candle go, when you blow it out? Wouldn't you like to know?' You could hear cynical hearts melting. Camera flashes flashed, and mothers cried at how sweet their children were.

At the end Mr Rivers came up to Sally and me, red-faced and in tears. 'I've never seen anything so funny in all my life,' he wheezed and wiped his eyes with a huge spotted handkerchief. 'You two should be so proud.'

But Mrs Benson was furious and accused us of being

unprofessional and childish. 'How could you go out of your way to make the children look foolish? What did you think you were going to achieve?' and so on. Then she turned and went back to the doting parents, shaking hands and agreeing with Santosh Gore's mother that he was the best soldier on the stage, and the way that he said, 'Company halt! Company dismissed,' held real authority.

'Bugger that,' said Sally as she lit a cigarette. We stood a little way from the group on the edge of the muddy playing-field. The rains were over now and when the children came back from their summer break the field would be baked solid and we'd be outside again playing rugby on rock hard earth, getting beaten by other schools and having complaints from parents about bruises to their children. Sally pulled her baseball cap lower. 'Bloody Benny. She knows we hate this shit, and she knows we are no good at it. The school never has been. She's the only one that thinks we should do it. If she wanted something professional she should pay a professional to come in and do it, not cheapskate around with us chimps.'

Geraldine led the 'Frog Monster' over, swaying and weeping. 'I am sorry,' he said to Sally. 'I so wanted to help you, but I was frightened. I have been such a fool,' and he hung his head in shame.

'You weren't so bad, and neither was the show,' said Ron, ever the diplomat, but then he started laughing. 'Actually, yes it was. It was awful, we all were, but at least she can't expect us to do it again next year.'

At the final school assembly of the year Mrs Benson announced to the school that next term would be Mr Rivers' last term as the sole head teacher at Greenfields. He would still be teaching and continue to be involved, she assured us all, but a Mr Peters would be joint-head from September. He was a New Zealander who had run a missionary school in northern Kenya many years ago. He, his wife, and their two children were very excited at the thought of coming back to East Africa, she said.

She turned to Mr Rivers who thanked the children for making this year so much fun. He said he knew that in their hands Mr Peters' family would have no trouble settling in, and he wished them all the best of luck. 'Next term will still be the same,' he said with dignity, 'and I will still be around in the future. Still teaching Maths, so don't think you have seen the last of me.' He tried to laugh but it got caught in his throat and came out as a gurgle. 'Thank you,' he said and sat down.

And then it was over. I had survived to the end of my first academic year in-country.

15

On the first day of the holiday, Sally, Ron, Geraldine and I borrowed one of Greenfields' four-wheel drive vehicles and headed north past Naivasha and Nakuru up to Lake Baringo and the heart of the Great Rift Valley.

As we crawled up the Nakuru Road out from the Kikuyu District of Nairobi, the Great Rift Valley opened up on our left. The Rift Valley is said to be the Cradle of Mankind, and Richard Leakey claimed to have found the earliest evidence of people here. The roads are lined with trinket shops set out expansively on dozens of wooden viewing platforms built out from the steep valley side. Once the shopkeepers got bored of us not buying their Masai blankets or postcards and went off to hassle someone else, the true scale of the Rift left us speechless.

With one of Ron's easy-listening tapes playing we sped north along the 104, windows open and stereo loud, watching rural Kenya the same as it ever was, with children tending small flocks of goats and sheep, donkeys pulling wooden carts piled high with sisal and wool. Women, in simple shirts and bright *kangas* and *mtandio* scarves, walked tall with pots perched on their heads, and fat men sat in the shade of scrawny trees and outside corrugated-tin shacks, watching the cars and colourful buses juddering by.

Children ran along the roadside holding rabbits by their ears and puppies cupped close to their chests. 'For you, *mzungu*!' they yelled, following the cars. Unmanned stalls of fruit and vegetables were stacked high and covered with dust and oil from the spluttering trucks which struggled up every incline and flew down every hill before them. No one has a stall on the downside of the hill. There is no point. Every vehicle goes by too fast.

Maize cobs, fresh from the roadside fields, are fanned with bits of cardboard and roasted above smoky charcoal. They taste of cardboard and sweating canvas. Water is sold in recycled plastic bottles collected from the dump and filled with water from the stream in the valley below. Danger – drinking this water may seriously damage your health.

We stopped in Nakuru to refuel and buy some provisions and then headed straight on up the B6 to Lake Baringo. Near Sandai we paused on the roadside and watched giraffe running through the low brush, their legs so long and gangly it looked like they were running in slow motion. Johnny Mathis played low on the tape player, and the savannah wind blew in through the open windows. Later we saw two male giraffe fighting, beating their necks against one another, the great thud echoing across the open plain.

We pitched our tents in the Roberts Campsite as near as

we dared to the Lake Baringo shoreline reeds. With the rains the lake was pretty full and we sat on a pontoon, taking slugs from a bottle of wine, watching crocodiles sliding across the top of the muddy water and listening to hippos chuckling away in the reeds behind us.

Over four hundred and fifty bird species live around the lake, and Ron was busy noting them in his bird book. The red bishop bird and weaver-birds were the most prevalent, but there were so many it was impossible to record them all.

In the evening the clouds piled in from the east, and our plans for a pasta supper cooked on my little paraffin stove by candle light near the tents were blown away as the wind picked up and rain came again. We huddled in the car, boiled the pasta in the vehicle's foot-well, and ate bread and cheese and the 'Slim Jim' beef jerky we had picked up in the Nakuru market on the way through.

During the night I woke hearing what sounded like cattle grazing, and I watched the shadows of adult hippos moving slowly round the campsite. I woke Sally who cursed me and turned over. It was her suggestion to leave the tent door open and just have the flysheet closed so we would see the hippos. Later in the morning she cursed me more for *not* waking her. 'Tonight,' I swore, fending off her blows. 'Tonight I will.'

As the dawn came up, the hippos strolled back to the coolness and security of the lake. I was transfixed, their size and grace like nothing I had ever seen before.

After breakfast, as we drove up onto a ridge above the lake, we looked out across the valley and were silenced by the pink sheen in the sky caused by the millions of flamingos on Lake Bogoria to the south. We were amazed by the colours of the lakes and the bush, newly lush with vibrant scrub after the rains.

'The Grand Canyon has nothing on this,' said Ron, and Sally nodded her head.

'It's a pretty bland canyon in comparison,' she said.

I pulled the car off the road and switched off the engine. 'I wonder how long it will be before someone tries to break into the car,' I said, and Geraldine laughed.

'Not up here. That stuff only happens in Nairobi.'

We walked and climbed higher and sat on a rocky outcrop high above the road. To the south we watched a cyclist grinding his way up the incline, passing a man and a woman with a quiet '*Jambo*' and a raise of his arm.

The cyclist stopped by our vehicle and took a good look around. Then he got back on his bike and continued up the road. The woman was lagging behind, the sack of meal on her back slowing her down, but when the man came level with the car he crossed the road and tried the door handles.

Our shouts of 'Oi' rang out in the stillness, followed by stifled giggles as he jumped from fright and looked round. When he saw us four *wazungu* high on the cliff above him he shrugged and raised his arms to say 'What? What's the matter? I didn't do anything,' in the same way a pickpocket would do down on River Road as you caught him with his hand in your pocket. He wandered off again, and Geraldine sighed audibly. 'Even up here. Even up here.'

In the afternoon we took a boat ride on the lake for a couple of hundred shillings and saw hippos close by, a crocodile catching and eating a huge fish and some fish eagles – the largest raptors in East Africa. They looked incredibly regal as they sat in the upper branches of the acacia trees on the edge of the lake, but their dignity vanished when the boatman threw them a fish, with wood jammed in its mouth to stop it sinking, and the great birds swooped down and plucked the fish from the water less than ten feet from the boat. It's a shame, we agreed, that these magnificent creatures had allowed themselves to become a human tourist attraction like this. But when we were there encouraging it and paying to witness the spectacle, we were as much to blame as anyone.

We ate out in the evening, *nyama choma* in the campsite bar, and sipped warm Tusker under their electric mosquito-zapping machine, which crackled and killed continually.

That night I managed to wake Sally, and we giggled in our sleeping bags at the bulk and gentleness of the hippos. She wanted to photograph them, but we were worried about the flash, so we just watched and engraved them on our memories, which give a far more exciting record than photos ever can.

The next day we drove the few miles south to see the flamingos on Bogoria. They feed on the algae in the alkaline water of the soda-lake, and their smell and noise are unforgettable, like a huge, musty fish-packing plant full of well-amplified chickens.

We watched from the shore as a fish eagle sat close to the flock on the salt flat, watching and waiting for its moment to strike. With its speed and power it is an awesome killing machine, and we watched as it hit a flamingo with a wallop, feet first, and then it sat on its neck and chest as the bird suffocated in the shallow water.

Several marabou stork, which had been watching like stern judges from a few hundred meters away, flopped down nearby and waited for the fish eagle to extract its choice pieces. Then they moved in to tear the bird to shreds. Later wild dogs came to clear up whatever was left, and all the time the flock of over a million flamingos kept sifting away in the murky water at a million smelly decibels.

We walked down to the hot springs half way along the lake and had supper just up wind from their misty sulphur cloud. That night we slept on the floor of an open-sided ranger's hut with a huge fireplace and skulls of big game on the walls. We watched an electrical storm bounce its way up the valley with thunder and lightning, wind and rain. It was the most violent storm I had ever seen.

We had spent the weekend talking like friends do everywhere, but as we lay there on thin bedrolls in the darkness, two men and two women, with the thunder crashing round us and wind and rain lashing the side of the hut, I reflected on our friendship for the first time. There was a bond between us now that I had never had before with anyone, not even family. We had shared fears and had seen things that tied us together. Things that would be inexplicable to others. When we got back home at the end of our times here and showed the photographs around, talking like travel guides or someone on a television programme, our descriptions would never be enough.

How could we share the smell of a million flamingos to someone who hadn't smelt it? Or the excitement felt on hearing the sound of a contented hippo grazing just feet from our heads with only a thin tent lining to protect us? Or the disappointment we felt when the walker tried to get into our car?

Then the storm passed as suddenly as it came, and the

night was calm, and the lightning bugs came out flashing their backsides in the stillness.

We drove back slowly south the next day, taking a detour through Nyahururu, watching the scarred African scenery around us become damper and greener, and by the time we reached Nyahururu it was like a rainy day in the Brecon Beacons. We stayed the night in a hotel overlooking the Thompson Falls, walking up to see hippos in a lagoon nearby. Then, after a day reading Laurens Van Der Post and walking by the river, we headed back to Nairobi before it got too dark.

16

I sat in a bus a few days later watching Yuri weave his Trooper through the crowds filling the road. It was eight-fifteen in the evening and the bus was due to leave at eight-thirty.

Outside people filled the street. Those with tickets, those without, those trying to sell biscuits, sweets, watches, peanuts and calculators, all clamouring, crushing and pushing to get onto the bus. The noises and smells of Nairobi's rotting heart drifted to me through the windows. The sweat, the grime, the dirt and anger of River Road at night.

I had met Yuri and Anya earlier for supper in Buffalo Bill's restaurant, but the place was so grim we didn't eat anything there. It was very dark, and Anya sat in some mayonnaise on the first bench we tried, and then, when we moved to another booth, Yuri and I found ourselves surrounded by prostitutes offering more than just the meal we were looking for.

We ordered food and bought drinks and looked across the

twilight of the restaurant to where a group of fat Kenyans were laughing loudly and pawing at the prostitutes. One girl had her hand down a man's trousers as he sat back laughing, bracing himself with his hands on the table and staring at the ceiling. Waves of delight bounced up and down his belly. When she was finished she wiped her hand on the bench, and he went back to his *nyama choma*.

'I don't think that was mayonnaise I sat on,' said Anya with a grimace, and we cancelled our food order and drove up the road to the Milimani Hotel, where we sat on stools by the bar and ate chips and *bajias*.

Anya showed me a piece in the *Daily Nation* about bandits shooting out buses' wheels to make them crash so they could rob the passengers. 'I only show you because I feel you should be taking the train,' she said. And I should have been, but the train ticket cost 2000 Kenyan shillings and the bus was only 340 shillings, and even if I hadn't already bought my bus ticket I wouldn't have changed my plans. What does a few hours cramped in a bus mean when I could tell people about the adventure afterwards? Why go to Africa if you hide in the safety net of being white and comparatively wealthy all the time?

'Anyway,' I said with a grin. 'What could possibly go wrong?'

'Rather you than me, man,' Yuri said as I climbed out of the Trooper and swung my bag over my shoulder. He took my arm and said, 'Take care my friend. Don't be brave now, you hear. Go well.' And I smiled as I left him and climbed the steps to the bus, taking the best seat there was, the one directly behind the driver on the front row. I began to relax.

I knew Yuri and Anya were good people, but they did go

on. Sometimes I felt they had no confidence in me, and part of this bus adventure was to show them I was as capable as anyone else. So what if only Andrew of the Greenfields staff would go by bus when he went to the coast? The rest shared the driving in Ron's little car, went by train or sometimes flew directly to Mombasa or Malindi from Wilson Airport.

With their experiences of working in East Africa, Yuri and Anya were highly cynical as to the amount of good they believed anyone was doing here any more. People tried hard, but very little would come to anything. And they felt there was no point in taking stupid risks when you didn't have to. The thought of the Nairobi-Mombasa Highway at night, with its potholes, upturned, smoking trucks, stoned and wayward drivers and, of course, the gun-toting bandits, brought out the worst in them.

I began to think of the few days to come, and I smiled and stretched out as best I could in the narrow seat. In my bag I had two classes worth of exam papers with me to mark while I sat on the white sands of the East African coast. Who of my teacher friends back home would be marking their papers on a beach?

One of the questions in the exam was a passage from the letter to the Ephesians, where St Paul writes of the mystery in the symbolic marriage between Christ and the Church. That had been one of the hardest lessons during the year to teach.

Teaching RE back home was a struggle, but so long as we concentrated on a good story or two it was easier to keep the peace. In Kenya having a faith was a social requisite, and even with most of the Greenfields' children not being Christians, many of them, and the majority of their parents, knew great chunks of the bible by heart. It kept me on my toes and made me think more about what I was teaching and what my faith meant to me.

The bus driver revved the engine impatiently as the ticket touts kicked off the hawkers who were still trying to sell their junk to the passengers, who still had no interest in buying it.

A man with a clipboard asked me for my ticket, which I handed over, and then, attaching it to the board, he walked up the bus checking other people's tickets. The driver smiled at me and put a handful of *miraa* twigs into his mouth, a stimulant he chewed to keep himself awake.

I glanced back along the bus and saw I was the only European, and fifty sets of eyes stared back at me from already tired black faces. I was used to children touching my skin and feeling my hair to see if they were real, but I still found the adult stare intimidating. It was good to be at the front of the bus, so I didn't have to sit through eight hours of faces turning round to look at me all the way to Mombasa.

Beside me slept a middle-aged man who smelt of cigarettes and alcohol. On the bus steps stood a mother carrying a small, light-skinned child that whimpered into her shoulder. She spoke very fast to the bus driver in Kiswahili, pointing at my neighbour.

The man with the clipboard returned and asked me for my ticket. Checking my pockets I said 'No, you didn't give it back to me. You still have it.'

'*Hapana*, no. Come, ticket, ticket.' The man said clicking his fingers in my face.

'No. No, you didn't give it back. You still have it.'

'No ticket, you get off the bus.'

'Did anyone see me give him the ticket?' I said standing now in the aisle, but all the faces were turned away.

'You buy new ticket. Three hundred and forty shillings.'

'Did you see?' I asked the driver who shook his head. 'How about you? Did you see?' to a man beside the door.

'No English.' He replied.

'You buy new ticket. Three hundred and forty shillings.'

'No, look. I gave you the ticket.'

'No one see. You buy new ticket. Three hundred and forty shillings. It is nothing to you.' He said with a smile.

This was clearly a common routine to the tout, and I knew I'd been stupid to let the ticket out of my sight, but now I could either buy a new one, or get off the bus and go back to school.

'I did give you the ticket.' I said with as calm a voice as I could muster, and I reached into an inner pocket for my wallet. But just as I was taking out the notes I heard the woman on the steps say, '*Mzungu*, I saw you,' like a voice from heaven. 'He has your ticket in his pocket.'

'Oh yes, here it is. I remember now. Sorry, my friend. Here it is. Here it is.' The tout was full of smiles. He gave it to me and clapped me on the back as an old friend might do. Caught, but unrepentant.

I took the ticket and sat back relieved as the tout woke the man beside me. He stood up and wobbled off the bus. He did not have a ticket; he just wanted a comfortable place to sleep. The mother on the steps carrying the child settled into the seat.

'What an effort,' I said to my new neighbour. 'Thank you.'

'*Hakuna matata*,' she replied. 'No problem. Most people blame the badness on the Somali refugees, but the truth is the *mzungu* is vulnerable to anyone. It leaves a bad image with the tourists.'

107

'Actually, I'm not a tourist. I am a teacher here in Nairobi.' And we talked about the city as the bus pulled out from River Road, weaved its way through the traffic, joined Mombasa Road and began hurtling east.

Rose said she had lived with an English research student for eighteen months outside Diani on the south coast, and between the two of them they produced a child, Faith, who was sleeping now, quietly on her lap. When his visa ran out he returned to England, promising he would send for her as soon as he was settled. 'That was two years ago, and I have heard nothing.' She was back working nights outside a beachfront hotel, offering the same thing she had been offering when she met him.

By the time we reached Ntito Ndai, Rose was asleep. I closed my eyes trying to sleep too, but the volume of the *lingala* music, which the driver played full blast to keep himself awake, and the bumps of the wheels as the bus veered off and on the edge of the uneven road, were too much, and each time I dozed off I woke with a start and resumed my staring into the darkness.

I thought of Laurens Van Der Post's descriptions of Kenya in the 1940s, of Carla Jones's recollections of thirty years before and Wahome Mutahi's embarrassed descriptions of his people today. Cultures change but as we drove through the Tsavo National Park I stared up into the clear sky, spotting the Southern Cross and Orion's Belt. It was such a different sky to the one back home, where there was light pollution from the houses and smog from factories around the cities. Here the stars are clear to see, and it's a truly magnificent sight, a mystery, really, how they all came to be and even more so what lies beyond them.

I bounced in my seat, head pinging on the window, and watched the lights of the buses, the lorries and the cars on the other side of the road and began to ponder the Sacred Mysteries. There was the miracle of creation. The conception of a child and the Immaculate Conception of Our Lord. Then there was Jesus' Ascension and the Assumption of his Mother Mary and all the glorious and sorrowful mysteries celebrated in the Holy Rosary. It was a mystery too how the Christian faith had survived through the years of persecution.

The bus weaved around an overturned lorry, flames blazing from its engine, and continued coastward without any reduction in speed. It was the fourth accident we'd passed, and we still had over three hundred kilometres left to go. I wondered how this major cross-country highway had fallen into such a state of disrepair. A lot about the Kenyan way of life and how the political leadership stayed in power seemed extraordinary, although once you scratched the surface the answers were all too clear.

Greenfields' French teacher, Peter Ochieng, also tutored students at Nairobi University. He was obsessed by Kenyan politics and was sure that President Moi's time was nearing its end. Mobutu had just been overthrown in Zaire, and in Britain the Labour party had finally gained power after eighteen years in opposition. In less than a year President Moi had to hold an openly democratic election, or the World Bank would withhold promised development grants. 'His time is up,' said Peter with a grin.

During Kenya's first democratic election in March, 1988, Moi's KANU party were the only licensed party and unsurprisingly won one hundred percent of the vote. At the next election there were dozens of tiny parties which were all swamped by KANU, and any leader that looked like a threat was either paid off, and experienced a Damascus Road conversion back to KANU, or died tragically in a car accident. There is really no mystery over how corrupt governments stay in control and degrade nations, Peter told me. There is an art to political corruption, but in Africa, generally, the Big Men are so big they have nothing to fear if they get caught.

We stopped near Voi for a twenty-minute meal break and moved on again, the bus quiet this time, the cassette player having chewed the driver's tape. Now he sat hunched over his wheel humming and chewing continually on his *miraa*. He spat dollops of gloopy green phlegm and twigs, which splattered against the bus window as we bounced up onto the road again.

Rose and Faith got off in Voi, and I watched them huddled beneath a canopy, leaning against a brightly-lit building waiting for their connection to take them up into the Taita Hills. Theirs would be a long wait.

Eventually I fell asleep, but when the crunch of the wheels on the grit and rocks on the edge of the road woke me, I was filled with a huge sense of regret. The bus bumped back onto the tarmac, and the driver reached for his bottle of Coke and put a few more twigs into his mouth.

In those few minutes asleep I had been reminded of the things I'd always meant to do when I found the time, and as I thought about it regret became more real. Mostly I thought of my divorce.

It is possible to convince yourself you are doing OK, claiming that mistakes and errors are so minor they are easy to ignore and soon forget, but there are moments when they all come back, and as I rubbed my eyes and began staring into the darkness, I realised I had so many loose ends that I wished I'd never left untied.

In front of me I noticed the driver's head nodding drowsily, and I climbed from my seat to shake him and wake him up, but I was thrown sideways as the bus careered off the road, crashing through the acacia thorn and coming to a thudding halt feet short of a great baobab tree.

The driver looked down at me curled up in the stairwell where I had fallen and smiled. 'Ah, *mzungu*,' he said. He shook his head and laughed, and pulled the bus back up onto the highway.

17

The bus got into Mombasa at 3am, and I found a taxi to take me to the Hydro Hotel on Digo Road/Kenyatta Avenue junction. I slept for a few hours and then went walking in the city.

Yuri told me that Mombasa reminded him of cities in Moldavia that he had flown to at the end of their civil war. It was hot and dusty, buildings flaked away in the coastal humidity and, like Nairobi, there were street-boys, beggars and huge piles of garbage all over the place. Without the Kenyatta Conference Centre and Westernised tower blocks and offices to distract you, Mombasa seemed even more run down. The salty sea winds didn't help the buildings but, more ominous than the decay of their structures, the city looked like it was falling apart. The smell from the city dump covered the city like a cloak when the wind was in the right direction. The imposing but increasingly decrepit European buildings around Government Square contrasted with the Asian Mandry

Mosque just a couple of minutes along Mbarak Hunawy Road. Mosques are built to last, and that fact was obvious in this coastal city where everything seemed temporary, with 'maintenance' a rare word.

Along the coastal strip to the north and south of the city, new hotels clung to the shoreline, built by Western money with the profit going straight back out of the country again. Westerners, and a minority of affluent Kenyans, enjoyed their all-inclusive hotel holidays, never having to leave the compound for anything. 'Oh yeah, I had a lovely holiday in Kenya. Two weeks of beautiful sandy beaches and coral reefs. No sign of trouble and beggars are a thing of the past.' And the only Kenyans they met were the mute waiters and warriors performing pseudo-Masai tribal dances in the evening, their skin tone and facial features looking for all the world like Kikuyus.

Beach-boys patrol much of the shore, selling trinkets and drugs and trawling for a white woman, or a white man, to take them home. Around the richer hotels, huge sweaty guards held them at bay, but elsewhere they hunted in swarms.

In Uganda, Idi Amin solved his street-boy problem by rounding them all up and dropping them into the Nile. 'No street-boys – no problem.' Twenty years of President Moi's leadership has left parts of this potentially wealthy country looking like they are in the middle of a war, with prostitution and robbery practically the only profitable occupations for the younger generation.

Yuri told me he once flew some doctors to Lamu to save the life of a German tourist with sword wounds. He was lying on the beach on the peaceful Muslim island when he felt a shadow cross him. Opening his eyes he saw someone reaching down to take his backpack, which lay by his side on the sand. He reached up and called out in surprise, and the man stood back, pulled a sword from inside his walking stick and slashed the holidaymaker's arms and shoulders. Luckily there was a nurse on the beach who stopped the worst of the bleeding using a lot of towels from sunbathers, and the flying doctors were called.

It is a simple, and by no means unique, story from a place which is 'incomparable with any other Swahili town anywhere along the coast. No where else can you find such a cultural feast, with uncorrupted style of architecture and blending of traditions,' as it says in the guidebooks.

But the risks are the same all over the world, Yuri said. In Johannesburg, New York or Delhi, London, Paris or Sydney you still have to be alert and aware of the dangers. I have seen things in Cardiff on a Friday night that I would prefer to deny ever happened in my homeland's capital.

I sat under a tree on a low wall in Fort Jesus, which overlooked the Ocean, and watched men fishing from dhows, children playing in the mud and a few whites shooting up and down the shoreline on jet-skis. It was exactly like the scene described in my guidebook, and I read about how the Portuguese built the vast Fort Jesus at the end of the sixteenth century to protect their trade routes from the rampaging Turks. Apart from the jet-skis it was a scene that could have been seen any time in the last four hundred years.

The Turks finally kicked the Portuguese out in 1720, and the Arabs regained control of the coast. Mombasa was an important stronghold for seafaring trading nations, being well placed to benefit from the trade winds which, at certain times of the year blew to, and from, the larger Indian ports.

A woman sold me some bananas and smiled at my stumbling Kiswahili gratitude – '*Asante sana Mama*'. Her features were much more European than her in-land cousins, and I read about how the trade routes brought in new blood-lines as well as trinkets, beads and spices. She grinned at me shyly from beneath her lilac headscarf. It's easy to see why these coastal-women, with their mix of Somali, Arab, Ethiopian and European blood are considered some of the most beautiful in the world.

Tourists came and went with dark glasses, bright T-shirts and some of the shortest of shorts, and I thought about how crap it is to travel alone. Then an attractive, middle-aged blonde woman climbed out of a battered yellow Mitsubishi and gave the white driver a mouthful about how he should grow up a bit. She turned and walked up the path to the fort. Seeing me watching, the driver smiled and shook his head, and pulled away from the curb.

Walking along a lane back towards the middle of Mombasa, a street-girl of about eight years old caught sight of me, and picked up a tiny baby she had been playing with in a mound of garbage piled up against the ramparts of the fort. 'Hey, *mzungu*,' she called and I kept on walking. She caught up with me, grabbed my arm, and said 'Hey, *mzungu*, you help us, *mzungu*. Howareyoufine.' I pulled away, and she lifted the baby higher up onto her hip, and the baby, with running nose and flies at her eyes, began to cry.

Up at a junction I saw more street-children and knew if I gave her anything I would be swamped with more; and with nowhere to take sanctuary I tried to ignore her and increase my pace.

'Hey, *mzungu*, she not my baby,' she tried a different tack and skipped round in front of me. 'Not my baby. Come on, *mzungu*,' pointing at my crotch, 'come on, *mzungu*, I do that. I do that,' and she smiled. It wasn't the first time she had used the line. 'You take me home. I do that.' I crossed the road and escaped into a tiny Asian mini-market.

I had planned to stay a few days in Mombasa, but my bed in the Hydro had bedbugs which savaged my feet. All the other beds in the dormitory were full of English tourists who spent much of the next night at the Mombasa Florida 2000 nightclub, and when they got back they spent the dawn giggling and throwing up in plastic carrier bags. In the morning I walked to the bus depot on Abdul Nasser Road and clambered onto a *matatu* heading up the coast towards Malindi.

By Kilifi my feet were itching so badly I got off the *matatu* and followed directions to a *duka* which had a chemist shelf. I bought some lacto-calamine lotion, Piriton tablets and a large bottle of warm water. I took a couple of pills and doused my feet and ankles with the water and covered them in the lotion. The next *matatu* was so battered that the breeze coming in through rust holes in the floor cooled my feet enough to get to Gedi without going mad.

I sat in a petrol station on the side of the dusty highway and waited for an hour for the next *matatu* to take me the two miles from Gedi to Watamu and along to my destination, Mrs Simpson's guest-house. On another day I would have walked, but not with these feet, not with this coastal humidity, and not at the hottest point of the day. I felt my spirits sinking.

I'm hot, tired and a long way from home, I sulked. I'm alone, don't really know where I'm going and my feet hurt.

This country stinks, the people don't help themselves, and they are all out to get me. What wouldn't I give for a cool pint in a pub back home?

When the *matatu* finally arrived I greeted the smiling driver with a frown, grunted where I wanted to go to and climbed into the front seat next to a Masai in full warrior's dress on his way to a beachfront hotel. The Masai shook my hand and tried to chat, but I looked out of the window at the thatch shacks, the goats and the spiky casuarina trees and ignored him. He said a few words in Kiswahili to the driver, and they both laughed.

I checked in at Mrs Simpson's, took another two Piriton, bathed my feet and sank onto the bed in my chalet. Tears started gathering in the corner of my eyes, and I couldn't remember ever being so unhappy.

Soon I was weeping, with great sobs and shaking shoulders, and nothing I could do or think of could change my mood.

Mrs Simpson was the only survivor of an attempt to cross the Sahara Desert in a Morris Oxford back in the 1930s. All the others in the group died, and it was only by chance that she was found alive. She spent the rest of her life in East Africa and had run a guest-house in Watamu for more than thirty years. There was nowhere else in the world like it, as she presided over meals and welcomed one visitor after another into her home.

In the early evening I heard the other guests gather on the veranda of the main building and go into supper. Mrs Simpson asked where I was and Jonah, her number one houseboy, came out to find me.

I crawled off the bed and splashed water on my face in

the tiny cubical bathroom with geckos on the ceiling, and by the time Jonah made his ambling way to my door I felt I looked as fresh as I could, or at least not as if I had spent the afternoon in tears.

Around the dinner table I found I had nothing to say, and I couldn't concentrate on what the others were saying. I knew I was rambling like a junkie street-boy when anyone asked me a question. Between the main and dessert courses I said I was really tired, took a bottle of water from the sideboard and went back to my room. I took two more Piriton and went back to bed.

I slept well, but by the morning my mood hadn't improved. I forced myself to get up and stagger to the dining-room, where I found I had missed breakfast, so I took some fruit from a bowl in the kitchen and walked down the sandy track to the beach and sat on the coral sand looking out across the Indian Ocean. The tide was in, and there were boatfuls of bright, life-jacket-wearing tourists floating about a hundred yards out, studying the coral and wowing at the size and colour of the fish.

A woman helped a huge American man pull himself up into a boat and stripped off his buoyancy aid. 'Geeze, Mary, it just don't get no better than this,' he yelled at his chubby companion, who was wearing a bikini so skimpy it looked like two elastic bands on an egg. 'It just don't get no better than this.'

I sat on the sand, ate a mango and began to feel better. My feet didn't itch as badly as before, and as I walked along in the shallows, following a huge flatfish of some kind, I began to feel like living again. My flip-flops flapped in the water, flicking water up my back, but I didn't take them off, remembering warnings of the weaver fish waiting to spike me just below the surface of the sand, and the poisons in the coral itself that can best be neutralised with human pee. If you are scratched in an inaccessible place you have to get someone else to pee on you, which is not easy if you are travelling alone, or if you are shy.

The best way to break down the proteins in the weaver fish sting is to douse yourself in boiling water. Apparently this hurts less than the sting itself, and I thought of this classic Kenyan scenario. It's a beautiful coastal region with incredible wildlife and climate. But you take your mind off the dangers for even the briefest of moments at your peril.

As I stood on the shore rueing the damn place, I watched a fish eagle take a fish from the sea barely ninety feet from me. I turned to look at the Americans in their boat and grinned to notice they were so busy taking pictures of each other they hadn't seen the eagle as it rose and wheeled away inland.

When I walked back up to Mrs Simpson's, I came to a yellow Mitsubishi car and saw the couple who had been arguing at Fort Jesus sitting with another woman on the front veranda. They called over and asked if I was feeling better, and I joined them for a cup of tea. I hadn't recognised them over supper.

Sitting on the veranda with the sea breeze on the back of my neck, I collapsed into the comfortable chair and began to weep, shoulders shaking and hand to the forehead. 'I'm so sorry,' I said. 'I'm just so terribly tired,' and I tried to stand up.

'Hey, what's the matter?' asked Trudy. 'A problem shared...' and I said I didn't know.

'I have bites on my feet, and I feel so pathetic. So tired. Maybe it's malaria?'

'There are other symptoms for malaria. Shakes and sweats,' she said. 'Do you have them?'

'Just the tiredness.'

'Have you taken anything for your feet?' said the man sharing a chair with Trudy, the blonde woman. 'Maybe it's a side-effect of your medication?' I passed him the Piriton packet and tried to breathe deeply. 'Here it is,' he said and smiled. '"side-effects – may cause drowsiness." I'm thinking you might be having an adverse reaction to your medication, sunshine.' And as soon as he said that I began to feel better.

He passed me a bottle of water, told me to drink it all to flush my system and then to go to bed. 'Sleep is the best thing for you. We'll be here all day. See you later. Yeah?'

When I woke it was late in the afternoon, and they were still sitting on the veranda. They welcomed me over, waving away my sheepish apologies as I sat down. 'Vasco da Gama set out for the Indies from Malindi,' read Trudy. She was holding an ancient book she had taken from Mrs Simpson's library. 'And Hemingway stayed right here in Watamu while he wrote a few of his books in the fifties. I never knew that, and I'm an English teacher.'

'Tusker was his favourite beer too, apparently,' said Andy, finishing a bottle and looking at the label intently. He spun the bottle on the palm of his hand and placed it gently on the floor beside his chair. 'Stick with me, man,' he said with a wink. 'Mine is a mind of incalculably valuable information.'

Andy and Trudy had been teaching in a mission school in Sololo on the Somali border for nearly three years and were travelling with a couple of other teachers before heading

121

home. They were young, tanned and their relaxed manner quickly put me at my ease.

Andy said they had planned to live and work in Kenya longer, but the cross-border conflict had become too much, and they knew it was time to leave. There was no bravado in what he said. Basic facts simply stated, with no intention to glamorise the stories.

'There has always been cattle-rustling and banditry up north,' he said, 'but the warlords have started stealing people too, and conflict is coming right into towns.' Even the mission school had become a target.

'A friend of mine told me he was offered an AK-47 for twenty dollars when he was up that way not so long ago,' I said.

'It happened to me. When we were up at Lake Turkana last Christmas. That happened to me. Everyone has a weapon of some sort. You're no sort of man if you don't.'

'Katrina and Caroline were targeted because they were two single women living together,' said Trudy factually with no hint of adventure in her voice. 'First words, then stones and stuff. Even though she seems so little, Katrina took it well, but Caroline suffered badly. I think she has always been the target of some sort of bullying.' These were the cold bare realities of life in northern Kenya. 'When our compound got shot up for the second time, we decided enough was enough.'

'I was sitting, reading by the window in our house,' said Andy. 'Trudy was sleeping in the backroom, and the doors were locked and windows open but barred, when we heard gunshots just outside. I lay on the ground like they do in the movies and waited. After ten minutes of quiet I got up and had a look around, and I found bullet holes in the back of the chair I had been sitting in.'

'They might have been ricochets, but you have to think about what your own life is worth,' said Trudy. 'Relationships become terribly strained.' She smiled at Andy and brushed some sand from his cheek.

'It was a nice chair too,' he said and cracked open another bottle of Tusker.

'We told the mission fathers we had had enough, and they told us they were grateful and surprised we had stayed as long as we did,' said Trudy. 'It feels unfair that we were just able to leave when things got too rough for us, when everyone else had nowhere to go. We were supposed to become part of the community, not just be teachers. That is why we were there, and yet when it comes down to it, we could pack up and leave the moment we wanted to and head back home to a place with running water, reasonably honest politicians and seriously restricted gun laws.'

I asked if they knew Father Marcus, who I remembered spent the school holidays up on the border, but they didn't. Trudy said they knew a Marcus Abdi, but he had a big family with children in the school, so it couldn't be the same man if the one I knew was a Catholic priest. 'His wife made us some curtains,' she said.

We spent three days together, bird-watching in the mangrove swamps, looking for elephants in the Arabuko Sokoke forest and getting drunk in the evenings on sweet coconut-milk beer that Caroline industriously collected by tapping green coconuts and fermenting the milk in the sun. The following mornings we crawled around hungover and swearing we'd never touch the stuff again, but by evening we'd be checking turtles nests along the high-tide line, with milk beer in one hand and papayas from a tree in the other.

'Will you be sad to leave?' I asked Andy, as we sat on the sand hoping we'd be there to see the turtle eggs hatch and watch the babies fight their way down the sand to the ocean.

'Sad? Of course,' he said, 'but all good things come to an end. It's been an amazing experience and we've seen things we'd never see had we stayed in East Anglia.' They'd seen everything, from the sun setting right into the crater of Mount Kilimanjaro from a campsite in Tsavo, to the 'Kenyan Handshake' in one of Nairobi's nightclubs. 'But life goes on. Just somewhere else that's all.'

'Best bits?'

'We fed giraffes by hand at the Giraffe Park in Nairobi and petted baby elephants in the Animal Orphanage,' said Caroline. She was a big lady with a tiny, almost comical, voice. 'We had a picnic in the shadow of the Ngong Hills, beneath the thorn trees at Karen Blixen's House in Karen Village.'

'Swimming with the fish right here amongst the coral heads was pretty amazing,' Katrina added softly. She and Caroline had been through so much. I couldn't help but think that heading home would be an anticlimax for them, after the simple tension of living they had experienced. They were an odd couple; with Caroline so big and Katrina frail and quiet, but if I felt closer to Sally, Ron and Geraldine after our shared experiences up in the Rift Valley, our friendship was nothing compared to what they had been through.

'The colours and sounds of the flamingos on Lake Bogoria as the sun came up over the hill is the best thing for me,' I said, and described how we had stood in silent admiration as the fish eagle killed a flamingo and was then forced from its prey by the pair of ugly marabou storks.

'And the people,' said Trudy. 'We've made so many friendships. Real friendships,' and the others sighed their agreement.

We went snorkelling over the reef twice a day and walked along the shore as a group late in the evening. The lights from the beachfront hotels and tinny *Lingala* music contrasted with the millpond ocean and clear southern skies.

We cycled up to Gedi and walked round some ancient Arab ruins, and at the Kipepeo Butterfly Farm nearby, Jayne, a pretty Irish girl, showed us round explaining how it was run as a conservation project to preserve the Arabuko Sokoke Forest.

'We buy pupae off farmers living in the forest at one dollar each and send them off to butterfly centres around the world,' Jayne said. 'It gives the farmers an income and they can see that they get more and healthier butterflies when the forest is healthy round them. It's in their interests to keep it strong and standing.' And the project was working. Illegal felling had diminished, poaching seemed to be decreasing and the number of forest-dwelling farmers who wanted to be part of the programme was on the increase.

The forest is the only place in the world that the golden-rumped elephant shrew is found, and it is in great danger of extinction. It is distantly related to aardvarks and elephants, rock hyraxes and sea cows and is a strange-looking animal. They practice facultative monogamy, so they pair for life, but they will mate with a 'widowed' animal, which has not yet found a new mate.

We stood in their butterfly cage with luminescent, blue-spotted charaxes and the golden, violet and black coloured gold-banded foresters landing delicately on our faces and hands. Jayne pointed out the rarest of the butterflies, saying how much they were worth on the international market. 'The foresters are the most common forest butterfly. They fly close to the ground and are easy to see on forest walks.'

'We teach the farmers to find eggs on leaves, train them how to handle and feed caterpillars, matching plants to creatures, and when to bring the pupae in to us for sale. All the profits are invested back in the communities,' she said. 'If we can encourage people to value the forest, they will do their best not to damage it. Then other animals like the elephant shrew have more chance to survive.'

'From profits made from the project we were able to fund huge rainwater tanks in a couple of villages, to help the farmers keep their equipment clean and make life easier.' Her face lit up and eyes sparkled when she smiled, like a small child squinting into the sun.

'In the past the women of the villages had to walk miles each day to collect water from boreholes in other villages, while the men sat outside their houses, gambled and smoked cigarettes.'

'This worked well for a while, until the village elders set up their *mancala* boards near the water tanks, put a lock on the tap and began charging their women for the water.' And so the women reverted to putting their five-litre jerrycans back on their heads and walking the same paths to the public boreholes that their mothers had done. 'We tried to talk to the elders about it, but they made it clear it was a local issue, and we shouldn't try to play the colonial with them. You really can't win,' she shrugged.

Jayne lived in a house on the shoreline, and motorcycled

to work each day weaving round the loose goats and children on the roads and piles of elephant crap in the forest. It was a good place to live, she said, but thought she might try New Zealand when her contract ran out in the spring.

That evening Andy, Trudy, Caroline, Katrina and I ate in an open-fronted restaurant on the roadside in Watamu, feasting on goat roasted on a spit in front of us and dollops of a maize and bean stodge with *suma-wiki*. Eating like Kenyans, we became a great attraction to the children who called to us from outside.

A woman came over from the pub on the roadside, hearing there were white men here, and she shooed the children away. Her smile faded when she saw white women sitting with us, her hope of a night at 'white-rates' disappearing, and she sat at a nearby table glowering.

'Why didn't you ask Jayne to come with us tonight?' Caroline asked me with a smile. 'She was nice.'

Andy gave me a wink. 'Yeah, think about it. If you play your cards right, you could have one life in the big city and a lovely girlfriend down here in this coastal paradise to run to on the weekends. Who could want for more?'

I said I thought every visitor would try to crack onto her and she'd be fed up with offers. 'I bet she has a boyfriend somewhere anyway.'

'Well, I reckon she was up for it,' said Andy, 'and it's a man's duty at least to try!' He smiled at Trudy's glare. 'Women love being asked out,' he grinned.

In the dark of that restaurant, with flies attacking the uncooked meat on the back shelf, giggling children sitting in the dust on the roadside and Somali prostitutes watching from nearby tables, I told them about my divorce. It was the first time I had spoken about it to anyone, and I explained why I felt it was best to be alone for a while.

The next morning Jayne ran her motorcycle into a stray goat and broke her leg. She spent one night at the hospital in Malindi, and then Mrs Simpson sent Jonah to bring her back to stay at the guest-house. 'She will only get an infection in there,' Mrs Simpson said, 'and we can take care of her as well here as anyone anywhere else.'

The following day at dawn her boyfriend, Jake, turned up having taken the night bus from Machakos, where he had a job managing a reforestation project. He spent the next day trying to pacify both the dead goat's owners, who demanded the value of a prize cow for their mangy beast, and the local police who threatened to charge her with dangerous driving. A little *chai* passed hands each way and all charges were dropped.

I walked up the path from the beach the next morning, and found Andy loading his yellow car before he, Trudy, Caroline and Katrina headed north to Lamu. 'Travelling alone is the easy way. There are no compromises to be made,' he said. The north section of the B8 and C112 were renowned for bandits, and they planned to link up with a police-escorted convoy starting in Malindi. 'It's like in life as a whole. Generally much easier alone, but it is never really as satisfying.' He said he would call me in Nairobi as they headed back home, but I doubted that he would.

In the afternoon I caught a *matatu* back to Mombasa and booked a ticket on the night train back to Nairobi.

That evening I sat in the train's dining-car writing postcards and staring into the darkness, imagining myself as Laurens van der Post or Ernest Hemingway, Karen Blixen or even Mrs Simpson trundling along these same lines over fifty years before. Back then the carriages would have been sparkling and new, the food as good as in any European hotel, and you could leave your carriage door unlocked at night with little fear of robbery.

It had been a good break, but I was looking forward to getting back to Nairobi, and to my little home. It was strange to think of Nairobi as home, but that was how I had begun to think of it, and I smiled. Kenya gets to you. It gets under your skin and you come to love the place. It will give you a scare – like my bus ride to the coast – and then reward you with the beauty of the reef, horrify you at the offers of the street-children and then introduce you to Mrs Simpson with her resilience and generosity. I thought of myself in forty years time, and whether I would have anything like the stories to tell that Mrs Simpson had. Somehow I doubted it.

A group at the next table were discussing their tours so far. A black American couple said they had been attacked down on Nairobi's River Road on their first day in Kenya. They were walking back to the Parkside Hotel from the Blue Market in the early evening, took a wrong turn and found themselves where they really did not want to be. They lost their souvenirs, three hundred dollars and, most importantly, their naïvety.

'I was looking forward to coming,' said the husband. 'Getting back to our ancestral home. But now the more I see I think, thank God for slavery. Thank God for getting my people out from this place.'

'Our ancestors went through hell,' his wife continued, 'but if they'd stayed here we could only dream of the lives that we have now in Georgia.'

'If we had ever even heard of Georgia,' said her husband. 'Let alone the good ol' US of A.'

The Canadian sitting with them said she had been pickpocketed on Nyali Beach and had lost all her money. The Australian sitting opposite me said he had been robbed while he slept on the train on the way from Kisumu down to Nairobi; he woke to find his bag slashed open and his cameras gone.

'Everyone I have met has been robbed at one time or another,' he said. 'Some include violence, but most sneakily by pickpockets or through scams at travel agencies or in hotels. That sort of thing,' he said. 'Every guide book should start with the line "Best watch your back at all times."'

I sat opposite Curley, who was an Australian working for an Aid Agency building water tanks for Somali refugees. He admitted he had a negative experience here. 'The national dependency on overseas aid and external development policy means the Kenyan will always think of the non-Kenyan as a meal ticket.'

'This country is great, and potentially greater, but with the poverty and sickness many of the people will rob you just to have enough to eat,' he said. 'I am sure most thieves regret the need for their thieving just as much as the person they steal from.'

And I think he was probably right.

Back in Nairobi I stood with a group of people at the side of the road waiting to cross the madness of Haile Selassie Avenue, and I was pleased to be back. The holiday had done me good, and I closed my eyes, lifted my bag higher over my shoulder and raised my face up to enjoy the warmth of the morning sun.

The road was as full as ever with the *matatus* and cars jockeying for position on the potholed circuit. One by one people fled across the road, knowing their jobs depended on it, and with ballerina skips or head-down charges they made it to the other side. Amazingly none were smashed to a pulp.

There were always a lot of people on Haile Selassie Avenue in the mornings, and they often jostle or nudge you if you are not walking at the same rate and direction as everyone else, but sometimes a push is quite deliberate, and as I enjoyed the sun on my cheeks, I felt someone grab my rucksack and shove me from behind, and I stumbled out into the road in front of a speeding bus and had to keep running just to stay alive.

When I arrived at the other side I was rucksack-less and fuming. I waited for the next break in the traffic and crossed the road again, but I knew that even if I was quick as Kip Keino my bag and attacker would be gone.

I cursed and swore, standing there on the dust-coated cracked pavement. Why me, for God's sake, and I felt for my money belt round my waist to be sure that this at least was where it should be.

All my clothes were gone. My walking boots, camera, the rolls of film, diary and the trinkets and junk that I haggled from the beach-boys in Watamu. All were gone. But I still had my passport, a small amount of money in my pocket, and thirty postcards that needed posting. And I still had my life. But for God's sake why the bloody hell does this sort of thing have to happen?

I stomped up Haile Selassie Avenue, starting to walk back to Greenfields scowling at everyone I passed. I ignored an old man with milky eyes who wanted money, told a couple of glued-up street-boys to fuck off when they started following me, and I nearly clobbered a tout who tried to coerce me on to his *matatu*.

I stopped in a soda shop and bought a cold Stoney and tried to calm down. 'You are a thief. You are a thief, and I know you,' I found myself thinking about everyone that passed, stopped and looked at this strange big *mzungu* with fury in his eyes. 'I know you are no different, and I know you are just waiting for your moment.'

As I handed back the soda bottle and started on up the road, I heard someone hissing at me. Kenyans '*pssst*' each other to attract attention, so I ignored it and kept on walking, with my head down and with rounded shoulders. I know that most Kenyans only earn about a hundred shillings a day, but why did they have to steal *my* bag? 'Why do they expect me to give them more all the time?'

The '*pssst*' followed me and I glanced round to see an old man staggering up the road behind me. 'Another bloody beggar,' I said under my breath and increased my pace.

The old man fell behind, but as I waited to cross Uhuru Highway, he caught up and thrust a ten-shilling note into my hand.

'You drop this when you buy soda,' he wheezed through a gummy grin. Then, as I stood there, open-mouthed and humbled, he turned and hobbled his way back down Haile Selassie Avenue again.

18

The next term passed quietly as Mr Rivers' involvement in the school decreased. He and I went to the Nairobi Club for cricket practice each Friday evening, and with the rains gone the club started playing friendly matches on Saturdays.

National League games take place on Sundays, with the ten Asian-owned clubs playing each other twice, and then once more again in the Kenyatta Cup. I started playing friendly cricket for the Nairobi Club with Yuri, David Brown and a few other Europeans and Antipodeans, and I played occasional games in the National League for Ruaraka Sports Club and was the only white man in the competition.

Playing friendly games at the Nairobi Club was fun, with all the petty-politics and dynamics of every small club back in the UK. You also had the novelty of games being halted, fielders diving to the ground when swarms of killer bees passed overhead, occasional gunshots echoing up from Uhuru

Park, and sacred ibis stalking round in the outfield where seagulls would be, back home.

Yuri and I opened the bowling, charging in full pace before the day got too hot, and then the spinners took over and got smashed miles as the pitch dried and died for the bowlers. The outfield developed so many crevasses after the rain that fielding in the deep was sometimes a hazard. Taking high catches out of the cloudless skies proved more difficult than I had imagined.

On Friday evenings, after practice, everyone sat in the pavilion bar, either in the deep leather armchairs or on hard wooden stools up by the bar. The retired players arrived at six and, drinking gin and whisky, they would be slurring over their often-told tales by the time practice was over and we arrived.

David Brown, the junior from the High Commission, introduced me to one of his superiors, Douglas Slater, who talked so softly and with such a lilting voice that it was impossible to concentrate on what he was saying. His words were like a lullaby, and you could see people drifting off to sleep as he burbled away. It was a relief that he ended most of his sentences with a three-note laugh, which woke you up to the state of the conversation.

Being the High Commission's representative for Kilimani District, Mr Rivers was my first port of call, should I have any major problems in Kenya, or if a civil war was to suddenly break out. Douglas Slater was his next in line. 'Ever since *Mau Mau* the High Commission has been pretty keen on worst-case-scenario exit strategies,' David told me. 'And things kick off pretty quick in Africa. If you go away for the weekend, let someone know where you are going, and be sure to keep a foot in at the club.'

The international agencies like UNICEF and World Vision took care of their own staff, and the British High Commission had a record of all British citizens registered in Kenya, keeping an up-to-date evacuation plan for real emergencies.

'There is a chance that things will turn nasty during next year's elections,' sang Douglas, 'so we need to be ready. Hopefully nothing will happen, but who knows,' he giggled.

'Probably a convoy to Uganda or to the coast,' said Yuri when I asked him what he thought could happen if there was trouble. 'The major airports will close, so once a flight leaves it will be tough to come back and ferry others out, and there is no oil here, so the Americans are unlikely to come charging in to save the country.'

'If Rwanda is anything to go by, there will be armed gangs on the major roads, no electricity, restricted fuel supply, and the country will be split along tribal lines depending on who is leading the trouble. It would be pretty fucked actually.'

'It could be a coup like in 1992, when the air force tried to oust President Moi,' said Glen Stevens, the Kiwi missionary who wanted me to do some coaching in the slums. He was a good cricketer himself, but already ran football and volleyball clubs in Kawongware, so it made sense to get someone else to start cricket.

'Or if Moi thinks he is going to lose the election,' said Yuri, 'then he might fund disturbances himself to displace people in opposition areas where they are registered to vote. They can't vote anywhere else, and he gets in again easily.'

'You shouldn't really talk like that, Yuri,' said David smiling. 'It's scaring our young Welshman here, and it is close to sedition to suggest the President might do anything so low.

Best just to keep your eyes and ears open, though. Be prepared and wait and see what happens.'

So I tried to spend a lot of time at the Nairobi Club, to become well known and get in on all the information loops.

'Your father is a landowner, I hear,' said Colonel Birkin-Rowley, a grandly whiskered old man, as we poured ourselves tea from a huge urn in the club's main drawing room.

'No, he is a farmer, but we don't own the farm,' I told him. 'We are tenant farmers.'

'Oh, I say,' he said and edged away, frowning. 'Jolly strange chap,' he mumbled, shaking his head as he helped himself to some Jammy Dodgers.

Copies of the London *Times* and the *Telegraph*, a couple of days old, and English magazines from the week before, were scattered around on a huge oak table at the far end of the room, while the log fire took up much of the other end. This was lit by the fire-boy every evening at six, burning massive pieces of knotted wood no matter how hot it was outside.

'It's a tradition,' said Mr Rivers, 'as is so much else at the club. You will get used to it in no time. It is reassuring to be able to turn off Haile Selassie and find yourself in a London gentleman's club which hasn't changed in fifty years.'

But a farmer's son from the Teifi Valley doesn't fit too well into the big leather-bound armchairs in the men-only drawing room, with the portraits of the Queen and President Moi looking down from the end walls and pictures of former club presidents watching suspiciously from the side. They know I am a fraud and don't have the breeding to be here. Their glares say I should be carrying a tray of gin, or clearing the old-school bread and butter pudding bowls from the tables in the dining-room – anything but sitting here with a neatly dressed Kenyan appearing silently at my shoulder, wondering if I would like a drink and whether he should put it on my tab. A white face goes a long way in Kenya.

So I drank in the pavilion on Fridays and played every game I could. I ran around the sand hockey pitch when it was too wet and slippery to run on the grass at Greenfields, but I stayed away from the main club. When I did go out in the evening, it was usually with Yuri and Anya, and we'd go to the Gedd Inn in Westlands or drive out along the Limuru Road to play pool at a bar out there. Sometimes the ex-pat Greenfields staff would go en-masse to the Carnivore restaurant and nightclub down on Langatta Road, where Sally always got drunk and Erica usually got lucky.

The Carnivore restaurant offered wild game steaks delivered to your table by sweating waiters carrying spitting chunks of zebra, antelope and wildebeest, pork, mutton and goat on great metal spears. After eating too much we'd go drinking and dancing in the nightclub, which was full of whites, along with a few wealthy Asians and Africans, and we all laughed loudly and forgot about where we were.

We were no longer in Kenya when we were in the Carnivore's nightclub. We drank imported bottled beer and danced to Western tunes far from thoughts of street-boys, poverty and President-induced riots.

But driving home at the end of the evening in one of the Greenfields minibuses brought us back to reality with a thud. With no enforceable drink-driving laws, Langatta Road became a speedway and, with the potholes and flooding on Mbagathi Way, as well as people running between the Madaraka and Kibera Highrise estates, you had to be alert.

Fires in oil drums on the roadside warmed street-dwellers, beggars and fifth-grade prostitutes so obviously riddled with disease that their only hope of finding work was to hide in the darkest places and feed off the most desolate of men.

Cardboard boxes on the road might contain breeze-blocks, and behind every wall might lurk a gang ready to rob you and your crashed vehicle. No one stopped at traffic lights, and everyone kept moving at roundabouts. Don't stop at crashes, and beep your horn as you arrive at your compound. Only unlock the car doors once you are safely in, and the *askaris* have locked the gate behind you.

Even with these rules of the road, trips back from the Carnivore were fun, dropping Geraldine and Ron at their flat on State House Road, next Erica, her latest boyfriend, and her housemates up in Westlands, and then sweeping up Riverside Drive and Mandera Road to drop a couple of teachers from Kenton College back in their school's compound in Kileleshwa. Finally back along Argwings Kodhek, where the drains were so full of sand that any rain filled the road, and we splashed along like we were heading up a river bed.

Sally was usually sick out of the window as we waited to enter the Greenfields compound, and she paid thirty shillings to any *askari* who would clean it off the side of the van before her uncle found out.

In the Carnivore a beer cost one hundred shillings. Back out in Kenya, an *askari* earned that at the end of a twelve-hour night shift, so Sally's thirty shillings went a long way.

19

I never liked teaching very much. At training college few of us could honestly say we did. We used teaching sports as a way to be kids in an adult world. After leaving school we figured that, if we weren't good enough to be professional players, the next best thing was to teach. We imagined ourselves running around in the sun or in a warm gym a few hours a day and then enjoying the long holidays. What could be more fun than that?

'If you don't respect what you are doing to fill your days, how can you respect yourself?' my father asked me, as I helped him in the milking parlour one evening during the Christmas holiday. I'd told him about my first, not very successful, term of teaching practice.

'But I don't live to work,' I replied with youthful arrogance. 'I work to live,' and we both knew what I meant – I could use it to get away from here. I didn't want to get stuck on the farm like him and Mum. He smiled and shook his head. 'It's a bigger world than it used to be, and there are more choices.'

'Make sure you make the right ones,' he said. Then a cow squirted diarrhoea over my back and he laughed. 'When you realise you've made a wrong one, do have the courage to do something about it.'

The next term I met Laura, and any thoughts I might have had of dropping out and going back to the farm quickly faded. Her family never would have tolerated her dating a college drop-out. It was bad enough that I was Catholic.

Eventually I became proud to be a teacher, of educating young people and sharing their experience of learning, watching them achieve things they knew for a fact they couldn't possibly do before you showed them how to, or gave them the courage to try.

In my first school, I introduced one girl to cricket, and she went on to play county standard for Hertfordshire as a left-arm spinner. She used to write me letters about how well she had done, and although her spelling never improved, it made me proud that through sport she had managed to find some self-respect, dignity and strength.

Some of the lads at Greenfields were quite good cricketers, and I took one of them, Rikesh Patel, to a national trial for a youth tour of South Africa. He bowled with a lovely loop, and with coaching he began second-guessing the batsmen, confusing them with variety, and by watching the batsman's footwork he became a fine spin bowler. But he was so small they didn't take him seriously at the trial, and he never made the tour. The selectors came from several of the main clubs and were more interested in getting their own youngsters into the touring party than actually picking the best players. They sat in the bar drinking whiskey and ginger and eating *bajias*, missing some top quality youth cricket from a group of young Africans who took a turn to bat and bowl after the Asians had had their turns and gone off for a cold soda. These boys had learnt to play cricket with a stick and maize cobs on the potholed tracks of their estates around the Sir Ali Muslim Sports Club. With natural talent and athleticism, many hoped cricket would help them find a better life and give them money to support their extended families. They looked far more like sportsmen than the majority of the chubby, privileged Asian children ever would.

I stood beside an African ex-captain of the national team who smiled and shrugged when I commented on how good they were. 'It has always been this way,' he said and turned away. I met him a few times, and he never said much. What he did say was worth listening to, but he seemed isolated in his speech, and his voice quickly faded into the security of silence. Later he moved to Jinja and became the Ugandan Cricket Association's Development Officer.

Uganda's gain was Kenya's loss, but ten years later, after the Kenyan government sacked the entire Kenyan Cricket Association's committee for a multitude of reasons and replaced it with a new organization named Cricket Kenya, he came back with the near-impossible role of Chief Executive Officer, joining in the unenviable task of getting Kenyan cricket back on track.

I started coaching in the Kawongware slum on Nairobi's west side with Glen Stevens, the missionary from New Zealand, who was also a regular at the Nairobi Club. Kawongware was a massive area where people lived in tin shacks, where there was no electricity, and water was collected from a tap near the road a little way up from the central dump.

The first three times I visited it was impossible to get to the area where we were due to play cricket, because the city council officers had sent their team to dig out the dump. But as no one had told them to take the refuse away, they left it in a rotting, stinking mess which covered the road, making it impassable.

Glen went to the council offices daily to complain, and it was only after he managed to get Nairobi's bishop to come with him that he got any action. It would have been different had he been willing to sprinkle a little *chai* around, but this was not the way his mission was run. He had never given or taken a bribe, and he was not prepared to start now.

'At least this didn't happen during the rains,' he told me, as we finally made it to the cricket area. He was a short, wiry man, who seemed much bigger than he was. He looked you in the eye when he spoke and was like a terrier when he was faced with a problem. I never knew him to back off when he was faced with a problem, and I envied his patience. 'We have enough sickness here as it is,' he said, 'but with that running into houses, we'd be sure to end up with cholera or typhoid.'

We walked past pigs and goats grazing on the tufts of grass growing out from the walls of the huts, and hopped over the drainage channels through the settlement. There was foul water and shit floating along in the bottoms, but by then I was used to the sweet pungent smell of it and leapt after Glen without thinking.

Across the wider channels men often sat beside a plank and charged people three shillings to cross. The alternative was to try to leap over the ditch and risk the humiliation of slipping on the side and falling in. This was a public service, Glen told me. The same guy sat there from dawn to dusk guaranteeing a strong and safe crossing like a ferryman over a river. If he ever left the plank, it would be taken and used for firewood or to build a house. After dark he went home, taking his plank with him, and you were on your own, but only a fool or a thug would be around here after dark, he told me.

When the South African cricketer Jonty Rhodes ran a coaching session in Soweto, South Africa, over a thousand children turned up to take part. In Kawongware I had one hundred and sixty. Me, Glen, four bats, two balls and one hundred and sixty kids running after every ball hit anywhere.

It was chaos, but it was also the most fun coaching I have ever had. With the grazing goats and circling black kites, tall, skinny acacia trees surrounding us and the adults sitting on the hill behind us laughing and wondering out loud, 'What is this cricket?' it was a surreal scene. The barefoot, raggedy children bowled with left arm high and sideways-on actions like Allan Donald, even though I only demonstrated it twice. The batters smashed the balls miles, and the fielders took amazing catches, leaping into thorn bushes and over sewage-culverts, anything to take a catch and get the next chance to bat.

After years of throwing stones at crows and goats grazing where they shouldn't, tiny children threw the tennis balls forty yards with flat throws to my hands, and when we packed up exhausted after the session, Glen and I were like Pied Pipers as we walked back to the school where his car was parked. The 'Mzungu, mzungu,' chant followed us all the way back like a swarm of bees, and the goats looked up startled and ran to the end of their ropes.

'*Asante sana*, Glen,' said Gerald, the mission school's head teacher, and he bowed as he shook my hand. In Kawongware they call Glen *Mtw wa watu* – Man of the People – which is a huge compliment, especially for a white man. They talked for a few minutes in Kiswahili about some money that had gone missing from savings for the street-boys' trip to Mount Kenya. The children gathered round me, touching my skin and hair, the '*Mzungu, mzungu*' changing to '*Howareyoufine*' to add a bit of variety.

As Glen drove the car back up the track away from the school, the children ran after us shouting, and the shopkeepers in the *dukas* lining the road looked around bemused. I laughed, but Glen frowned and talked about the street-boy rehabilitation program which was his mission's main focal point.

'For every child that is saved there are a thousand who don't make it,' he said. 'So many come so far, but don't have the strength to stay with the program and they end up back on the street.' Beggars can make a good living in Kenya, and thugs an even better one. There are stories of politicians and Big Men collecting boys off the street to run errands and to do 'personal favours' for serious money. One way of curing yourself of Aids, the story goes, is to sleep with a virgin, and tiny street-children were picked up, raped and infected by grown men. There were rumours of government ministers practising this trade. Desperate fathers were known to have raped their own newborn babies.

Glen's program was small, but it was honest and sincere, and the skills learnt – making postcards and carvings and learning English, Maths and Carpentry, would last the young people a lifetime. 'Our mission father in Auckland told me there would be frustrations, but that if we even touch the life of one child and make that better, then we should be satisfied. It is hard, though, and there is always so much to do.'

We left the slum and turned on to Gitanga Road. Passing Valley Arcade, Glen slowed the vehicle and pointed out two lads sitting on the grass surrounded by some white people who took photographs and studied the icons they had carved. 'They were two of our boys,' he smiled. 'With us for three years, then got fed up and went solo. The mission buys all the work that our youngsters make, and then we sell it in registered places. These guys got fed up with their art being thought of as only good enough for sale through a charitable outlet. Brendan came to me and said he appreciated the profit from these sales went back into the mission. He said that they would give money to support us when they could, but he and Alfred wanted their work to be compared on a level with other craftsmen and not as charity, and that was that.'

We watched as the icons ended up in the tourist's luggage, and the shillings ended up in Brendan's pocket.

'Donald Otieno brought these lads to the mission years ago,' he said softly. 'They were glue-dependant and Alfred was almost blind.'

'You should be pleased, Glen,' I said. 'You've made a difference to them for sure.'

20

I spent most of my holidays in Nairobi coaching and playing cricket, and while many of the Greenfields European staff flew home, and the Kenyans headed off to their home-places up country, I stayed in my little bedsit. Glen gave me a lift into the slums four days a week, so I was in Kawongware on Tuesdays and Wednesdays and in Mukuru to the south-east of the city on Mondays and Fridays. The rest of the time I walked around Nairobi and took trips out of the city to Karen Village, the giraffe farm and the animal sanctuary, or I borrowed one of Greenfields' vehicles and crawled around Nairobi National Park. I sat on a bench on Hyrax Hill watching the small hairy rock hyraxes scuttling around near my feet. They looked like large guinea-pigs but, in some strange evolutionary twist, are more closely related to elephants. They made pleasant companions as I finally found the time to finish *Tales from a Fragile Continent* and histories of Nairobi.

Nairobi is a capital city that developed from a railway depot midway along the Mombasa-Entebbe Railway, paid for by British money and built by the sweat and lives of labouring Indian 'coolies'. It is high enough to be malaria-free and cooler than the Great Rift Valley to the west or the Athi Plains which swept out eastwards. The Masai called it *Ewasso Nairobi* – Place of Cool Water – and the British named it the 'City in the Sun'. The soil suited their gardens, and the seasons reminded them of home, so the British settlers thought they had landed in heaven.

From the smart hills of Muthaiga, to Happy Valley in the Central Highlands, the European settlers led privileged lives and had wild times. With the sweep of a general's pen across a map of East Africa, Uganda, Tanzania, Somalia and Kenya were created, and the different tribes in each of these 'countries' became one nation. The Luo, Kikuyu, Masai, the gentle Giriama people on the coast, and around forty other tribes who had little in common, became Kenyans.

Eventually Kenya developed into what it is today – the flawed but magnificent jewel of East Africa, with enough good agricultural land to be self-sufficient in food, and a tourism industry to compete with any in the world.

Kenya's potential is limitless, but with no word in Kiswahili for 'maintenance' and the tradition of overseas aid handouts and officials creaming off *chai* at every level, Kenya is full of half-finished, externally-funded projects. They are abandoned, as international agencies and charities invest and then pull out regretfully when they see their money being frittered away. When Clare Short, the then Secretary of State for International Development, visited Kenya in 1997, President Moi told her it was Britain's duty to always support

Kenya as a parent has a duty to support a child. Self-sufficiency and true freedom for the nation were never Moi's top priority.

Day-to-day living is the same in Kenya as everywhere else. It is filled with the struggle to find shelter, feed the family and make it through until morning. There are different ways of going about it in different countries and cultures, but the goal is still the same. Simply food and shelter. The same as it ever was.

If you can build a house between dusk and dawn and have a fire in the grate with smoke rising before the sun does, you have squatter's rights, but no actual deeds to property. It gives you shelter but no security, which is better than nothing.

The slums filled up with people moving in from rural areas, coming to the city in search of work and the hope of a better life. The *El Niño* rains flooded fields and villages, harvests and hopes, and despair replaced pride and optimism.

Men pulled carts along the roadside, ten miles a day, knowing for sure that life would be better in the cities, and buses streamed into Nairobi, Kisumu, Eldoret and Mombasa. *Matatus* arrived with lives tied up in hessian sacks strapped to the roof and sides, as families sat silently inside, never having been so far from their home-places before.

One day an old man turned up at Father Matthew's church-house in the middle of the Mukuru slum, dazed and disorientated. He was a Kikuyu from Meru two hundred miles to the north, and his son was a truck driver. His son had invited him to go on a trip with him, taking coffee to the coast, and had let him out on the roadside for a pee at the Athi River Junction. He then drove off, leaving his father stranded. The old man waited a day and a half for his son to return, and then he started walking. He didn't know where he was walking to, he was just walking, and it was luck that brought him to the mission. Luck, or the hand of God, and Father Matthew gave him a bed and a hot meal and listened to him mumble and cry long into the night. The next day the old man died.

Like every other country in sub-Saharan Africa, Kenya's debt to the international community included repaying loans at impossible rates. This led to subsistence farmers being forced off land so that it could be used to grow expensive cash crops for export to the Western world, with the income used solely to service the debt. This reduced the quantity of food produced locally, leading to hunger and starvation, and so more aid was needed, bringing with it increased debt, the need for cash crops, and the everlasting cycle of poverty and hunger.

The incomers included many Aids-orphans and refugees from Somalia, Ethiopia and the tribal conflict in northern Kenya, and great areas of the slums used Somali as the primary tongue. Many people arrived with a bundle of possessions balanced on their heads, or slung over their shoulders, having walked five hundred miles to the perceived security of the city.

Father Matthew's church and mission station was overwhelmed with children dumped on the steps, as tearful women walked away from their offspring, believing they had more hope there than anywhere else.

Others cobbled bent tin and cracked branches together as they tried to create shelter for themselves and their families. Shelter is everything, and as the rain came down disputes broke out over who owned each and every piece of corrugated-tin roofing. Priests and nuns ran to prevent anger boiling over into a fight. 'Think of Jesus. These are the trials that are sent to test us.' And usually the men shook hands, shamefaced, and returned to work side by side, building rows of houses rather than detached ones, so halving the materials needed.

Women collected water and boiled it for three hours, but still the disease came. Dysentery killed the weak, the young and the old, while the depressed sought the warmth of prostitutes and potato wine. Others wandered off, leaving families, security and loved ones. There must be something better somewhere else.

Flies gathered in the warm and the wet, and exposed food became piles of wriggling maggots in days. There was typhoid, but at least Nairobi was too high for malaria.

The mission station had pit latrines. They were the first things built after the church, and they offered a demonstration of cleanliness and encouraged others to think about hygiene and build their own. Every three weeks the mission paid private contractors to come to the mission house with huge tankers to suck out the latrines and dispose of the waste elsewhere. Often it ended up in Athi River, which was already stinking with pollution from the rubber factory and tannery.

And in the mission station the nursing rooms were filled with nuns working double shifts and, when they could, sleeping fully-clothed on pews in the chapel. Father Matthew Kali prayed as he changed the nappies of squitting children and refilled plastic beakers of cold boiled water. 'You must drink,' he said, and blessed the sweating form curled up in a blanket on the earthen floor.

One time, Glen Stevens didn't go home for six days. He

used his Subaru estate car to ferry building materials around until the earth became so loose that it sank up to its axles and it had to be abandoned where it sat. Then he set up a pole travois and dragged equipment behind him. He, too, slept in the chapel, and he ate with the nuns. His clothes stiffened with the layers of ingrained dirt, and his face became bearded for the first time since he was a teenager, but he was positive and bright and supported Father Matthew the best a white man could. Support can never be complete when you are a white man. Not when you can leave at any time and head up the road to a hot bath, a cold beer and a good meal.

Father Matthew Kali was a Luo from Western Province. He was educated in a missionary school pre-*Mau Mau* and studied at Edmund Hall in Oxford shortly after his friend Jomo Kenyatta had been at the university. Rather than join the New Kenyan Elite after independence, Matthew chose to live and work in the slums already forming around Nairobi. Once every two years he toured Europe and America on fund-raising trips, and his was one of few charities that published audited accounts unclouded by any misunderstanding or deviousness.

Under big umbrellas Glen and Father Matthew walked the shanties together in the evenings, consoling families and offering support where they could. Father Matthew prayed with groups, while Glen discussed practicalities of getting hold of more building materials that weren't stolen.

Four days after Greenfields' new head teacher, Mark Peters, arrived in Kenya he drove me down to the mission in the largest of Greenfields' 4x4s. He had had his fill of unpacking and decorating and needed a change, he told me.

So, after phoning Glen's wife to see what they might need, we filled up the back of the truck with sacks of maize-flour and fruit at the Uchumi supermarket on Ngong Road and headed off to Mukuru.

It was early afternoon and the earth steamed as the heat of the sun evaporated the night's rain. Glen was sitting on his haunches with a group of orphans near the chapel as we climbed out of the truck and walked towards him. He was telling them the story of Noah and trying to explain how *El Niño* fitted into God's promise that he would never send another flood.

There were large groups of people milling around the gate, some carrying children and others leading the elderly by the hand. Women waited with battered jerrycans and jars near the water-tap, and men sat smoking on the roadside, defeated by the heat and the wet and the flies which gathered and fed at the damp in the corners of their tired sunken eyes. Flies swarmed round the overflowing drainage channels, the sides of which had caved in with the rain, and the liquid faeces and foul water slopped around your feet.

'Your wife was wondering where you were,' I said to Glen with a cautious grin. 'She sent us down with some food.'

I raised the tarpaulin on the flatbed back of the 4x4 and lifted out a sack of maize-flour and passed it to Glen. 'She's a good woman, that wife of mine,' he said, but he was too tired to carry the sack. He leant against the side of the vehicle as Mark gently took it off him. 'I'm sorry,' he said. 'I'm done in.'

Father Matthew came over to join us with a group of men who helped unload the truck, storing the sacks in the chapel. 'You go, Glen,' he said. 'You have done enough here for now, and you will be no use to us if you collapse,' and Glen didn't argue.

Mark lifted a kilo bag of boiled sweets out of the cab and handed them out to the children and the adults, grateful eyes looking out from once proud faces. He smiled sadly as hands reached up to his, clamouring for more. When the bag was empty the children ran giggling into the corrugated-tin maze, leaving a blanket of plastic wrappers in their wake. I watched my new headmaster wipe his eyes and turn away. His broad shoulders were damp with sweat from unloading the truck, and his face and hands were filthy. He reached into the cab for his dark glasses, and when he eventually turned back to face me I saw his cheeks were wet with tears. I tried to look away, but he caught my glance and shook his head. 'It breaks your heart,' he said softly and reached up for another sack.

I stood on the back of the pick-up and passed down the sacks of maize-flour, looking across the shanty town.

Back in the 1930s, my grandparents were already adults and living on my family's farm in west Wales. In North America, the poorest people on the continent were gathering in California looking for work and a chance for a better life. My father was born only a little later. It was no time ago. Back then they fled the Great Depression and the over-farmed fields of the Midwest dust bowl. Today in Kenya they flee the drought, the famine, the *El Niño* rains and floods and the national need to grow cash crops which cover the once small-scale, farmable land.

The black clouds built up in the west, and the sun beat down through clear skies onto tin roofs and bareheaded Kenyans. Black kites circled and dogs and goats snuffled through the garbage piled up against the high mission station fencing, the wire sagging under its weight.

Each sack brought a sincere '*Asante sana,*' and a white-toothed smile. '*Hakuna Matata rafiki,*' – 'No worries friend,' – I replied. This flour would provide a barely nutritious *ugali* meal to a tiny percentage of the people here, the gloopy dollop of starch providing high-carbohydrate energy but little else, and I knew when I got back to school in the evening, we were going to celebrate Ron's birthday down at the Carnivore where we were going to eat, drink and dance 'til dawn.

In a few hours time I'd get drunk with the rest, and I'd drive the vehicle back up to Greenfields through the rain, dodging the potholes and garbage loosened by the rain, which will have slipped in great, stinking avalanches out onto the road. We would have the tape player on full blast, playing Rod Stewart probably, and the windscreen would steam up with our singing.

I told myself, as I stood on the back of the Greenfields' 4x4, that tonight I must remember Mukuru and the white-toothed hungry smiles, and thank my lucky stars for my life. 'The roulette wheel of birth,' Yuri called it, and here, but for the grace of God, go all of us.

We sat around a fire in front of the church and shared mugs of sweet *chai* with the ever kind and optimistic Father Matthew and some of the nuns. We talked quietly and promised to be back with more provisions soon.

I felt like a crow bringing more and more worms to her newly-hatched chicks, only these chicks don't grow in size, just in number. People streamed in from the country regions where there was too much rain and too little food.

I tied a tarpaulin down on the back of the pick-up truck

and turned to shake Father Matthew's hand. 'I knew a Father Matthew when I was young,' I said. 'He was a good man. Along with my father, it was him who taught me to play cricket.'

'There are many good men here today,' he said with a smile and nodded.

21

I asked Donald about the civil disturbances that had begun
happening around the country, what they might mean and
whether life had always been this way. We were walking to
the Yaya Centre after school one evening at the start of the
September term. Sally smoked her Marlboro Lights; Donald,
his Roosters, and we all sipped warm Fanta Orange bought
from the *duka* on the corner. 'I heard there were government
instructions behind the troubles,' I told him, but he hushed
me to silence.

'Even talk like that is sedition,' he told me, and he looked
hurriedly around. 'The punishment for sedition is death.'

'Nobody is going to hang us for talking like this,' Sally
laughed. 'Now you are being paranoid.'

'Not you,' Donald whispered. 'Nobody would hang you.'

22

Over the Moi Day celebration in October I caught a bus north and camped alone in the Hell's Gate National Park near Naivasha.

The Park Wardens shook their heads and laughed at the crazy *mzungu*. But the walk through the cliff-sided valley surrounded by giraffe, gazelle, wart-hogs and zebras made their ridicule worthwhile.

I pitched my tent high on a plateau overlooking the park, and after strange noises in the night I woke at six to find bovine hoofmarks around me.

Through the open front of my tent I watched the sun creep up over the cliffs and climb higher, pushing back the shadows, exposing the herbivores grazing on the valley floor and a herd of buffalo winding their way down a trail away from my campsite.

By seven it was warm enough for me to sit in shorts on a

tree stump and sip herbal tea boiled up on my small paraffin stove. A flock of swallows crashed over my head as low and loud as any jet as they swooped down into the valley and along towards the geothermal plant at the end of the gorge.

A troop of thirty baboons appeared from some rocks behind me and sat watching as I ate my breakfast. The lead male ambled towards me with an arrogant air and a couple of younger males on his shoulder. Baboons can be vicious and violent, and I'd read about how they rip tents to pieces to steal food inside. Never, the book said, never ever give them any food or you will be over-run. A bite or scratch from a baboon is sure to go septic, and with the threat of rabies, caution is by far the best policy.

So I stood up and reached for a stick, and they stopped, sat down and looked at me without backing off. I picked up a stone and gently threw it to land short of the lead male. The stone landed at his feet and splintered with a crack, and he shied away. I hit the second baboon with a smaller stone, clipping his shoulder, and I got the third on the head as they moved back to the safety of the troop, where they stopped and stared at me.

I had visions of a Hitchcock film and me being ripped to pieces as they rushed me, so I went on the offensive and approached them, flinging stones and yelling. A few stones connected, but most went wide, and they loped away back up into the rocks with their flabby pink bottoms mooning me in the morning sun.

By the middle of the day I was back near my tent, reading *Grapes of Wrath* in the shade of some scrubby thorn trees, but I spent the morning down in the valley, watching animals taking turns at one of the watering holes. There were wart-hogs charging around in families, barely higher than the grass, and a dozen giraffe, gangly and graceful and nearly silent. I sat on a rock beneath a big white hat and watched in awe.

A guidebook's description doesn't come close to matching the excitement of watching animals in the wild, and a sixteen-inch television screen can't compare to three-hundred-and-sixty-degree vision. How can television capture the smells, the breeze, the scale and feel of the dusty valley floor blown up against your cheek, as the wart-hogs searched for roots and rolled in the sand?

With no camera to seduce me, and no companion to worry about, I sat for hours watching, and then just listening. Thoughts of Nairobi and Greenfields faded as the sun climbed higher and the animals grazed and drank and wandered away into the scrub when the day became too hot.

I thought of my father walking through a field of our Welsh Black cattle back home, combing one after another with a curry-comb and whispering to them. He learnt his cattle skills as a boy when he worked on a farm at Tal-y-bont in mid Wales during the war, and I never met anyone who generated so much confidence from the animals as he did.

I imagined him here, walking out from behind me towards the antelopes. I saw him stop short and watch as they moved and grazed, and then he walked forward and stood among them. The impala and hopi barely glanced at him – no danger there, and the Thomson's gazelles came over like jealous young heifers vying for his attention. Only the zebras leapt away from his touch, like skittish and unpredictable limousans. My vision of my father stayed away from the buffalo, as I knew he would. These are the most dangerous herbivores on the savannah. They weigh over a ton and are

161

quick and cunning and sometimes work in pairs. No, even my father would have thought twice about making friends with them.

Back up by my tent I dozed and finished Steinbeck's novel under a tree as the heat of the day passed and shadows came again to my valley. I was ready for the baboons when they called by again in the evening, sending them quickly on their way with a hail of small sharp stones. After a pasta supper, I sat under a moonless sky as satellites silently traced their way through the heavens above me.

In the morning I watched the sun rise across the valley and then packed up my tent for the journey home. By eight I was walking back towards the main gate, following a group of ostrich who stalked ahead of me like chickens running ahead of a car. Then I rode in the back of a ranger's truck with the ghost of Tom Joad, the hero in Steinbeck's *Grapes of Wrath*, sitting beside me, bouncing along the lakeside road towards Naivasha, past the vast glass-houses and poly-tunnels and collections of mud-walled *bandas* in high-fenced worker's compounds.

Tom Joad's ghost reminded me about the American Great Depression and how the same suffering is happening in other parts of the world today. This time it is the West that is persecuting the Developing World, in the way that the growers did to the workers back in the '30s.

'My family fell apart in the search for work,' Tom's ghost said with a shake of his head. 'We buried my grandpa by the side of Route 66 seventy years ago. You have put a man on the moon, but you can't put food on their table.' And when he said 'you' he meant 'me' and my generation, and all of us who don't spend every day fighting for equality and against the injustices of the modern world. What sort of Christian am I if I spend my time teaching young people in the slums something as insignificant as cricket and not making sure they all get at least one good meal a day? What lessons do I keep failing to learn, and at what cost? It is not easy to justify your life to the ghost of a man whose family died of hunger.

We drove through some of the best agricultural land in East Africa, farmed with an intensive system to match the efficiency of any in the Western world, but, like many farming systems in the West, completely dependent on chemicals, which run off the fields and pollute the nearby watercourses. Lake Naivasha becomes more damaged each year, and during years when the rains fail, the level of the lake drops as water is extracted to irrigate the thousands of acres of export-quality beans. These will soon be picked and sped to Nairobi in huge refrigerated lorries, where they are processed and packed in plastic and flown to the supermarket shelves for sale the next day to consumers in the affluent West. You can buy lovely, fresh, green beans on Christmas day in Safeway in Basingstoke that were grown here in these vast mono-culture fields.

The workers couldn't afford to buy the beans, even if they were on sale here.

Each worker's compound had its own grower-owned shops, bars, medical schemes and basic schooling. Rents were reasonable, and credit was available in the shop if it was needed. Once a worker was in debt, they were able to pay it off with money coming straight out of their wages at the end of the week. Sure, the shop's prices were a little higher than shops in Naivasha, but then no one *had* to shop there, and no one *had* to get into debt.

163

No one had to work in the camp either, but when there is so little choice elsewhere, if you want to feed your family, you have to go where the work is, no matter what.

I sat on the veranda outside the La Belle Inn in Naivasha and watched an overloaded truck full of white backpackers struggle to overtake a donkey and cart on the dusty road below me. The ninety-five-shilling ice-cream stuck in my throat as I watched the skinny children run along the road beside the truck, their '*Howareyoufine*'s' lost and ignored in the wobbly sound of the truck's stereo.

I walked round the corner to Kariuki Chotara Road, stepped over a couple of men dribbling and dozing on the steps of a lodging house, and got a bus back to Nairobi.

23

Early in November, Mrs Benson, Greenfield's deputy head, came to me one lunchtime, just as I had started battling with Father Marcus over whether the children at our table would get even the smallest piece of meat with their smearing of gravy. 'There are some friends here to see you,' she said. I followed her out of the dining-hall to the school office, and there, beaming, were the couple that rescued me from my Piriton hell down in Watamu.

'We are flying out tonight,' said Trudy. 'Thought we'd come and say goodbye.' She gave me a hug.

'Got a favour to ask, actually,' said Andy as we shook hands. 'We need a lift to the airport at eleven and wondered if you were up for it?'

'I don't have a car,' I told them.

'No, but as it happens we have one for sale,' he said with a smile.

I found them a couple of spare places in the dining-hall on Sally's table and brought over plates of food. 'Too late, mate,' said Andy. 'Sally's just bought it.'

'You'd only dither,' she said. 'And anyway, it's yellow. That's hardly a bloke's colour is it?'

I laughed. 'You haven't seen the heap of junk yet. The colour is the least of your worries.'

'For fifty quid, I've got no right to complain.'

After Lamu, they had headed south to Tanzania to climb Mount Kilimanjaro. Katrina and Caroline flew back to the UK from Moshi, while Andy and Trudy headed north-east through the Serengeti to Lake Victoria. They had just driven back from the Ugandan Border after six weeks in Mount Elgon National Park and camping in Kakamega Forest.

'You can say what you like about the colour,' said Andy. 'But the Yellow Peril has done some mileage and never once let us down. She's done us proud.'

The meal ended, and children started streaming out of the dining-hall. Donald came over and joined us and asked Andy about Kisumu. He was too shy to talk to Trudy. 'A cousin of mine worked on Rusinga Island,' he said. 'It is a hard place,' he frowned.

At the far end of the dining-hall Father Marcus stretched, rubbed his belly and heaved himself to his feet. As he waddled towards the door, he looked down at us and smiled at the *mzungus* seated together. Then as he got nearer his smile became confused and he tried to look away as if he hadn't noticed us there.

'Father Marcus,' I said standing up. 'Father Marcus,' more loudly, 'these are some friends of mine. Trudy and Andy. They used to teach up your way, near Moyale, wasn't it?'

'I do not know them,' he said.

'In Sololo,' said Trudy, and she turned to look at him. 'Hey, I know you? Your wife made me some curtains.'

'No, not me,' Father Marcus said backing away. 'It is an easy mistake, *mzungu*. We all look the same to you, no? No offence taken.'

'Marcus Abdi?' Andy got to his feet. 'Yeah, I know you. You ate all the barbecue at that *harambee* fund-raiser when that kid got run over. How are you?' He reached out to shake Father Marcus' hand.

Father Marcus stumbled over the corner of a table as he stepped back and sent a pile of plates crashing to the floor. 'I do not know you,' he said.

'Hey, hey. What's all the noise?' shouted Mark Peters as he stuck his head in through the dining-room door. 'Oh! I'm sorry guys. I thought it was a bunch of kids mucking around.' He smiled, and I introduced him to my friends.

'We know Marcus from northern Kenya,' said Trudy. 'Although he is pretending we have never met.'

'Father Marcus? Really? It is unlike you to be shy,' Mark grinned.

'Only he wasn't a Catholic priest then. He had a wife and many children.'

'Father Marcus? Really?' Mark was frowning now.

Donald said something to Farther Marcus in Kiswahili and he spat back viciously.

'You have wronged the wrong man,' he forced through gritted teeth and pushed his way out past Mark in the doorway. 'You will regret this.' And he never came back.

'That was strange,' said Sally.

'Wow, life in the city sure ain't dull,' Andy laughed. 'And

167

it seems we've added our little splash of excitement. Sorry about that.'

'Where am I going to get a new priest?' said Mark scratching his chin, and then the bell went, and he turned and headed off to class.

'What did Father Marcus say to you?' I asked Donald, as we bent down to pick up pieces of the broken plates. 'It looked pretty rough.'

'He said, "Never take the side of the *mzungu* against your own people. They will always desert you."'

The lights on Sally's new car didn't work, so I drove Trudy and Andy to the airport in one of the Greenfields 4x4s. We shook hands and smiled, and I envied them going home, while not really wanting to go home myself. It was a strange emotion.

24

The Yellow Peril misfired and mistimed and had a leaking front window and boot. The brakes squeaked and the front door could be opened with a penknife. Worst of all was that the ignition key was so worn it fell out as Sally bounced the car along Nairobi's roads.

One Saturday we broke down with water in the spark plugs as we drove up to Westlands. The rains were at their worst, and the drains were blocked with sand and dirt and couldn't cope with the downpour, leaving the potholed road more like a river bed.

We sat near the Museum Hill roundabout, hoping that if we waited long enough they might dry out, and we argued over who should get out and dry them off with a cloth.

'Go on then,' Sally said with a grin. 'I'm a damsel in need. Just what you always dreamed of.'

'Yeah, right! But it's your car,' I pointed out, taking a towel and an adjustable spanner from the glove box. 'And anyway, what about equality of the sexes?'

'You are supposed to be a gentleman,' she said punching my arm.

As I opened the car door to get out, a man tapped on the window. 'Hey *mzungu*,' he said. 'I will help. I am mechanic.' And he took the cloth and spanner from me and disappeared under the bonnet, taking out the old plugs cleaning them with petrol that he sucked from the fuel pipe, held in his mouth and spat at the plugs.

He closed the bonnet and tapped on my window. 'All done *mzungu*,' and Sally turned the engine over. It coughed and then kicked in. 'All done. That is two thousand shillings.'

'Two thousand shillings!' Sally yelled. 'You're joking, man. I'll give you two thousand shillings!' and she floored the accelerator and sped away along Uhuru Highway. '*Mzungu* rates are one thing but that's taking the piss. There is no bloody way I'm paying the equivalent of twenty quid to have some joker clean my plugs!'

Yuri's Trooper wasn't a much better vehicle. The window on the driver's side was jammed shut, and the air conditioning didn't work, so he drove with the passenger's side window wound right down. The dust affected his sinuses, and he spat great lumps of phlegm out of the window in front of the passenger, which wasn't a pleasant experience. But he did give notice, so passengers always had time to get out of the way. A street-boy once got in the way, and caught the lot between the eyes. He ran after us for a quarter of a mile along Ngong Road yelling, with Yuri laughing like an idiot and me cowering in the seat and giggling in embarrassment.

In the Nairobi Club bar after Friday night cricket practice,

Yuri laughed again as he described the face appearing at the window, and the way the stoned grin had changed to a furious frown in the briefest instant. I sipped my Tusker with a furrowed brow. Is that funny, I asked myself? Should I really be laughing at this kid's misfortune? And I was shocked to realise I had started to see the street-children as little more than a pitiful annoyance in everyday life. In my head they had just become another of the trials of Kenya, rather than actual individual human beings. I had stopped caring about what happened to them as people.

The week before, David Brown, the junior from the High Commission, had lost his sidelights when he refused to give money to some street-boys. A gang of them surrounded his car as he waited in a jam on Moi Avenue, and they rocked the car from side to side while he sat there refusing to open the window. Passengers in a *matatu* beside him laughed and pointed as he got redder and redder, and just as the cars started moving again one of the boys walked round to the front and ripped off the sidelight. He held David's gaze and showed him what he had done, then he smashed the light on the ground and stepped aside with a nonchalant shrug.

'I was in tears by the time I arrived at the High Commission,' he whispered. 'Tears of frustration and anger. But what could I do?' He was balding and wore horn-rimmed glasses and had the air of someone who had always been bullied.

'You could do nothing,' said Yuri resting his hand on David's shoulder. 'Back home in Johannesburg my brother lost a truck. He was sitting at a junction when someone opened the back door, took out a can of petrol and ran away with it. It's never been in his nature to let things go, so he got out and gave chase. The thief dropped the can after about fifty yards, but when my brother got back to the junction his truck was gone. Even though there were many people, not one person would admit to seeing anything.'

Friday nights were always like this, gathering in the Nairobi Club pavilion after practice, sharing a beer and swapping stories. Each week something extraordinary had happened to someone, and we'd sit shaking our heads and saying, 'Ah, Kenya,' and wondering what we were doing here. I heard everything as the weeks went by, from a carjacking, to an *askari* security guard stealing fruit, or a High Commission driver phoning the office to say all the wheels of his vehicle had been stolen in the Yaya Centre car park while he was posting letters.

Another Nairobi Club member, English engineer John Rogerson, told a tragic story. His *askari* ended up seriously ill in hospital when he tried to stop a robber stealing the covers to some of John's garden furniture. 'I pay him one hundred shillings a night and he was prepared to be killed to defend my property,' said John. 'Hell, man, I wouldn't do that for anyone.' There were tears in his eyes, and we shared his melancholy as we wondered at the loyalty and honour of so many of the people here.

Trying to pick up packages from the post office without paying more *chai* than the package was worth was another favourite, especially around Christmas time.

Mr Rivers delighted in telling his story about when he overtook in a no overtaking zone. 'A policeman flagged me down and mumbled, "No overtaking here, *mzungu*," and pointed down at the road. "There are no lines," I said, "you can't give me a ticket for overtaking here." "There are lines," he told me, "they are worn away, and you can't see them, but they are there. Two white lines. No overtaking."'

'I refused his demand for *chai* and said I wanted to see a senior officer, so off we went to the Kilimani police station, where the senior officer nodded and said, "Yes, that is a no overtaking zone," and he made me pay a fine.' He always laughed at this point, delighted by the absurdity of the situation and the story. 'There haven't been lines on that stretch for ten years.'

Later, as we waited for our pizzas and looked out through the dirty glass of the pizza shop, giggling at the enticing poses of the hideously infamous prostitutes of Kirinyaga Road, I moaned to Yuri how dull my life had become. 'Nothing ever happens to me,' I said, not realising the stupidity of my complaint. 'I never have anything to say up at the club.'

'You saw enough adventure in your first two days here to last many a lifetime, boy. Don't forget it, big guy,' he said with a fraternal grin. 'I shouldn't go hoping for any more.'

25

My first Christmas in Kenya was a depressing affair. Donald went back to his home-place in Kitui; Sally's mother came over and they went up country with Mr Rivers, in an attempt to heal their family tiff. Geraldine and Ron went to Lamu; Yuri was in Rwanda, and Anya was in northern Uganda where the Lord's Resistance Army were kidnapping children, forcing the boys to become child soldiers, and the girls, sex slaves. I was left to house-sit Yuri and Anya's house on Ralph Bunche Road and drink myself crazy.

At the Greenfields carol concert on the last day of term, Mary Odinga played the hymns the same way she played everything – at three-quarter pace. They took forever as we dirged our way through 'In the Bleak Midwinter' and 'Good King Wenceslas' who looked out on the deep and crisp and even snow, as the African sun streamed through the chapel windows. We sweated uncomfortably in the heat, as we remembered the poor man gathering winter fuel in the frost so 'cru-el'. Father Matthew led the service and swung the thurible with gusto to add a bit of atmosphere. The kids fidgeted, longing to get out, because once the service was over the holiday had begun, and we were all free for three weeks.

Towards the end of the service Sally faked a coughing fit, and she stumbled out along the pew to get some fresh air. 'It's the incense,' she wheezed to her concerned uncle as she passed, and when the service was over she was sitting on the steps outside the chapel calmly smoking a Marlboro Light with her baseball cap pulled down low.

There was a Christmas tree with tinsel and fake snow just inside the bay window of the school's Great Hall, which you could see from the rock-hard cracked earth outside, and the crib in the chapel entrance was complete with Balthasar, Melchior and Gaspar, bent-legged sheep, plastic Friesian cattle and a black Holy Family.

'In the Bible, when it says that Delilah cut off seven locks of Samson's hair, it means seven dreadlocks, not golden blond Charlton Heston California sun-bleached ones,' Andrew Greeley said when I questioned the black figures. 'Samson was David's ancestor and David was an ancestor of Jesus. Also, Jesus was a Nazarene, and they were dread-locked Ethiopians, which is why the Jah Rastafari faith makes such sense. Christ was an Ethiopian, therefore a black man, complete with dreadlocks.'

Yuri nodded later when I asked him about it. 'Richard Leakey found the earliest sign of human life in southern Ethiopia,' he said. 'The geography of this region was very different of course. Back then Egypt and Israel were joined, with the Hebrews originally coming from Ethiopia, and with Ethiopia, Egypt and Israel all being one big place, before the lands drifted. If you go back far enough, by historical rights the Ethiopians have every right to live in Israel; they were the original Hebrews just as much as they are present-day Ethiopians.'

'Times change, though, just as much as continents. I don't think the Israelis would be all that welcoming if a shipload of Rastas turned up on the shore claiming it as their own.'

On Christmas morning I went to church on the University Way roundabout which had a crib in the doorway with a Joseph who looked liked Robert Powell, a Mary like Jean Simmons and a Holy Child so white that it glowed in the gloom of the crib.

The service began at twelve and took hours, and I nearly fainted in the heat and claustrophobia, with all the benches overflowing and the aisles packed. Instead of celebrating the birth of the Prince of Peace, a guest priest, Father Gerald Halliwell, used his sermon to remind us that it would only be a few months before we strung Jesus up again on a cross and that we should never forget it. Sometimes there isn't a lot of fun in being a Catholic, even on Christmas Day, but at least the hymns were uplifting with so many fervent African voices belting out the words.

When I got back to Ralph Bunche Road I found a message on Yuri's answering machine from Erica inviting me to a party that evening with a few of her friends. My spirits rose, finally having something fun to do, but she went on to ask me to bring Yuri's barbecue, and some beer, charcoal and any meat that he had in the fridge, because they were out of food and were too hungover to get more.

I deleted the message, rang home and talked to my mum. It was my first-ever Christmas away, and I missed our traditions of midnight mass and drinking packet-made chicken noodle soup when we got back home. Even the Christmases when I was with Laura were spent on the farm. We spent Christmas in Wales and New Year in Surrey with her parents. The same reassuring thing each year.

It was about ten in the morning in the UK, and they should be getting ready for the traditional walk. On Christmas morning we always opened one present at breakfast and then took a walk to the old church by the river to visit my grandparents' graves. I imagined my parents doing the same thing, but, instead of talking with me, they'd talk about me and hope I was OK out here so far from home.

My mother picked up the telephone with a giggle. She said she had just got up and was getting ready to head out to a drinks party in the village. My father had hired in a relief-milker for the whole Christmas period so he could have a bit of a break. He was having a lie-in, my mother said, because they went to a party last night and didn't get in until late, or early, depending on how you looked at it, she chuckled. She sounded like she had already had a couple of glasses of sherry to start the day.

I asked about the things we always did at Christmas, and she laughed saying they only did them because they knew how much I liked them, and since I was away they thought they would make a few changes. She said she hoped I didn't mind.

My dad was still in bed and couldn't come to the phone. She told me to call back the day after Boxing Day, as they had a lot to fit in, and she didn't like the thought of me phoning an empty house.

So I sat in Yuri and Anya's house on Ralph Bunche Road, watched MNET and drank my way through to New Year.

26

The Catholic church on the University Way roundabout was packed full each Sunday, and not just at Christmas time. Voices rose in magnificent celebration of a collective faith, and my white skin brought smiles and shaken hands. Whites were pretty rare, and apart from me there were three old nuns seated way up front and the Irish priest, Father McIntyre, who had been here for thirty years. Then there were eight hundred Kenyans squeezed together on narrow pews and sweating in joyous communion between the red-bricked walls.

The services were spoken in English and sung mostly in Kiswahili, and even though I didn't understand the words, the singing was like none I had ever heard in a church before. The power and emotion in the voices was more like Cardiff Arms Park back in the 1970s than the sparsely-filled churches back home, and the passion and celebration would have made the disciples cheer.

'Some churches make you suffer *in* your faith rather than *for* your faith,' Father McIntyre said during one service, 'and there is a difference. Some churches make you crawl on your belly through your poverty before they'll grant you admittance. Some will use your brokenness as a weapon to trap you in your hope of another way.' He bent his head in sadness and said in barely more than a whisper, 'Jesus would have been so ashamed.'

And that's how it usually was – a celebration of faith and, despite the hardship outside in Kenya, the church was filled with positivism and gratitude for what we, as a communion, had. It wasn't much sometimes, but it was better than it might be. We had to try to do the best we could, in honourable preparation for the after-life to come.

'I saw a young man I recognised outside of church last Sunday,' the priest said, to begin his sermon. 'I knew him as a child and think I might even have baptised him. He stood proudly beside a beautiful young woman and they made a beautiful couple.' He slowly nodded his head in recollection. 'A picture of how we all might hope our next generation will look. Well educated, well off and attractive young people. It made me smile to see that this young, handsome and wealthy couple were still keen to come to church, and that their faith still mattered to them.'

'"Father," said the young man, "It is good to see you," and we shook hands as honestly and openly as two men should. "I am back from university in London with an education and a fiancée. God has been good to me." And what a smile he carried.'

'And by any chance is this beautiful woman your fiancée?" I asked him. "No, father," he said abruptly. "It is not by any *chance* that this woman is my fiancée. There was no chance involved in the eventuality. It was by my design and through God's generosity.'"

'"Many years ago, Father, you taught me that there is no such thing as chance. Things happen by design and for a reason. The reason may only be known unto God, but there is a reason and by God's great blessing rather than by mere chance this beautiful woman is now my fiancée. I do not know the reason God has blessed me so, I only know that he has. That," said the young man "is good enough for me."'

Father McIntyre smiled and moved away from the lectern. 'He is qualified as a doctor now, and his fiancée is a teacher. They are moving to Kisumu to settle and work for the people.'

'In all my years as a priest, first on Achill Island on the west coast of Ireland and then during the thirty years that Africa has been my home, I have seen many things and talked to many people, but very few have spoken of their faith with such clarity and simplicity. I feel greatly humbled by the meeting.' He smiled and walked down the few steps in front of the altar and stood between the first rows – now truly a member of the congregation celebrating the mass together.

'I wrote this sermon last Wednesday with a great deal of joy, and I was delighted with it when I read it back. But when I reread it this morning, I notice that what was to be my last line was very wrong, and it reminded me how little I know of my faith and the way my God works. What I had written was, "I feel greatly humbled by the *chance* meeting," but nothing happens by chance, my brothers and sisters. It happens by design. By God's design.'

'I am sometimes asked how is it that God's great design can include the suffering that we see on the streets around us and read of in the paper, and I reply I do not know. But when I am asked why God does nothing about it, I say that he does do something. I can look out at you, my brothers and sisters and know what God has done to help those suffering. He has put us here to work with and for them, and he has given us the knowledge that it is our destiny to do so.'

'So let us stand and put our hands together and pray forgiveness for what we have done, and for the strength to do his will with greater commitment in the future. It is not by chance that we are here on this day, it is due to God's blessing that we are here to celebrate, and it is through his kindness that we are able to help others.'

Waiting on the steps outside the church after the service had ended, I met Yuri who had arrived late and had stood just outside the doorway at the back.

'I didn't know you were a Catholic,' I told him.

'You don't know many things,' he smiled.

'True,' I nodded and we started walking back up to his house. 'How have you been?' I asked. 'I've hardly seen you since you got back after Christmas, and you haven't been to cricket for a while.'

'I have been working. There are bad things happening in Rwanda,' he frowned and shook his head. 'Sometimes it is better not to talk. So what has been happening here with you, my friend?'

But nothing much had been happening with me. I told him about school starting up again, and a dreadful six-a-side cricket tournament I played in up at the Rift Valley Sports Club in Nakuru, and some goofy headlines in the *Daily Nation*, but then that was it. 'Not much else, mate, sorry,' and we walked on in silence for a while.

We walked past Uhuru Park, full of people enjoying the sunshine on a Sunday afternoon. Young Asians played cricket while the elderly Africans watched. Young Africans played football while the street-boys watched. The street-boys ran off with empty soda bottles left on the grass, and elderly Asians watched them and grinned at their industry. With a small deposit on each bottle they were well worth collecting.

'There is a park in the part of Johannesburg where I lived where people meet on Sundays,' said Yuri. 'When I was a child it was to play cricket and touch-rugby. It was in Hillbrow, a multi-cultural district. The kind of inner city area that immigrants are drawn to all over the world, like the East End of London. It was a good place for us back then, but a frightening place too, with great poverty and crime. Prostitutes, gangsters and drug dealers living right next door to young families like ours who could not yet afford to live anywhere else.'

'On Sundays we all played together in that park. Whites, Blacks and the Coloureds, no problems. A few years later the park was the site for many anti-apartheid demonstrations. Then there were police with dogs and sticks. It was not a good place to be for anyone at any time. We had moved out by this stage. To a much nicer and whiter part of town.'

'What is it like now?' I asked. 'Hillbrow?'

'Now? How the hell do I know? I am stuck here flying from one disaster to another. I don't know my country any more. And I can't go home to work. I apply for jobs I could do blindfolded, but I am never even called for an interview. Apartheid was revolting. I agree one hundred percent. But now things are stacked so heavily against young white men and the positive discrimination for black people so rigid that

I can't get any work at home. And then I go to church to pray for help, only to hear some dumb Paddy priest telling me everything happens for a reason. I'm well and truly buggered if I can see it.'

'Well, I am glad you are here, mate. Maybe that's all there is to it. You saved my life once already, and I hadn't even been here twenty-four hours. You are here to be a good mate to me.' I looked up at his face with a smile and saw he was crying. 'Oh *mate*,' and I led him across the road to sit in the shade on the low wall of the Panafric Hotel, and I ran to a *duka* for a couple of sodas. 'Here you go, Yuri,' I said handing him a bottle of warm Fanta Orange. 'I'm sorry. It's all they had.'

We sat and watched the people stream into the cathedral on the other side of Lower Ngong Road. 'So many people and so many faiths,' he said eventually. 'The last church I was in was in a tiny village in Rwanda on Christmas Day. I was with Al, a cameraman from New Zealand and a woman reporter, Cathy, who was from Wales like you, but she sounded English, yah? She was tiny but so strong.'

'We had a guide with us, but when we landed on the runway, he wouldn't even get out of the plane. He was scared shitless and saying it was a bad place. And it was a bad place. That was why we were there. No one is interested in stories from good places. It was in the middle of God knows where. I went with Cathy and Al into the village. There was no way I wanted to be alone with that jabbering bastard in that place. Not a hope in hell.'

'From the plane we could see smoke rising from the village, and as soon as we left the plane you could smell the death. Hutus or Tutsi? I don't know. They were people like you and me, and like him,' he pointed to a street-boy dancing in the

184

road and sucking on a small glue-filled plastic beaker.

'The village was empty. Flattened houses. Dead animals with necks slashed open. But there were no people. And the flies. Jesus Christ. The cameraman filmed. Al filmed the village, and Cathy spoke notes into a dictaphone, and I walked behind them like an idiot. But there were no people anywhere.'

'We took an hour. And it was a slow hour. Turning over every house, looking in every pile of garbage. Sometimes people will hide their babies, you know, if they think an attack is coming. Babies have been found days later, dehydrated but alive beneath their parent's butchered bodies, so we looked everywhere.'

'The only building left untouched was a stone church. Its doors were barricaded closed and there was a headless goat rotting on the steps. I found a bar and levered the doors open.'

'We knew what we would find. Jesus Christ, man. The smell was incredible even outside. There were piles of people on the pews, in the aisles. On the altar. Every-fucking-where. And the black stain of blood. Sticky. Everywhere. Al took pictures, and Cathy was sick again and again. We all were. The bodies were melting. Like wax. Melting in the heat. Oh God, I can't sleep, man. Like melting wax.'

'And then this woman. This wailing. There was a woman still alive in a corner. Cowering in the corner. She ran at me, and I pushed her aside. She slipped and fell into the bodies, and then she ran out blindly into the daylight. She stumbled over the goat and lay there in the dirt.'

'Cathy went to her. Gave her water and a sedative, and Al and I went back to the church and looked for survivors. Al said the people were three or four days dead, but with that heat it is hard to tell. We tried to turn over bodies with a stick, but they were stuck to the ground and burst open when we prodded them, and in the end we couldn't do it. The flies were unbelievable.'

'We were crying, man. Two grown men and we were crying and vomiting.'

'We carried the woman back to the plane and flew back to the base.' He finished his bottle of warm fizzy pop and spun it on the palm of his hand like a cocktail waiter would do. 'And I don't know if there were other survivors there,' he shrugged.

'You did your best,' I told him, but he shook his head.

'How do I know that?' he snorted. 'And then the very next time I go to church the priest tells me everything happens for a reason. You have got to be joking me. Yah?'

'You did your best, mate,' I whispered. 'You did your best.'

27

Sometimes at the Nairobi Club we didn't go straight into the clubhouse after practice. Sometimes someone would start a story outside, as we packed up our cricket kit, and they'd continue talking until well after dark, while the rest of us stood around, listening quietly on the edge of the cricket field. Listening to the sound of a lone voice, with the hum of early evening Nairobi in the background.

One evening, Glen Stevens told us about the clearances in Mukuru slum that none of us had even heard about. It was nine days before they were reported in the newspapers.

Glen was there, and watched as the diggers and bulldozers arrived at dawn one day and drove paths clean through the corrugated-tin shacks and wooden shelters. Armed police and soldiers stood silently by, as families rushed to gather their possessions and children, and then stood back aghast as their lives were crushed into the mud.

The machines coughed diesel smoke, and their juddering wheels spread waves through the churned-up filth. It was unhurried but steady progress. The number of machines meant the destruction was quick. The community of hundreds of houses was flattened in hours.

The slum dwellers had travelled to Nairobi from all over East Africa, surviving genocide, famine and flood, and now they were dispossessed again, under the eye of armed government soldiers and officers of the law. And even if there were no gunmen, the machines were too big to stop, and the drivers followed orders to get on with it and not waste time checking that the homes were empty before they razed them to the ground.

Father Matthew reproached some policemen. 'How can you do this to your brothers? Do you not claim to be saved? How can you do this and claim to be saved?' But the officers shrugged and turned away. The priest ran over to the diggers and shouted up at the drivers in their cabs high above the ground, but the drivers simply ignored him, concentrating on revs per minute and oil pressure. Glen had run over to him, taking him gently by the elbow and leading him back to safety.

Orders for the clearances came from the top, from the Big Man who owned the land and wanted to demonstrate his strength. He flexed his muscles, and the machines went in. The police stood by and watched.

'When the police and the army and the diggers left, the families went back to the piles of rubble that had been their homes,' Glen said. They stood in the oily, slicked mud and started searching for the courage to rebuild their lives. Then they returned to where their houses had been, and they began again. They helped neighbours straighten bent nails and hammered them through damaged corrugated tin. They sifted through the debris to find pieces of timber strong enough to make a reasonable lintel. Most of the wood was so shattered and splintered that it was suitable only for firewood, if it wasn't too wet from the rain and the mud. There were rarely windows in the single-roomed shacks anyway, so there was little broken glass to worry about, and they hung sheets of colourful cloth over openings to act as doors.

The diggers moved on to clear other areas of illegal dwelling, on the far side of the river, the hum of their engines swamping the sound of the house-building, but not stopping it. Eyes rose from the work and glanced over. Heads shook and sweat dripped as the brows furrowed in sympathy, but the rains would be back before nightfall and new roofs must be complete by then, so they cracked on and tried to ignore the far side of the river. Those on that side would never get their homes rebuilt by dark.

The mission station in Mukuru remained untouched. Perhaps it was the makeshift crucifix high over the wooden chapel that intimidated the drivers and shamed them away, or maybe the Big Men were scared of disrespecting God, or at least the wrath of the Kenyan churchgoers. Either way, the power of God protected the mission. The people inched nearer, and the services were fuller than ever. The orphanage grew as children were left in the compound or were found wandering, stray, through the broken houses.

The diggers crushed the communal pit latrines along with everything else. Waves of slurry ran along the tracks and gullies, working their way downhill and into the streams and contaminating drinking and washing water. Women pulled bedding and clothing from the mud and washed it in the river, while men re-dug trenches so the sewage could run away and find the river downstream from the women's washing.

A bluey sheen of diesel-oil streaked the foul water, and the sweet composting smell of effluent filled the air, the sweaty cider-house scent enveloping everything.

The night rains flooded the trenches that the men dug daily, sides caving in as the earth became more viscous. No point in putting pipes in. The diggers would only break them next time.

'The mission complex had one tap on a concrete tank that collected rain run off from the roofs of the buildings,' Glen said. 'One tap can't supply a thousand families, though, and although the women queued through the daylight hours, others collected water from the river and boiled it above damp and smoking wood that was too smashed up to be usable for anything else. They boiled the water for a long time, praying above it for its cleanliness, but many people still fell ill with dysentery and weaker children died of dehydration.'

'I was sitting in the long drop pit latrine last Thursday evening,' Glen said, 'and I was singing. I always sing in there.'

'Hell ain't no hotter than a Kenyan slum in summertime,' he had sung quietly. It had been a long day, and through the gap above the door he could see the blackening clouds rolling in from the west. 'Hell ain't no hotter than a Kenyan slum in summertime, no.' He had frowned at a cockroach that climbed out of the hole between his feet and ran off into a corner. 'Hell ain't no hotter than a Kenyan slum in summertime, Baby. And soon, soon I'll be going home.'

'I reached for the pages of the newspaper I had brought in with me and had jammed in the door frame to keep it dry and out of the way.'

'There was a headline saying "*Fourteen die in bus crash*,"

and as I ripped off a page I read a quote from Reginald Njuna, the police officer in charge, who said, "We could have saved more but for the onlookers getting in the way." The bystanders had helped some people get out of the bus, but they had then robbed them as they bled on the roadside and as others were dying inside.'

'The noise of the slum was the same as always, but I could hear crying and whimpering pretty close by, and I guessed there must be someone in the queue with a baby, but when I opened up the door, there wasn't.'

He walked around the wooden structure, looking for the source of the noise but couldn't find it. He rinsed his hands beneath a dribble from the tap on the rainwater tank as a young woman balanced her clay pot upon her head.

'*Jambo, mama*,' Glen said to her with a smile. '*Hibari*?'

'*Nzuri sana*,' the girl giggled, embarrassed and delighted to have the white man asking how she was.

'I popped into the nursing room to say I was going home,' Glen said. Sister Heather, a senior nurse, smiled at him, and moved to stand by his side. One of the other nuns tended to a woman, barely more than a girl, who had just had a baby out there in the slum. She had no family, she said, and she held the child tight to her chest.

'It's a lovely sight,' Sister Heather said. 'Despite all of this, a perfect child is born and is loved.' She smiled at the mother's natural concern and reaction, as the baby lost its toothless grip on her breast and let out a whimper of disapproval. Sister Heather smiled and looked up at Glen, but his face held a look of realisation and horror.

'Jesus,' he said, as he turned and ran back towards the pit latrine. 'Jesus Christ!'

'Matthew, quick,' shouted Sister Heather turning to run after Glen. 'Father Matthew, come quickly. Something is wrong!'

When Sister Heather and Father Matthew caught up with Glen, he was lying on the ground in the pit latrine with his head and shoulders over the edge of the half-full pit. He had pulled the door open and pushed the woman peeing aside. She crouched in the corner pulling up her skirts mortified, watching as Glen had ripped up the wooden flooring and leant in as far as he could. 'The smell was appalling,' he said, 'And I vomited.'

Father Matthew grabbed his shoulders and pulled him back. A group had gathered around, and as he gasped for fresh air, Glen saw white teeth in astonished, black, sweating faces. '*Wazimu mzungu*' he heard as he retched and threw up over himself. 'Crazy white man.'

'In there,' he choked to Father Matthew. 'In there. A child. I heard it cry.'

Father Matthew shouted some orders in Kiswahili, and a man came running with a ladder, which he pushed down into the pit. He giggled as he stepped onto the rungs and it sunk further into the faeces. 'You are not joking with me, my friend?' Father Matthew said, taking a step down into the darkness. And then he had heard the baby's whimper.

'Father Matthew reached down and gently picked up the baby,' Glen said. 'I watched him from where I lay. The most incredible thing I have ever seen. I watched him lift out this tiny form, wrapped only in a ripped, black plastic carrier bag. He cradled it in his arms, and he smiled.'

28

At the start of the Spring term I paid a *jua kali* metalworker to weld us a basketball hoop, and I fitted it to a wall in our accommodation compound.

Sally played basketball to county-level in her youth and captained the University of Brighton ladies team during three of her four years there. She also played football and cricket for the college and had a couple of games of cricket for the Sussex Ladies team, but then she got into drinking and began to smoke and her sport faded away. Student Union bars have a lot to answer for.

'This term you get fit,' I told her, as I threw her the ball for the first time. 'I'm tired of carrying you,' I said with a smile. 'Time you gave up smoking and sorted yourself out. What sort of a role model are you for the kids anyway, with all your puffin'-and-a-wheezin'.'

'I'll give up smoking when I get pregnant, I told you.' She

dribbled past me and sank the ball before I had turned. 'One-nil,' she said. 'First to twenty for the game. First to five games for the match and first to five matches for the series. And I'll put two hundred shillings on it.'

'Quit yapping and get on with it,' I said.

She threw me the ball, blocked my charge, flipped the ball between my legs, skipped around me and sank another basket. 'Two-nil!'

The *askaris* sat watching by the gate and laughed at the '*wazimu wazungu*' – the crazy white people running around in the heat.

Sweat didn't drip, it streamed down my face and my back, as Sally beat me again and again, turning and twisting and rising high above me with the smallest puff of dust – her tread was so light, and she patted me on the shoulders as I crouched, bent double and breathing heavily. 'How's that for your male ego,' she jeered. 'Get up, you're wasting good drinking time.'

Day after day when school was over we met beneath the hoop and played one-on-one for an hour, or until I was shaking so much I couldn't stand straight. Then we went to the swimming pool where Donald was tidying up after classes, and he sat on the side with his feet in the water as Sally and I lay in the coolness, talking, sipping sodas and swimming the occasional languid length.

'Very few Kenyans swim,' said Donald proudly. 'What is the point of learning when, if you are not eaten by crocodiles or hippopotamuses, the chances are you will catch bilharzia? Learning to swim is not a top priority.'

Occasionally I saw Donald with the basketball trying to slam-dunk. He came loping up to the basket, leaping high, and I'd hear the thunk of the rubber ball on the metal rim as the ball bounced away from him and rolled towards the gate, where the *askaris* picked it up and threw it back. Other times he sat in the shade, cheering us on and keeping score.

One day Andrew joined us for a game. He'd spent weeks watching from his room, like a ghost in an attic wanting to come out but not sure how he would be welcomed. Sally told me not to, but I beckoned him down. 'It's not healthy to be stuck up there all the time,' I told her. 'He's done his penance surely?'

'It's your ball. You choose who you play with,' she said.

So Andrew came down and stood beneath the hoop, with his newly shaven white chin and nervous grin, as we ran through the rules. Andrew and I made up one side, while Donald went with Sally.

Andrew and I took an early lead and Sally became frustrated when Donald fumbled easy balls and our lead grew. Donald got worse as he became more nervous. In the end all the points they scored were from Sally shooting baskets from extraordinary angles, and the scores levelled at sixteen apiece.

At nineteen all, with the next point the winner, I turned to shoot but found Sally leaping above me, and she punched the ball down and away and straight into Andrew's face. The ball bounced towards Donald, who panicked and jumped and sunk the ball with his first and only slam-dunk.

Andrew's glasses shattered, and his face exploded with bleeding nose and screaming profanity. 'What the hell are you doing,' he yelled through his smarting tears. 'What's the matter with you, you crazy bitch?' and he stormed off towards his room.

'It was an accident,' she said with a shrug and pulled her

cap down low, but I didn't believe her, and I turned away in shame.

The ball rolled away towards the gate, where an *askari* picked it up and grinned. The next day the ball had gone, but none of us were in the mood for basketball any more. Maybe that was my greatest success in helping Kenyan sport to progress – not complaining when an *askari* stole my ball and took it home with him to the slums. Perhaps in years to come Kenya will have a great basketball player who becomes the pride of his nation, and it will be because of Sally's temper and Donald's dunk.

And poor Donald, the only slam-dunk of his life, and we were all too embarrassed to congratulate him.

29

Mark Peters called him Danny, after the President. The child he adopted. I don't know if it was ironically meant, but thinking of him still makes me smile. The child rescued from a pit latrine wearing nothing more than a ripped plastic bag. There is something almost biblical about it.

Danny was a very smiley child, and he deserved the secure home life, great sisters and loving parents he found himself with. He joined the Peters family as a three-month-old black boy, and became the son of two proud white New Zealanders.

Nia and Anna smiled when Polly, their mother, asked them how they would feel about having a little brother. They had met Danny a couple of times already and were delighted when they heard it was to be him.

We sat on the grass just outside the boundary of the Nairobi Club's cricket field in the shade of the acacia trees, Mark, Polly and me, watching a team of youngsters from all over Nairobi playing against a school from England who were visiting Kenya on a cricket tour. Mr Rivers had put the Kenyan side together made up of Africans, Asians and a couple of white children whose parents were members of the club. We watched the hard-fought battle, and Mark told me the saga involved with adopting a child in Kenya. He acknowledged this was just the start of difficulties for Danny.

'Nia and Anna are too young to realise the issues involved with foreigners adopting a Kenyan national,' he said. 'We have to think of the future. We have to think about what happens when we go back home, whenever that is.' Auckland might be more open-minded than it used to be, but there are things like that to think about.'

He had picked up the relevant documents from the government offices on Haile Selassie Avenue, paying duties to the ministers to get the correct forms and appendices. He paid more *chai* to get the forms looked at, and more again when the first set went missing somewhere in the wheels of bureaucracy. In the end, Mark dished out eight different bribes before he could get the papers signed and in front of the correct official.

'It felt like we were buying him,' Polly told me with a resigned shrug, but she didn't grudge a penny of it.

Then there were the interviews with the ministers, to see if they were suitable.

'They asked what makes us think living with us would benefit Danny,' Polly said, glancing behind her to where Danny slept in a carry-cot. She brushed away a fly that was circling near his head. 'And that's pretty obvious. From the minister's office you could see street-boys lying in the sun on the dusty pavement. In the distance was Uhuru Park with

Station Road and Kabira slum beyond. There are over a million living under tin roofs down there. No electricity and only a little running water. How could anyone think he wouldn't be better off with us?'

'We had to be careful,' Mark said. 'It was so hard to concentrate on talking ourselves up, and not the place down. They didn't want to hear us bad mouth their country. If we had done that, we wouldn't have stood a chance.'

But six months later, the paper process was complete, and smiley Danny had a family.

30

To say corruption was an issue in Kenya would be an understatement. It went from the bottom to the top of society, from the request for *chai* in exchange for a parking spot on Mama Ngina Street, to importation taxes, consultancies, kickbacks and other cons played by MPs, policemen, judges and senior members of society.

It is not solely Kenya's problem of course, as any number of other politicians can demonstrate. It is similar around Europe and North America, as well as the rest of the developing world. But in the West, when someone is caught they usually lose their standing and occasionally go to prison. In Kenya they are able to buy off their accusers, terrorise juries, or simply be so untouchable that accusations never even make it to court.

A Big Man needs to be all-powerful and above the law to feel secure. In the whole of sub-Saharan Africa over the past fifty years only the Ivory Coast has not had a bloody coup, while the rest of the continent has had over seventy.

In 1975 JM Kariuki led a revolt in Kenya, fighting against the social inequality he and his followers saw in President Jomo Kenyatta's government. He was betrayed and shot by one of his own followers, and it led to Kenyatta reinforcing his authority, using the police and the military to restore order and maintain stability. When Commander General Jackson Mulinge tried to use the army against President Moi's KANU government in 1982, Moi claimed there were foreign powers trying to overthrow him and 'grooming a certain person' to take over from him, without specifying who this person might be. This generated suspicion throughout the country, and there were over 150 lynchings of opposition sympathisers. This made people even more terrified of honestly speaking their minds, and all the more vocally supportive of Moi and everything he stood for, even if they didn't believe a word of it.

As he became more secure, high-level corruption became a defining part of President Moi's leadership style, and he often used his family for secretive deals, land transfers and negotiations. One of the many examples happened in 1988 when, on 'order of the President', building rights were granted on reserve land to Tristar Investments Limited, whose directors included President Moi's own son, Philip, using his pseudonym Philip Kipchirchir.

The majority of the police and judiciary were so involved in corruption that it was not in their interests to rock the boat, even for the benefit of the nation as a whole. From the ten shillings given to the policeman on the side of the road when he says you have been speeding, to the extra thirty percent added on to building costs that are needed to get a minister's signature, it is all part of life in Kenya, and there is little point in doing any more than shrug and get on with it.

Yuri told me that when President Moi's entourage came with a great fanfare to open the new wing of the AMREF – the flying doctor's offices near Wilson Airport – he and his minions were given use of the VIP suite for half an hour before he gave a speech, shook hands with the Director of AMREF and drove away again back up to State House in a nine car convoy. During this half hour they managed to dismantle the whole suite, stealing all the gold-plated taps, light switches and handrails in the bathroom, clearing out the complimentary drinks cupboard – not drinking them and leaving empty bottles, but just taking them all for later – as well as taking two standard lamps, three pictures off the wall and a telephone from the main reception room.

In sport it was no different, as I found out when I worked on the PA system during the tri-nations tournament between Kenya, South Africa, and Pakistan, towards the end of 1996.

Around the ground there were dozens of advertising boards for banks, businesses and beers keen to benefit from the television coverage, which would beam the games all over Africa as well as the cricket-mad sub-continent. The Kenya Cricket Association commissioned the promotion company MediaP as the agency to broker a deal for this television coverage, the advertising boarding, and much of the rest of the promotion of the series. MediaP, paying the KCA a fixed fee for the honour, then negotiated the best figure they could with MNET television and the sponsors and advertisers themselves. At the end of the tournament the Kenyan Cricket

Association found they had lost money on the whole event, while MediaP did very well out of it.

A few years later, in 2004, after repeated government orders, for the first time in nearly a decade the Kenyan Cricket Association turned their books over to independent auditors, and revealed they had debts of over forty million Kenyan shillings (US$650,000). In June of 2005, Guy Shyster, the Association's former chairman and marketing manager, and also Director of MediaP, was charged with corruption by the Kenyan Police for theft of US$3.3million of sponsorship money from the tri-nations tournament, much of which was intended for grassroot development of the game. Incredibly, the case was thrown out when the KCA's current chairman, Raymond Jiminy, told the judge he didn't believe that Guy Shyster had a case to answer. Shyster was a whale of a man, as wide round his waist as he was tall. It was unbelievable to learn that in his youth he had been an East African table tennis champion.

The Kenyan government sacked Shyster, and his entire committee, disbanded the Kenya Cricket Association and replaced it with a new organization named Cricket Kenya. The new committee is doing its best to sort out the mess left by the KCA and are striving to take Kenyan cricket forward.

While sitting behind my PA microphone I overheard a conversation between one of the Kenyan Cricket Association committee members and a member of the cricket board of another country. The Kenyan was trying to blow the whistle on Shyster. He told his friend that very little money was getting to the players and to the coaches, and absolutely none was filtering down to the youth development programme because Shyster was taking it all himself. The foreigner smiled deeply and put his arm round the Kenyan's shoulders. 'We know this, my brother,' he said. 'Even our chairman knows this. It is the way that cricket works.'

The following year, when another international side toured Kenya I found myself with the chance to speak to their chairman, and told him what was happening in Kenya. Although there were many people working really hard to develop the game at grassroots level, I said, they are battling against others who had their own interests at heart. The chairman smiled, patted my arm patronisingly and said he knew. 'That is the way the game works out here,' he said.

A couple of years later Hansie Cronje, the much respected South African captain, was convicted of match fixing and an inappropriate relationship with a bookmaker. 'It's not cricket,' people said. 'Football is one thing,' and they mentioned Grobbelaar, Maradona and others, 'but not in the gentleman's game,' and the world of cricket was outraged that corruption could find its way into the sport. But if the chairmen of two separate national cricket associations both knew about the corruption inherent in the Kenyan Cricket Association's then committee, and they still supported it, one has to wonder what else is going on around the world.

You come to wonder who the winners and losers in a game of cricket are, quite apart from those performing on the field.

But corruption in cricket, as in the rest of Kenya, is part of life. There is a book to be written about it I am sure, by someone braver and more committed than me.

31

Baby Danny had only been living with the Peters for a week when their house was broken into. Over a cup of tea in the Greenfields' staff room, Mark told Sally, Erica and me what had happened. 'They came in through the bathroom window,' he said.

He had said the same thing to Sergeant Josphat Mboya as he showed him round, and the policeman had nodded. 'I told him I thought there had been three of them because they had left three empty soda bottles in the kitchen.'

'He asked me to show him the kitchen, so I did, and he picked up an empty Fanta Orange bottle, scrutinised it and put it back down again carefully on the work surface. He looked around the kitchen. It must have looked so white and clean and different from his police digs.' Mark shook his head. 'His whole living space would probably have fitted into our kitchen. Anyway, I pointed to the pile of faeces on the kitchen floor, and he looked up at me grinning.'

'"They drank the sodas and left you a present," he said. "What else did they do?"'

'I showed him where I thought the men had climbed in through the bathroom window and crept along the corridor, past the bedrooms. I pointed out where Polly and I sleep, then Nia and Anna's room, and Danny's on his own on the end, but I said I thought they probably went down into the lounge room first.'

'He agreed and said he thought they most likely got the drinks on their way out, at the end, when their confidence was highest.'

'Polly and the children waited in the lounge room as I showed him round. The girls sat on a sofa yawning beneath a blanket while Polly held Danny in a shawl in her arms. Sergeant Mboya greeted them with a smile and started to say hello when he stopped, startled at the colour of Danny's skin.'

'He asked if he was our son and Polly told him Danny was adopted, but that, yes, he is our son.'

'I told him the thieves had taken the television and video and compact-disc player from the desk and our video camera and stills camera from the bureau. I was waving my arms around like a dervish and watching him lick his pencil and write details in his tatty notebook. Then there was my wallet and our passports from the desk drawer. I remember thinking that each of these things is probably worth more than his annual pay.'

'Polly pointed out that the cushion covers were missing too. Neither of us could think why they wanted them. There can't be much of a demand for cushion covers on the black market. The school provided them, and they weren't even very nice.'

'"Cushion covers?" the policeman nodded quietly. "To carry things in, Madam." Then he turned to me and asked what I had in my wallet? Was there a lot of money, Sir?'

'I told him there was nothing more than a couple of hundred shillings maybe. Perhaps a thousand. All I have here is the change in my pocket, and I took out the handful of coins and looked down at them mournfully and said not a great deal of money was taken because we try not to keep a lot in the house. He shook his head again. A thousand shillings is a couple of week's wages for a policeman, and I winced at my insensitivity as I said that. There was also my driving licence and card from the video store, I told him. I didn't think that either of these was a big deal, but replacing the licence will be a pain.'

'He repeated, "Your driver's licence?" a few times and made a note of it in his notebook, and then asked me to repeat how the whole thing happened, which I did. I had already told him twice, once over the phone and once more after I had picked him up from the police station.'

'I told him I woke about two, as I often do. A lingering bowel infection makes sleeping a full night through a rare occasion. I saw the bathroom window open but didn't think anything of it, but then after I'd used the bathroom, I went for a glass of water in the kitchen and saw the pile on the floor. I thought it might have been left by one of our dogs, but then I remembered we had lent them to a friend whose husband is overseas to give her a little more security.'

'The policeman asked me if many people knew about the dogs not being here, and I told him that some did, which was pretty stupid, as inside jobs are not uncommon. We *wazungu* think our staff should be loyal to us, but really why should they be? We pay them a dollar a day and expect them to put their lives on the line to protect our property. It's crazy.'

'Anyway, I told him I saw the empty bottles on the sideboard and knew something was up, so I called Polly, who went to check on the children while I checked the lounge room and noticed all the stuff was missing. Then I telephoned the police, and, because they can't afford petrol to fuel their cars, I drove down to the Kilimani Police Station to pick up Sergeant Mboya.'

'Once he had written it all down, Polly asked him whether he thought the thieves would be caught. He smiled and shook his head. She asked if he was going to look for fingerprints or something like that, and he held up his hands to say it was impossible. Out of his control. He wasn't from the Pinkerton Detective Agency after all. Hardly Sherlock Holmes or Eliot Ness.'

'I told him I'd drive him back to the police station, and we walked out to the car. At least with a police report the insurance company might be a little more forthcoming. There was nothing more we could do.'

'The sun was coming up as we bounced passed the YaYa Shopping Centre. People had already begun their walk into town. Black face after black face smartly presented in suits and shiny shoes and brightly-coloured polyester dresses – you know what it's like that time of day.'

'When we got to the police station, Sergeant Mboya turned to me and smiled, "You lost a lot, sir," he said. "Yeah," I replied. "It's annoying," and he agreed saying, "Yes, yes. What a shame."'

'"Still, at least no one got hurt," I said. He just sat there in the car, flicking through his notebook. "Your television and cameras and money," he said tapping the notebook on his knee and then, very theatrically, putting it away in his pocket.'

'"That's right," I said.'

'"Passports and driver's licence?"'

'"Yes."'

'"Your driver's licence?" He looked across at me nodding. I knew something was rotten in Denmark. "You know it is illegal to drive in this country with no licence?" he asked me.'

'"Yeah? Really?" I said.'

'"Yes. Illegal." He held my eyes for a moment and with calculated movements reached again for his notebook. Before he opened the book he stopped and said, "I tell you what. You and I, we might be able to come to an arrangement so I do not need to take this thing, this driving with no licence, further."'

'I couldn't believe it. "Illegal?" I said. "An arrangement?" I shook my head, laughed, and reached for the coins that are always kicking around in the ashtray. What a country. I have got to tell you, nothing could ever surprise me now.'

32

The High Commission agreed that the robbery at the Peters'
house was probably an inside job. There was the simple fact
that most crimes of this kind were, and the thieves seemed
to know the layout of the house so well.

Using Donald to translate, and me and Ron as bulky
backup, Mike Peters questioned the *askaris* on duty that
night, and they quickly admitted everything, relieved to have
the guilty secret taken from them. It was not their idea,
Donald said, but Father Marcus's. They were from the same
region as him, and he had found them the job at the school
in the first place. They owed him, and this was how he
wanted the debt to be repaid.

So they were all fired, and shuffled away with an apology
to Mike Peters and a glance at Donald that made me shudder.

Glen Stevens found us more reliable, church-going *askaris*,
who smiled and danced by the gate to keep themselves warm

during their night shift. One was the brother of Benjamin, who worked at Yuri's compound and always greeted me with a smile, asking about the state of Kenyan cricket even though he admitted he didn't know the rules. 'So, Mr Cricket,' he'd ask. 'What is this cricket?' and we'd talk for a little while, me naming the better teams and players in the national leagues, and telling him how Kenya were doing on the international stage. He'd nod, smile, and then admit he had no idea what I was talking about.

Felix, one of our new *askaris*, came up to my step and sat with me one evening, while I watched the new rains fall and the termites take flight on their one night of activity a year. It was a major event the first night the rains came. The termites crawled out of the earth and woodwork, flew heavenward, had sex, dropped back to earth, shed their wings and crawled under-ground until the next rains started. The Kenyans ran around grabbing them by the handful, stuffing them into pockets, so they could fry them up and eat them later. They make a good source of protein, but they didn't appeal much to me.

'*Jambo*, my friend,' said Felix, sitting down close beside me. 'When do you arrive in Kenya?' he asked me.

'About a year and a half ago,' I replied. The termites were fascinating and I wasn't in much of a mood for chatting. Sally was out on a date with a teacher from the Banda School and that bothered me, but I wasn't sure why, which also bothered me.

'How do you like it?' How many times had Kenyans started conversations with me this way?

When I first arrived in the country I tried to be friendly when strangers approached me. I'd politely refuse the five-times-a-day requests for money to bury a dead relative, to put a child through school, to build a water tank or pay a hospital bill. Pretty soon I started smiling a sad smile and simply shook my head, and more recently I found I became ruder each time I was approached.

'Do you like it here?' the *askari* asked again.

'Do I like it here? No, actually. Not a lot. Since I have been here my friend's house has been broken into with the robbers crapping on his floor and him being threatened by the police. I witnessed some of your mob-justice, been frustrated by the roads, the lack of water, the electricity shortages and the general corruption. I have had bad guts for over a year and that doesn't look like stopping. My friends and I are verbally abused pretty much every day, white children aren't safe outside of their houses, and I am tired of the constant begging and the fact your leaders don't help those that need help. No, I am afraid I don't like it here all that much at the moment.'

'Oh,' said the *askari*, a little unnerved by the tone of my answer. Normally people reply 'yes' and the conversation moves on. His face fell and I began to feel guilty about my tirade. It wasn't his fault after all. He was only trying to be friendly, and he was a friend of Glen's.

'Do you like it here?' I asked him more gently.

'Who? Me?' said Felix. There was no one else around.

'Yes. You.'

'Oh,' he said. 'About four thousand kilometres.' And he got up and walked back downstairs to join Nyambura and Robert, the other *askari*, chasing termites around the yard.

I shook my head. 'Four thousand kilometres?' I walked into my room, shut the door and went to bed. It was a relief, though, that he probably hadn't understood a word I'd said.

Later that night an African woman's voice called from the landing outside my door. 'Mr Griffiths,' she whispered. 'Mr Griffiths?'

I crawled out of bed and stumbled through the darkness to the door. 'What is it?' I asked. 'Who's there?' There had been shuffling feet and voices on the landing for ten minutes, so there was little chance of me still being asleep. 'What do you want?'

'It is me. I have come.' I opened the door a little and switched on my light. It was Nyambura, who worked in the school kitchens and was taking care of her sister in her room next to Donald's. She looked smaller than ever. 'It is me,' she said.

'What can I do for you, Nyambura?' I looked at my watch. 'It is very late.' She had never been up to my room before, and as she began to cry I realised how scared she was to be there. I opened the door wider and tried to smile comfortingly, but with my bed-hair and wearing only shorts, I can't have helped much. 'Hang on,' I said. 'I'll put some clothes on.'

'My sister,' she said. 'She is dead.' I dressed quickly and followed her down to the compound, splashing across the yard to the servant's quarters.

Donald was in her room, kneeling beside her narrow bed with his head bent in prayer while the *askaris*, Robert and Felix, hung around outside, looking at their feet and whispering in Kiswahili.

The room smelt of flowers with a bunch of fresh frangipani in a dented can on a chair beside the bed, where Nyambura's sister was covered in a thin white sheet. She was so small that it was hard to believe she was there at all. I had never met her and didn't even know her name. To me she had only

216

ever been Nyambura's sister, who was dying of Aids in the room next to Donald's.

Nyambura went in and knelt beside Donald, who put his hand on her shoulder reassuringly, and stood up. He smiled at me and took my hand. 'I must stay here with the body,' he said, and I nodded. 'You must tell the police what has happened.'

So I found myself driving one of Greenfields' minibuses along Argwings Kodhek Road towards Kilimani Police Station, with Nyambura weeping on the front seat beside me. We stood in front of the reception desk as the sleepy policeman stretched in his chair and grunted a monosyllabic response to my '*Jambo*' and Nyambura's tears – the silent language of her grief.

I told him what had happened and he shrugged. 'What do you want me to do, *mzungu*?'

'My friend's sister is dead,' I told him. 'Surely you should do something.'

'Like what?' he shrugged. 'She is dead. There is nothing I can do.'

'But don't you want to check her to be sure she is dead?' I said.

'Is she dead?' he asked.

'Yes. I think so.'

'Then I can do nothing,' and he smiled at my stupidity. *Wazimu wazungu* – crazy white men – they are so sentimental.

'What about checking she wasn't murdered or something?'

'Was she?'

'No, I don't think so,' and he shrugged again. 'I can give you a lift if it helps,' I said. 'There must be some checks you should do or something.'

'*Mzungu*, in Africa people die and she has died. It happens.' He held his hands wide and smiled. 'She has died and there is nothing I can do. I am a policeman, not a magician.'

So we drove back along Argwings Kodhek Road to school, where I explained to Donald what happened and he shook my hand. 'You tried, my friend,' he said. 'Tomorrow we will take her to the city mortuary and arrange for her to be taken back to her home place. Tonight I will pray with Nyambura.'

In the morning the *askaris* wrapped her body in the sheet and propped it up in the back of the minibus. Nyambura had run out of tears and sat in silence beside me at the front. Donald sat in the back beside her sister to stop her body toppling over as I bounced the vehicle along Ngong Road to the city mortuary.

We waited for an hour in a queue before we were registered and the body was taken in. Another two hours and nine hundred shillings in *chai* while 'processing' took place, and then I drove us back to school.

It is Kikuyu and Samburu tradition that if a person dies in a house then the house should be destroyed to free the person's soul. Often, just before they die, the family of the dying person will drag them out of the house and leave them to breathe their last in the dust. Once dead, they carry the body back, and the funeral traditions take over. If they mistimed it, they must burn down the house, even if it is their only one, and they have no other shelter.

The servants' quarters in the Greenfields compound were made of stone, and when we arrived back Felix and Robert were arguing about what should be done. I pointed out that neither Mr Rivers nor Mr Peters would be pleased if they burnt the block down. Nyambura burst into tears at the thought of her sister's trapped soul, screaming in limbo, and she slumped down in the dust exhausted. Donald said he knew prayers to release trapped sprits and asked me to sit with him while he said them.

He told the *askaris* he could absorb the trapped spirits inside himself, like a sin-eater, and then come outside the room and release them to the great outdoors. It was hard, he said, but worth doing. He didn't want her to be in limbo for long, he said, so he and I sat and prayed in the room and then again, kneeling beneath the frangipani tree near the gate.

Nyambura knelt with us outside but would not go back into her room, so Donald swapped his things with hers and her room became his, and his became hers. Then she packed her bag, put on her best clothes and headed up country to tell her family what had happened and to arrange a funeral fitting for her beloved sister. She had ten siblings still living, Donald told me, so it would take some organising. In a few days the body would arrive and the preparations must be made before then.

A few days later Donald told me he made up his spirit-absorption routine. He said he knew God was far more powerful than stone walls and a corrugated-tin roof, and he grinned. He said he was sure God would be able to find Nyambura's sister's soul without his help. If it kept Nyambura happy and stopped the *askaris* burning the place down, then so be it.

33

One weekend during the Easter term Mark and I played a game for the Mombassa Sports Club, who had a cricket match against an Indian development team from Mumbai.

We left Nairobi after lunch on the Friday, Mark driving, me in the passenger seat and his family in the back of the double-cabbed pick-up. We made it down to the Traveller's Beach Hotel to the north of Mombasa just as night fell. In the morning we ate fresh fruit on the veranda overlooking the golden sand and millpond Indian Ocean.

We stayed at the hotel that day, playing cricket on the beach and speeding across the surf on 750cc jet skis, being blinded by the spray, with knees buckling and ankles knocking as the machines took off over the wake made by other skiers.

The tide was out in the afternoon, so we went up the coast to a small leisure park with some water-flumes and took turns with the kids on the slides and swings and bubbling hot tubs. The weather got hotter and more humid as the day went on, and in the evening a tropical storm lashed down on the coast, and we watched the lightning dancing across the ocean from the safety of the glass-fronted hotel restaurant.

In the evening we took a waiter's advice and chose a goat curry, which I threw up all night. I stumbled down to breakfast weak and exhausted. The morning weather was still again after the storm, but the day was already hot, and I sipped bottled iced water wishing I didn't have to play cricket and cursing the sunshine.

Polly and the children played on the beach, while Mark and I drove to the Mombasa Sports Club for the game.

The Mumbai development team fielded three ex-international players and several youngsters who would go on to play for India in the future. They won the toss and batted first and Dilip Joglekar, Mombasa's captain, threw me the ball to open the bowling from the pavilion end.

'I'm feeling a bit rough,' I told him, but he wasn't listening.

'I asked Rivers to send me a bowler, so you will bowl. Yes?' he said, so I measured out my run up and tried to concentrate, but I felt so weak. My first over was a maiden, the second went for ten, the third for twelve and my fourth for nine as a pair of fifteen-year-old left-handers smashed my best efforts to all parts of the ground.

Mark took over from me, and I was relegated to sweat on the boundary in front of the pavilion where one of the club waiters brought me a big bottle of water on a battered silver tray.

Mark bowled his first over and then came running off the field towards me. 'I just pooped myself,' he said as he ran past. 'It's that bloody curry. I could hold it in when I was just fielding, but not bowling. Won't be a moment.' He ran into the changing room and straight into the shower, dropped his trousers around his feet and washed himself clean without even removing his boots. Then he pulled on his trousers again, ran back outside and was ready to start his next over.

'I'm sweating so much anyway I'm no wetter after my shower than I was before it,' he said, heading back onto the field. 'What a country!' and he laughed.

Luckily for us the heat grew into a storm and the game was abandoned in the early afternoon. Mumbai scored 2-276 from their fifty-overs, and we were 3-80 after twenty when the rain came and the Indians ran for cover.

'Shame,' said Mark grinning with relief that he wouldn't have to run around in the heat any longer. He had opened the batting and scored a solid thirty, and was just starting to get on top of the bowling. He stood in the rain with his pads and helmet on. 'I was looking forward to smashing those Indian seamers miles.' He twirled his Newberry bat with a flourish.

Back at the Traveller's Beach the sun still shone, and as we packed up the car for the long drive west we watched the black clouds creeping up the coast towards us. Polly drove as far as Voi, when it got dark, and then Mark took over, slipped a Pearl Jam tape into the stereo to keep himself awake, and got us safely back to Nairobi.

I slept most of the way and hardly remember them dropping me off, and crawling up the concrete steps to bed. When I was woken by the call to prayer next morning, I found I was glad to be back in the city again. There was a lot wrong with Nairobi, but it felt like home.

34

Some weekend mornings during the rains, I lay in bed listening to the *askaris* talking, to Nyambura singing as she swept pools of water off the compound, and to the weaver-birds working away in the frangipani tree outside my window.

Working such long, tedious hours for so little money, Kenyans are an amazing race. There were so many kind people we never mentioned in the Nairobi Club after practice sessions, and I felt sorry about that. Why do we only talk about the madness and so seldom the kindness?

Though the country is in danger of falling apart, people concentrate on struggling through the *El Niño* rains and getting enough food to feed their families, while not antagonising any of the Big Men or government-backed thugs. It is much easier for someone with nothing to become a thug, and to steal a few things to get by, when there are so few options and you have a family to feed. It must be tempting to pack up your possessions and abandon your family completely, and start again somewhere else without any dependants.

As I looked around my little room at my radio, cricket bat and books, which together cost far more than a Kenyan's annual income, let alone his disposable income, I felt ashamed by my anger and frustration at the country. After all, I was enjoying a far higher standard of living than a teacher could ever hope for back home. I was having an incredible experience, seeing amazing sights, teaching obedient children with a supportive head and reasonable facilities, and I could leave this life for my old one at any time I wanted, without even so much as a backward thought. Really, what was there to complain about?

I'd stretch and yawn and roll out of bed with nothing to do all day. Sometimes I took a book off the shelf and tried to drift away, sitting in the half-light of my room with curtains closed and light off, in an attempt to read myself away from the present and my guilt at my token involvement in it.

What right do I have to criticize a people and a place when it's so easy for me to leave, and when my bad attitude really doesn't help anyone anyway? It is so much easier to be critical than to be optimistic, and my mood darkened at my weakness.

I thought momentarily about the street-boys and how my reaction to them had changed in the time I had been in Kenya. Once I had chatted to them, but now I had more time for the dogs that guarded the school gates. Other people, like Mrs Simpson down in Watamu, Mrs Carla Jones who helped set up the arboretum, and especially Mr Rivers, were far more compassionate than me. They had been in Kenya for years and always saw the beauty of the country and the Kenyan people before they saw the potholed roads, the piles of rubbish on the corners and the tales of corruption in the newspapers. They had the strength to accept the journey that every culture makes, recognising the thousand years of social evolution that the developed Western world has imposed on East Africa in just one century, and acknowledging their responsibility to help the country move forward.

Everyone knew that President Daniel arap Moi would eventually be ousted and would be replaced by one of his former henchmen, who would promise an end to corruption and real changes for the Kenyan people. There would be free primary school education and better health care, with nurses in hospitals who didn't steal the patients' food. A wave of optimism would sweep the nation.

But even in the most developed countries there is corruption. In the UK, a vast number of children leave school with no qualifications and only the faintest grasp of the written word, and even in the United States, the last great superpower, where huge numbers of people can't afford health care, they still have wealth, possessions and standard of living that the average African could only dream of.

So what hope for Kenya and the rest of the developing world? The West needs cheap labour and wants cheap food and turns a blind eye to the poor people who stay poor so that we can stay wealthy. That is the bottom line, and it always will be.

Sometimes, reading in a darkened room helped change my mood, and then I'd drift away for hours, following John Steinbeck's description of Tom Joad and his family crossing America in their old jalopy, or Hemingway's Robert Jordan planning his explosion in the high pine forests of the Spanish sierra. Hours later, I would remember my surroundings and be surprised to find myself in Kenya.

Other days, the words wouldn't focus, and I'd drop the book on the bed beside me before I had read half a dozen pages, and I'd pull on my hundred-pounds sterling lightweight trainers and go for a run around the school playing-fields. Only the mud from the night rains would have turned the earth into a soup, and I'd slip and slide and struggle to stay upright and breathe a sigh of relief when I made it back to the compound without breaking an ankle. Then I'd hand my filthy trainers to Nyambura and watch her from my hot shower, washing them with Omo at the cold-water tap by the servants' quarter pit-latrine.

When she returned them to my room, cleaned and dry later in the day I gave her a twenty-shilling note, which was enough to be worth her while, but not so much as to unbalance the pay structure. I would have willingly paid one hundred shillings – one pound sterling – but that was what the *askaris* got for a whole day's guarding, so paying her the same amount for twenty minutes' work was sure to cause trouble between them.

35

In August 1997 the British Foreign Office reported that thirty-three people had been killed in Mombasa. The violence was politically motivated, and while it was not targeting tourists the suggestion was that it 'could become indiscriminate at very short notice'.

They recommended tourists stay away from Kenya's Northern Province, the Tana River District, Marsabit, the coastal strip north of Malindi, and the road between Shaba and Samburu, so in their view great swathes of Kenya should be considered no-go areas.

In the Nairobi Club on a Friday night Douglas Slater had trouble defending the British government's advice.

'We at the High Commission are suggesting that people exercise extreme caution here,' he sang. 'That's all. The atmosphere is changing in Kenya, and that cannot be denied.'

'Moi could start thrashing like a wounded tiger, if he feels under threat in the elections come Christmas time,' David Brown said, supporting his boss. 'And as the elections get nearer, more groups will try to exert pressure on him, and more opposition groups will rile up their supporters to behave in the most unusual ways.'

'Mankind is a confused and fearful beast,' said Reg Gerald, who worked for a shipping agency and had been making regular short trips to countries all over Africa for years. He enjoyed the role of having seen everything and survived to tell the tale. On his next trip to Nairobi, however, he was paralysed during a carjacking, with three bullets shattering his spine. 'Your worst case scenario is less than a speck of sweat against the ocean of chaos that might ensue,' he smiled.

'It doesn't help the Kenyan if the tourist industry collapses,' said Wally Dawkins, a South African who worked for the Serena Group and claimed to have once played cricket for the great Natal side of the 1960s, when the likes of Mike Procter and Barry Richards were the stars. 'That would cause more poverty and more people with nothing to lose. If anything can destabilize a country it's people losing all they had and seeing no peaceful way of getting it back. Anyway, Nairobi is no more dangerous than Moscow, New York, areas of Sydney or London, let alone Johannesburg. So why pick on Kenya? Tens of thousands of people come here and never see a single thing to worry them.'

Douglas Slater nodded. 'True,' he said, 'but you can't suggest we should say nothing when it has got to a stage that government troops can storm a church in Mombasa and beat up a bishop as he talked to his parishioners, with no charges being made against these soldiers?' He looked round at the group of us with sorrow in his eyes. 'I love this country. You all know that,' he said, 'but it's lunacy to suggest that things won't *potentially* be allowed to get worse.' He owned a house in Kilifi and planned to retire there in a few years. 'What good would it do the nation to have a major atrocity with Western tourists being killed or taken hostage? How can that help anyone here in the long term?'

'It's one thing if Africans all over the continent kill each other in their battle to find democracy. Every nation on earth has done that over the years, and they always will. I am not devaluing the importance of each and every human life when I say this, but that sort of thing makes a twenty-five-second spot on the mainstream news worldwide, and perhaps takes up ten minutes before a *Newsnight* arts review, but to the general public no one will notice. You know that this is true. But if a European or, God forbid, an American gets blown to smithereens, or even caught in the crossfire of someone else's battle, it won't be off the screens for weeks.' Douglas fell silent and shook his head mournfully.

'And we at the High Commission will be held accountable for not warning the world of the risk,' said David Brown. 'Caution is a far more responsible emotion than regret.'

David, Yuri and I stood in the car park a little later, watching as people danced around an overturned and burning *matatu* that had capsized in a crater on the edge of Ngong Road. I felt like we had been here before. Many, many times.

'President Moi is a corrupt and vicious egomaniac,' David said. 'He tortures dissidents and is suffocating his country's growth with his greed. It is only right that he will get his comeuppance.'

'He who lives by the sword,' said Yuri.

'Exactly.'

'Do you think we should be going to bed with our bags packed and ready?' I asked.

'Not yet, big guy,' Yuri laughed. 'But keep your eyes and ears open. You will know when it is the right time for you to go. And when you know, you go. No matter what. Alright?' Yuri put his hand on my shoulder to make sure I was really listening. 'All that regret and caution talk is true. I have no time for brave people who are also dead people.' He turned to David who nodded in agreement. 'David has orders to stay to help others. I have to stay to fly sick people to safety, but ask yourself if it really matters whether any of these children learn to play cricket or not?'

And how small did I feel later that evening, sitting on Yuri and Anya's balcony, eating pizza and watching a dreadful American movie on their television? And as the reality of life in a developing country again sunk in, I thought of my parents' farm and their Welsh Black cattle and the cereals that they would soon be starting to harvest. I knew how much my father would wish for another pair of willing hands and a strong back around the place.

My home called out to me then, and after Yuri dropped me back at Greenfields, I sat on the steps up to my room and looked down at the *askaris* huddled around their *giko*, wearing thick coats and woollen balaclavas. I watched the smoke from the charcoal rising and circling over the high compound wall with the spikes along the top, and I felt the tears coming.

It is hard to define the longing for home, but I felt it then so strongly.

36

At the start of the autumn term, Greenfields' deputy head teacher, Mrs Benson, flew back to the UK after a botched operation to remove some polyps from her nose. Somehow the doctors in Nairobi Hospital managed to puncture her cranial membrane, leaving cerebral fluid seeping out and her with the real danger of catching meningitis. Kenya was no place for her, so she packed up tearfully and went home.

With more control over what happened in the school, Mark Peters thought up the idea of inviting an outside theatre company to come in to run an interactive workshop and performance with the top two years.

He apologised to Sally and me, saying that he understood how hard we worked on the last pantomime and hoped we wouldn't be offended by not putting a play on this year. We smiled graciously and said we'd come to terms with it. He said he had spoken to the 'Association of People with Aids in

Kenya' about doing a health-related play, which would be educational and fun too.

Three representatives from TAPWAK visited him the next day with plans for the workshop. Their graphic posters silenced Mark as they ran through the storyline, which strove to change age-old Kenyan custom.

In tribal tradition, if a man dies leaving a widow, she must sleep with his brother to cleanse her of his spirit, while if a couple are childless for a long time, one of his older relatives must sleep with her to cleanse her 'barrenness'. A brother cannot marry unless his older brother is already married. Even if a husband or wife know they have Aids, if they are childless, they must still try to conceive, as they believe it is immoral to die childless.

After dark, in northern Kenya around Marsabit, couples copulate in the street as they have done for centuries, and health educators are run out of town and accused of trying to weaken a tribe by saying free sex is wrong.

The representatives left a video for Mark to show to newly in-country staff, and he sat with us in the staff room while we watched and tried to eat biscuits during the morning break. There were pictures of men with syphilis, genital sores and the emaciated forms of people nearing their deaths.

If I did have any plans to have unprotected sex with prostitutes, the images of scabby rockeries growing out the end of so many penises would have reversed them, and looking around the room at my pale-faced colleagues, it was clear they felt the same.

At the end Mark stood up and smiled. 'Well, I think we are going to have to rethink the theme of this production.' He took the tape out of the video machine and put it high on a shelf. 'If anyone can think of a suitable time to show this to their pupils, do let me know.' He stopped in the doorway and smiled back into the room, 'I'll tell the cooks you lot might be off your lunch.'

So he and Polly wrote and directed a play called *Solomon and the Ant*, while Sally and I spent the rains in the gym happily teaching badminton and dance. Anything was better than being involved in another pantomime.

37

Donald had just got back from a trip to Kisumu in western Kenya, where he was dropping a student at a family funeral. He had driven one of Greenfields' newer four-wheel drive pick-up trucks with a twin cab and anti-lock brakes. It was the top of the range and had just been serviced, and he loved driving the thing.

He leant against the wall outside my door and blew a long stream of cigarette smoke out into the clear night sky and smiled toothlessly. 'My friend, I did not think I would ever get home,' he said and grimaced.

The roads out west are even more potholed and cracking than the roads around Nairobi, he told me, and the bus and taxi drivers were a good deal more reckless. Many seemed to have a date with death, as they weaved through traffic and overtook on the left, over road kerbs and on blind corners. Some drove with a '*Mash Allah*' attitude – 'it is the will of

Allah' – saying they will die at their own appointed time. If they died in a smash at three-thirty on a Tuesday, then that was their time, and even if they hadn't been driving like a lunatic with twenty-three people crammed into their minibus on the outskirts of Kitale, but sitting quietly behind a desk or smoking absent-mindedly in their *shamba*, they still would have died, just in a different way. '*Mash Allah*' – 'the will of Allah'.

Donald often prayed as he sat behind the wheel; he was proud of his voice and sometimes sang hymns to pass the time. As a member of the First Church of Kenya, he was proud of his faith too, and often thought about it deeply when he was out on the road. The First Church of Kenya preached charity, compassion and consideration, which were three things he knew to be lacking in his country, despite the religious claims of the majority.

'It drives me crazy to see some of the things I see out on the road,' he said, and would be tight-lipped and fuming when he got back to school, still gripping the steering wheel in anger, after being carved up by a *matatu* or an overladen push-bike wheeling dangerously across the road. He would try to breathe deeply, say a prayer to the Almighty for patience, and tell himself he should not let the few who frustrated him get him down. He regularly admitted he found it hard sometimes, but he was proud to be able to say he had never sworn in angry circumstances. He had always managed to keep control and remove his negativity with a prayer.

As he drove back from Kitale, Donald said his mind was not entirely on his driving. There were surprisingly few vehicles on the road, and he was thinking of the colobus monkeys stealing charcoal from the piles on sale by the side of the road, and the huge numbers of butterflies in the woods. He was no lepidopterist, but he did like butterflies.

'I had dropped down into a valley just after Kakamega Town,' he said. 'The road veers to the left and then goes over a bridge.' He nodded as he remembered the bridge all too well. 'On another day I probably would have seen the lorry with the broken axle on the other side of the road, and I possibly would have slowed down and perhaps asked if I could be of assistance.' Donald was that kind of man. 'But today, today, I didn't see the broken-down lorry, and I didn't see the Akamba bus hurtling down the hill on the far side of the valley. I didn't see it swing out, trying to get around the lorry without losing its momentum.'

When Donald did notice the bus, it was too late.

'I tried to swerve the pick-up truck off the road and out of the path of the bus. But the wing of the bus clipped the tail-end of the truck, which spun and turned over and the next thing I knew, I was dangling by my seatbelt upside down in the maize, eye to eye with a bleating goat.'

People started to gather round and he was helped to a boulder where he sat, dazed and confused, and was sick.

Eventually he pulled himself together enough to need a cigarette, and he felt in his pocket for his lighter. But he couldn't find it. Thinking it must have fallen out during the crash he staggered back to the cab to have a look.

'The crowd had thinned out a little by now. A couple of young men went off to find their cousin, who had a tractor they could use to right the pick-up. A few other people hung about doing very little other than looking and talking.

'I looked all over the cab for the lighter. I looked in the glove compartment and then on the ceiling behind the sun-visor.

Perhaps it was caught beneath the seat, I thought. Even in the map pocket in the door, but it was nowhere to be found.'

He found his jacket and went through the pockets to see if he had inadvertently put it away at his last stop, but it wasn't there either.

In fact there was nothing in his pockets. No ID pouch. No small family photograph album. No loose change and no wallet. He had been completely cleaned out.

Donald Otieno had always tried his best to think kindly of his fellow man. He believed that the bad stories he heard were merely isolated incidents, and that generally men were decent beings. But as he stood on the side of the Kitale to Kisumu road holding his jacket in one hand and an unlit Rooster cigarette in the other, he swore like he had never sworn before.

'I will tell you my friend, Griff. It was as if I had been saving up all the profanities that I could have justified using over the years for this one moment.' He smiled. 'Yes, I want to tell you, they poured forth so fluently I would have made a drunken sailor in a Mombasa bar proud.'

38

It was nearly 1am when the telephone rang.

I was asleep on the sofa in Yuri and Anya's front room and the phone was two feet from my head. Half asleep I mumbled '*Jambo*' into the receiver.

'Hello? Mr Yuri?' shouted an African voice down the line.

'No, no it is not Yuri. I am not him,' I said. 'Hold on, I'll call him. Who is it?'

I climbed the stairs and whispered 'Yuri?' through their bedroom door. 'It's the phone, for you.'

'Who is it?'

'Solomon Ochieng.'

'Never heard of him. Tell him to piss off.'

'He wouldn't call this late if it wasn't important,' murmured Anya, and I heard Yuri shuffle out of bed. He followed me downstairs and picked up the receiver, as I crawled back under my blanket on the sofa.

'Hello?' he said and there was a pause as he listened to the caller. 'No,' said Yuri. 'No, I'm sorry. I don't know who you are; it's very late, and I won't give you twenty-five thousand shillings,' and he hung up the phone.

As he stumbled back up the stairs, I heard Yuri's despairing voice. 'It's one o'clock in the morning,' he said. 'Hell, man. I really don't understand this country.'

39

Civil disobedience increased as the elections neared, and violence became more common. There were stories in the *Daily Nation* about unarmed gangsters stealing the guns from armed police and holding them to ransom at gunpoint. The police are charged for every bullet they fire, so they load them backwards because they don't want the guns to go off by accident and waste half a day's pay through clumsiness.

There was a spate of daylight ram-raider robberies around Nairobi, followed by stories of armed police running away. The robbers sped away in their ex-military vehicles, triumphantly waving their AK-47s at passers-by. And there were never any witnesses. Everyone knew better than to be a witness.

President Moi swore in great numbers of additional General Service Unit officers, who sped around the city in big old blue trucks. They picked up suspected troublemakers, broke up disturbances and supported the police when they were out-numbered or inadequate. Some policemen rode horses because they couldn't afford fuel for their vehicles, while others clung on to the outsides of *matatus* that were going their way.

David Brown from the High Commission got caught up in a gun battle as he drove along Langatta Road one lunch time. He curled up weeping in the footwell of his vehicle after a stray bullet had broken his windshield. Another killed a rioter who was standing in front of his car.

'They ran up the road towards me,' he said, 'with house bricks in their hands. I watched one of them break the windscreen of the car in front and then turn to me laughing as he raised his arm to throw the stone at me. I saw him look up as the police on horseback rode up from the Nyayo Stadium and his grin froze. Then the shooting started and he got hit.' Three mounted policemen galloped down the road, brandishing short clubs which they were not shy about using. 'The car was covered in blood, which stained the seats. It smells in the heat of the day, and I can't get the marks out. I don't know how I am going to sell the damn thing.' He tried to laugh. 'I just don't know,' and his voice trailed away.

Ron found Carla Jones on the side of State House Road, after she was beaten up walking home from the arboretum early one evening. He hid behind a tree and watched the gang of robbers steal the elderly woman's shoes and sunglasses, and wander away chatting, unperturbed. Then he ran over, picked her up and carried her round the corner to his flat, where Geraldine treated her, and they took her to Nairobi Hospital by taxi.

Despite all of this, we tried to live normal lives. The children kept coming to school, and we kept teaching them.

We still gathered at Nairobi Club for Friday evening practice, and we still played cricket matches on the weekend. But we all listened to the radio for news of disturbances and changed plans to avoid them.

I stood outside the Greenfields' gate one afternoon after school, waiting for Glen Stevens to take me up to a part of Kabira slum that I hadn't visited before.

Kabira is Nairobi's biggest shanty town, with many distinct districts, and Glen was keen to get some sport happening there.

'Where in Kabira is this place? I asked the *askari* sitting on a rock by the gate.

'Not far,' he said and waved his arm vaguely south towards the centre of town and beyond.

Argwings Kodhek Road was quiet. The radio told me that down in town all hell was breaking out at an Opposition rally in Uhuru Park, where KANU activists were doing their best to ensure that it didn't pass off peacefully.

'Yes, but where is it?' I ask. 'Where actually in Kabira? How do you get there?'

'Nairobi Dam. Near the dam!'

I breathed a sigh of relief. We could get there along Mbgathi Way without having to go anywhere near town.

'The radio says there are roadblocks here and there,' I told him. 'People being stopped and cars being stolen.' He nodded. He was an old man and had lived through this sort of thing many times before. He must have been a boy during *Mau Mau*. 'It's pretty safe around here though?' I asked to boost my confidence.

'Yes, yes. Pretty safe around here,' he echoed and smiled a toothless smile.

245

One of the African teachers, Mary Odinga, called to me from the main school building, saying that I had a phone call.

'Hello there,' said Glen Stevens. 'The radio says the highway is full of "disturbances" so I think we'd better put the clinic off for another time. Is that OK? I'm not planning on even leaving my compound this evening.' He lived much nearer to town, and with a wife and children it was wise that they all stayed there together.

I walked out onto Argwings Kodhek and turned right to go up to the Yaya Centre to buy some food, but as I left the school gate a large blue General Service Unit truck pulled to a halt thirty yards up the road. Six officers leaped out of the back, grabbed an old man standing by the road and beat him with sticks until he lay flat out on the ground.

I ran back into the school compound and helped the *askari* to close the gate. We peeped out through the fence and watched the officers climb back into the truck and move off towards town. After a moment the old man struggled to his feet and hobbled past us in the opposite direction. No one came to his aid. No one was that stupid. You didn't know what he was supposed to have done, and you didn't want to be caught up with him however imaginary his crime might be.

The *askari* opened the gate and sat back down again on his rock.

'Oh yes,' he said smiling up at me. 'It is pretty safe around here.'

40

Many Kenyans were amazed when the Conservative Government lost the UK election and John Major quietly packed his bags and moved out of Downing Street. If he had been in Africa, he would have barricaded himself inside No.10 and not come out without a fight, I was told on numerous occasions. The youthful Mr Blair and cheesy-grinning Cherie would have had more of a battle on their hands to get him out of the building than the one they had to get him out of office, but that is not the British style. The Kenyans were pleased that Blair had got in. He spoke of change and promised an ethical foreign policy. He had special affection for Africa, he said, and, along with everyone at home, the Kenyans started the long wait for him to be true to his word.

I had letters from friends at home, expressing the delight in our new leader. My generation couldn't remember a time before the scary Thatcher and dullard Major Conservative Governments, so to have a guitar-playing family man now leading the country had to be a good thing. He even had Noel Gallagher round to No.10 for tea, after all.

But in Africa no one gives up anything without a struggle, and it is rare that any change comes about without violence. In Uganda, for example, Milton Obote used bloodshed to come to power twice and was twice forced out in the same way. Idi Amin's use of violence to solve a problem was even worse. Today it is safe to walk most of Kampala's streets day or night, but a lot of innocent lives were lost in getting there.

As a Kenyan citizen, if you don't like the way your government runs the county, the best way to let them know is on the streets. Suggestions that you should write to your MP generated laughter, and the thought of being openly critical of President Moi or his policies carried the threat of sedition, particularly if you did it in writing. Providing your enemies with a signed letter complaining about some issue would lead you to disaster. The only way to show dissent is to join together with a mass of others and run around in the dark throwing stones and setting fire to things.

I ran a few early-evening coaching clinics for Kenyatta University, a little way out of town along the Thika Road. The plan was to teach cricket to trainee teachers, so they could take the game with them all over Kenya, away from its traditional centres of Nairobi, Kisumu and Mombasa, introducing it to the bush.

This was at the same time that there were riots in the city centre, led by the Nairobi University students. They were protesting about stories in the *Daily Nation*, that many lecturers were taking bribes and sexual favours from students to improve their grades, and that this year's results should not be taken too seriously.

The students were furious and their anger spilled over into violence. Many lecturers feared for their lives and retired from their university posts halfway through the term, disappearing back up-country to their home-places. This led to rumours that many of the exam papers would never get marked, and newly-graduated teachers were drafted in to replace the experienced ex-lecturers. The students rioted again at this insult, and the violence spiralled.

When I collected up the tennis balls from around the gym at the end of one of my coaching sessions, I found some fist-sized pieces of breeze-block of perfect throwing size and shape which a student had brought in with him should trouble break out.

I mentioned this to my contact at the university, who smiled and patted me on the shoulder. 'In teaching, there is nothing worse than being unprepared,' Mr. Kimaiyo said. 'It is good to see we have taught them something.'

A week later, on the rainy evening of the 1997 Budget Day, Sally and I drove around State House Road on our way to the movies in town.

There had been rumours that riots were being planned to coincide with Budget Day, but these had come to nothing, and as parents picked up their children from school, there was a feeling of relief that the day was passing off so quietly.

Sally beat the Yellow Peril's steering wheel in time to Sheryl Crow, singing, '*This ain't no disco, this is LA*' on the radio, and we drove along University Way, past the left-hand turn for Arboretum Drive, heading down the hill towards the youth hostel.

It was about 7pm and there was a large group of people

gathered together on the side of the road outside the Nairobi University residential halls. Neither Sally nor I thought twice about them, imagining they were a group of students coming home after a lecture or a university function.

'*All I want to do is have a little fun before I die, says the guy next to me out of nowhere*' sang Sheryl, and Sally reached for the cigarette lighter. Then there was a crash on the door of the car and the people had gathered round us, shouting, throwing stones and waving sticks.

'What the hell,' we chorused.

'What do I do?'

'Go on, go, go,' and she put her foot to the floor.

We couldn't stop. It would have been insane to stop, so we sped down towards the Catholic church on the corner. In the distance I saw fire and more people, and as we came nearer we saw a burning tree blocking the road.

There was another car close behind us, and the narrow road was lined with people. As Sally pulled to a halt just short of the tree, a young man jumped out in front of our car. He climbed onto the bonnet, and another banged on my window. Someone opened Sally's door, hauling her out into the street. She called my name, and the man laughed and took the cap off her head and started dancing round the car laughing at her. '*Howareyoumzungu? Howareyoumzungu?*'

I unlocked my door and pushed it open standing with one foot on the road, not knowing what I could do and remembering stories about carjackings and people being stripped and left to run home in their underpants. I wondered how long we would have to beat on their door before the Catholic priests would let two near-naked white folks into the safety of their presbytery.

Then one of the Kenyan national-team cricketers was there. I recognised his face in the light of the fires. '*Hapana*, Jonah,' he called in Kiswahili. '*Nina ha-jua. Yeye ni mwanaume nzuri.* He is a g-good man,' he shouted to the man dancing round Sally and gestured me back into the car. 'Y-y-you go, you g-go,' he stuttered in English and pointed back up the hill.

We climbed back into the car and locked the doors behind us. Sally pulled a three-point turn and sped back up the hill as fast as the battered yellow car could take us, weaving round the rocks in the road and the branches ripped from trees, which would soon be added to more fires as the riot spread towards State House.

As we passed the crowd of stone-throwers outside the youth hostel, there was another crash as we were hit again, this time on the vehicle's roof, just above Sally's head, but then we were gone, down Arboretum Drive and away. '*And all I want to do is have some fun, can you tell me I ain't the only one*,' sang Sheryl Crow.

We took the long way back to school, driving slowly through Westlands and along James Gichuru Road, where we were carved up by a barely roadworthy *matatu*.

We went to my room, drank tea and cried. Sally slept there that night, and the following one, and by the middle of the next week her toothbrush was in the mug next to mine on the basin in my bathroom. It seemed the most natural thing to do.

Later we heard that the students' protests had been entirely peaceful, simply waving placards and singing songs. Then the police received orders to start baton charges and to use tear-gas on them. Then the students got angry and violent.

41

Donald was delighted Sally and I were together.

'You are my good friends,' he smiled. 'This is very good.'
But Geraldine was more cautious.

'I always thought you would make a good pair,' she said,
'but not like this. It's nice to have someone to wake up with,
but we will have more need for friends than lovers if this thing
goes wrong,' she frowned.

'It just feels right, that's all,' I told her.

'People who come together in crisis often need crisis to
keep themselves together; you do know that don't you?'

'Well, we should be fine here shouldn't we? If the words
"Kenya" and "crisis" don't go together well, I don't know any
that do.'

'Just be careful,' she said, and I promised I would.

But she was right.

Using our new closeness, we tried to build a wall around

ourselves to avoid what was going on 'outside', but Kenya always crept in. Where in the past we had supported each other, but thought first of ourselves, we began worrying more about each other and realising the risks we were taking, and it wasn't comfortable. As quickly as our friendship developed, our fears grew, and we started to blame each other for the worries we felt and for the loss of our old, easy friendship.

Sally became Kenya to me, and I lost the person I could complain to about the real Kenya. I knew she would worry more about me, especially when she was lying warm in my arms and needing me to be strong and supportive for her, just as I needed her to be strong for me.

Each moan against the country became a complaint against our situation, and it was easy to take that complaint as a criticism of each other. So we spent days falling out and making up, and in the end we avoided conflict by not really talking.

In many ways it had already become a typical marriage.

When the Christmas holidays came, we took a train west to Kisumu and a bus ride north to Kakamega Forest, the last piece of rain forest in East Africa. The trip was our last attempt to save our relationship, to see if we even still liked each other any more, away from Nairobi's stressful environment.

You can find a type of peace amongst the trees that you can never find anywhere else, and we hoped that a week together with nothing but trees, birds and peacefulness was all we needed. But we were both in foul moods when we woke on the train and argued over breakfast in the otherwise silent dining-carriage, and we didn't speak to each other until we were in the forest late in the afternoon.

We made friends again in the earth-walled *banda* that we had hired for the week. Using sex as a conciliatory act was awkward and restraining, but afterwards we felt better and sat outside in the dust drinking warm beer and watching waves of ants remove the body of a tarantula which lay squashed on the concrete step by the door. We burnt citronella candles to keep the mosquitoes away. I will always remember Kakamega Forest when I smell citronella.

Our walks in the daytime lasted hours, and we'd come back to the *banda* exhausted and delighted by the forest and fall asleep together under the mosquito netting, with the 'cheeps' of the geckos on the walls lulling us.

On our last morning we sat together on a high rock outcrop and looked out over the forest southwards towards Kisumu and Lake Victoria. Over a hundred miles away to the south-east lay Nairobi, and although we couldn't see it, the dread of Nairobi and our lives there came back to me, and I felt myself shiver.

Sally leant beside me on the warm rock, wearing just her shoes and shorts, using her shirt as a pillow. She had never bought another cap to replace the one that was stolen, and her hair grew long now over her shoulders.

She smiled when I stroked her head and said, 'We could stay here forever you and me, couldn't we? And just never go back.' She took my hand and kissed it, but my heart was filled with trepidation.

On the night-train back we made love on the narrow plastic seating of our first-class carriage, and I cried silently as she cuddled up beside me afterwards. I was too hot to sleep and feared what would happen back in Nairobi when reality kicked in. The sound of the rails beneath the trundling train reminded me of the rhythm of the pumps in my parents milking parlour back home, and I longed to be there then. I longed to walk with my dog in the woods and to be wet from the rain and not from the rain-forest sweat.

I thought of how we had been in Nairobi before our Kakamega trip, how little either of us liked the other, and then I tried to imagine Sally in years to come living at my parent's farm, wearing a big old raincoat and wellies, and smiling out at me from beneath the rim of a wide-brimmed hat. My tears dried as I realised it wasn't too difficult to imagine.

I stood by the train's window, and Tom Joad's ghost joined me, and we watched the sorrowful kerosene lights dotted beside the railway. Extended families gathered there in community and poverty, living under plastic sheeting with no income and nothing to look forward to except the hope of a train stopping on their piece of track and a white face looking down at them. Prayers answered when white hands passed down biscuits, sweets, biros or small amounts of money.

And when the train did stop, the smells of rot and heat and sweat came in to us through the window. We heard the whistle of the train and the shouts from the guard, as he cleared the line of cattle or branches or whatever the obstruction was. In South Africa trainjacking is common, and it was surely just a matter of time before it came here.

Things will get worse before they get better, Tom Joad's ghost told me. 'Can you handle it?' he asked. President Moi had the people on the knife-edge between having nothing to lose and having enough to feel empowered and the desire to strive for more. Tom and I agreed that being here when the balance tipped one way or the other was not a good plan.

It probably wouldn't, but if revolution did come, the Asians would be first to be targeted, just as they had been in

Uganda. African tribes would battle for supremacy, as Kikuyu and Luo sought political dominance, and the Masai and Samburu peoples put pressure on white landowners to return their tribal lands. And we temporary white residents would sneak away, leaving friends behind, running back home to safety with our collection of stories to tell in warm country pubs, and to our grandchildren in years to come.

I don't want to run away, I told Tom Joad. I don't want to leave loose ends. I want to go home, but I want to go properly. I smiled at the thought of Sally and me having a future after Kenya. This thought had never crossed my mind before, but then I frowned at the responsibility this feeling held, and I pressed my forehead against the cool dirty window and sighed.

My sense of anxiety grew as Nairobi drew nearer, and as the sky lightened I lay down on the bunk beside Sally and pulled her close.

'You OK?' she whispered, as she put her head on my chest.

'Just thinking,' I said. Tom Joad's ghost looked down at us from where he stood by the window. *Go on*, he urged. *Tell her.*

'Mmm?'

'Just thinking we should hand in our notices when we get back and get hold of a TES and apply for jobs back home. Give Greenfields time to find some replacements. We could go to interviews over Easter and get ourselves jobs that start in September.'

'Mmm?' she murmured, but I couldn't tell if she was really awake.

'If we have an end in sight, it might help keep us positive when we get back, you know? Make Nairobi easier?' She was silent. 'Just a thought, really. Might help?'

'Where would we go?'

'Anywhere. New Zealand maybe, or back home to Wales or Yorkshire. We could even live halfway between in Birmingham. We could live in Sutton Coldfield and work in Handsworth Wood or some place ordinary. Anywhere to get away from here.' I kissed the top of her head, and in the low light of the dawn I saw Tom Joad's ghost grin.

'Are you serious?' she asked. 'You and me together after this?'

'Why not?'

'Good,' she said.

In the dining-carriage over breakfast we said nothing but smiled at each other and at the same attendant that had served us cold scrambled eggs during our stress-filled breakfast on our way to Kisumu just a week before.

We got a taxi back up to school, and I went to bed. Sally packed up all our stinking clothes and drove to the Yaya Centre to do the laundry. 'I'm not doing this all the time,' she said from the door, 'so don't get used to it. Next time it's your turn,' and she came back to the bed to kiss me.

42

In 1992 President Moi's re-election campaign cost over US$250 million, four times what Bill Clinton spent to win the presidency in the United States of America.

Opposition leaders were threatened, gassed and 'had accidents', and great areas of the country became no-go areas to anyone with anti-KANU tendencies. There were huge pay rises promised for public-sector workers, and a massive vote-buying campaign meant the result of the election was assured long before the election day.

Teachers in the state-run schools went on strike for weeks and were rewarded with the pay rise they had been promised for several years. Seeing this, the nurses in Kenyatta and other state hospitals walked out demanding a five hundred percent pay rise to keep them in line with other workers of a similar standing.

In the maternity wards expectant mothers helped each

other give birth in the absence of the trained nurses, and visitors changed the sheets and dressings of the seriously-ill patients. At the best of times Kenyatta Hospital was a nightmare, but during the strike patients went two to a bed with another on a mattress under the bed. The dead were piled up in cleaning cupboards until relations came to take the bodies away.

Opposition newspapers criticised President Moi's handling, and his denial, of the Aids epidemic, saying he was using it to control Kenya's booming population and the disastrous economy. 'People are dying and the President does nothing,' said one headline while other stories echoed Frank Zappa in blaming the Americans for creating the disease and releasing it on the African population as a way to get rid of black people. There were whispers that Moi was undergoing treatment for Aids himself, including both the latest medicines and witchcraft, and there were reports of young virgin girls being kidnapped and taken to State House in Nairobi and President Moi's palace up in his home town of Nanyuki, so he could have sex with them as part of his cure.

In the Coastal Province, Sheikh Balala preached mass disturbance and revolution and made his way onto the front pages of the newspapers, but he had such a small following that Yuri and Anya laughed him off, describing him as the Kenyan equivalent of the Monster Raving Loony Party in the UK.

When the election finally came on Monday 29th December 1997, it was never likely to be free or fair. In the run-up to it, great areas of the country that were not KANU supporters descended into mini-war zones, with displaced voters pulling their lives on carts behind them, heading back to their home-places and tribal lands, where they would be safe from violence, but where they were not registered to vote.

In Mombasa's Likoni Region the ferry almost sank, beneath the weight of people fleeing their burning homes. These were mostly Luo people, who were originally from Lake Victoria but were living on the coast where there was more work in the Asian-owned gift shops and *mzungu*-managed hotels. Many people wanted change, but knew they wouldn't get it in this election.

'The country is ripe for change,' wrote Wahome Mutahi in the *Daily Nation*, 'if only we have the courage to take it.' Journalists wrote articles that publishers would never have dared to print even a few years before, and many ended up beaten as a result. But at least the papers were being printed. The KANU-owned *Standard* newspaper carried stories of the corruption of many Opposition leaders, while concentrating on President Moi's donations to worthwhile projects (which were usually owned by his sons, cronies, cabinet ministers, and senior army officers).

Other articles reminded the reader how dignified John Major had been over leaving Downing Street. 'Will President Moi be the same,' many wondered in amazement, 'when his time is finally up?' But most people doubted it.

It was a new concept that democratic elections *could* actually bring peaceful change! Many people hoped that President Moi would win, if only because the fear of his hard men wreaking revenge in the areas that backed the Opposition before he handed over power was too awful a thought to consider.

The violent suppression of the demonstrations did force some constitutional reform, but this only led to bureaucratic delays, and three million of Kenya's first-time voters were left off the new official register. With the youth being the most vocal about the need for change, this wasn't much of a surprise.

In other areas the record number of voters found they couldn't vote, because the ballot boxes and papers had failed to arrive. In Vice-President Saitoti's Karen Region to the west of Nairobi, helicopters were seen delivering additional boxes to the polling stations. In typical Kenyan fashion one plummeted to the earth and exploded with a sea of completed ballot papers blowing across the road. They all had an 'X' already printed in Saitoti's box.

The not-very-independent Election Commission declared there would be an extra day for voting on the Tuesday in regions that had experienced logistical problems, which only increased confusion, as it was unclear where the voting could continue. Many rural stations didn't have ballot papers even then. The elections were described as 'Chaplin-esque' and even President Moi complained over the incompetence of the Election Commission, suggesting that they were involved in rigging the election in favour of the Opposition parties.

His anger came from the Commission's efforts to disrupt KANU's efforts to 'organise' the vote, and although it was within his constitutional right to annul the election and call a re-run, he knew the thirteen opposition candidates had so divided the country that he was sure to win, even if the vast majority of Kenyans voted against him. So he didn't bother.

On election day, Sally and I stayed in Greenfields and went swimming behind the school's high compound wall, and we worried about Donald, who was out on the streets helping the local Democratic Party candidate with his campaign.

Up in the Westlands area of Nairobi, Betty Tett was one of the first Opposition candidates to beat their KANU rival. There was joyous celebration when the returning officer declared her the winner by a handful of votes. He went for a break before he made the formal announcement, but when he returned he announced he had overlooked eight hundred votes for the KANU candidate, who was instead declared the winner.

When all the results came in, it was announced that President Moi's KANU party had indeed won again, receiving forty percent of the vote, with Mwai Kibaki's Democratic Party coming second with thirty-two percent, and the rest being scattered amongst the other parties.

The Opposition finally stood together and called for the Commission to void the results, but the Commission Chairman, Samuel Kivuitu, said he was satisfied that the poll was free and fair. 'The Commission does not have the power to nullify parliamentary or presidential results, anyway,' he said. 'This is a matter for the courts to decide.' He later pointed out that the Court process would take years.

With sixty percent of the six million voters voting against him, it was not in President Moi's interests to reject the results, so he sat tight and said little. The Opposition planned to push for constitutional reform and work together for a clean and united election within two years. But, as it warned in the British press a few days later, 'This flawed and rigged election of Mr Moi threatens to further destabilise Kenya over the next five years.'

Moi was sworn in again at a big party in Uhuru Park, even as some ballot boxes were still held under siege in polling stations all over the country. Up in northern Kenya others had not yet left airstrips or police stations, where they were stored after voting closed and were still waiting to be counted. In the Tana River District, the region's two voting officers were washed away when the river burst its banks, the election results going with them, so there was no official record of who won there either.

Mwai Kibaki, who received 1.9 million votes to Moi's 2.4 million in the presidential vote said, 'We told you before that we do not recognise the result. It is phoney because it is based on rigged and incomplete figures.'

Mr Kivuitu admitted that his Commission had received many hundreds of complaints over the election process from all over the country, but 'these votes won't make any difference, anyway,' he said with a smirk.

The following month a wave of genocide swept through communities that voted for opposition parties. In the Rift Valley over a hundred were killed, and Parliament was full of MPs from all sides waving placards and blaming each other for the bloodshed. Moi was accused of a 'legacy of killing' and for supporting 'gangsters to do his dirty work'. He responded with a few disparaging gestures and blamed the Democratic Party for the clashes.

Mombasa's Likoni region and Transmara in the west suffered violence, and in the Rift Valley gangs murdered, looted and burnt property with no reaction coming from the security forces. In areas that backed the Democratic Party around Nairobi you could pick up flyers left on *duka* counters threatening the eviction and murder of residents, while other flyers recommended that targeted communities should arm and defend themselves or suffer the consequences.

And while these scores were being settled around the

country, behind our fences at Greenfields School we kept our heads down and got on with life pretty much as we had done before the election. A police car started hanging around outside the school, but we noticed few other changes. Only a small number of whites were registered to vote, so we didn't feel any more targeted during the post-election repercussions than we had done before, in fact it was a relief that the day had passed without our worst fears being realised.

School pupil numbers did continue to fall, however, and when Sally and I handed in our notice Mark Peters decided one Games teacher would be able to cover the work that the two of us had done, with a little more help from Donald.

'I will be sad to see you go,' Donald promised, but the thought of being known as a teacher, and of being driven to sports matches by a driver, delighted him. 'You will come back to visit won't you?'

Come back to Kenya? I couldn't wait to get home, and the thought of coming back again made me frown as if the idea was simply inconceivable.

With the Easter vacation coming Ron and Geraldine planned a trip to Lake Turkana, and Mark Peters booked a chalet on the Likoni beachfront for his enlarged family. Sally and I trawled the TES, sent off our CVs and kept our fingers crossed.

'Come with us to the coast,' said Mark. 'There is a Nairobi Club tour going. Everyone will be there. Be a great chance to say goodbye.' But money would be tight when we got home, we told each other, and it was best for us to stay in Nairobi and take a couple of cheap trips to Naivasha and Hell's Gate when the city got too much. Save money, take care and keep positive. These were the only things that mattered now.

43

One morning at the start of the Easter holiday, Sally walked back to Greenfields from an appointment with Doctor Somen in the middle of town and then picked up a package from the post office on Haile Selassie Avenue.

As she crossed Uhuru Highway at the lights a street-boy latched himself onto her. 'Give me ten shillings,' he mumbled as Sally sped up, ignoring him.

In the past Sally and I had taken to giving cheap biscuits to street-children instead of money when we were in a vehicle, but when we were walking we usually ended up mobbed as they swarmed in from all around, so we tried to ignore them and keep safe.

'Give me ten shillings,' the boy said more firmly, keeping pace with her.

'*Hapana*. No. You go home. Go home,' she said, and the boy smiled. He had gained her attention. The first battle was won.

'Mama. *Rafiki*. My friend. You give me ten shillings.' He began tugging on her sleeve and Sally pulled away, not angry, more disappointed. 'You take me home,' said the boy taking hold of her arm. 'You take me home. I be your boyfriend.'

'No. Go away.' Sally tried to shake him off, hoping one of the men she passed would step in and get the child away from her.

'I be your boyfriend,' the boy shouted, dancing round her.

Sally felt herself blushing. People had stopped walking and stood now just watching this scene. A young white woman with a box under her arm was being hassled by a scruffy young beggar. This was a rare situation, and something not to be missed. Maybe she would lose her temper.

'Go away,' Sally said, her voice rising. 'I already have a boyfriend. Leave me alone.'

'I be your boyfriend,' said the boy. 'I make you pregnant.' A man nearby laughed a horrible, toothless laugh.

'I make you pregnant,' yelled the boy. 'I make you pregnant in six weeks. I have hot sperm.'

At the University Slipway junction she managed to get away from him.

'If anybody ever speaks to me like that again, I'm just going to flatten them, bugger the consequences,' she said late in the evening as we sat on the step outside our room.

'We will laugh at a lot of things about this place one day,' I said. She looked at me doubtfully, and I smiled. 'I mean that's a grim thing, but nobody died. And it is quite funny, really, isn't it?'

'That's it with you, isn't it? So long as nobody dies, then it's not a problem,' she said. 'You don't think that maybe once someone has died, then it's a bit late to worry?'

'I do worry, Sally. Course I do. But one day we will look back and laugh at the stinky little kid offering to get you pregnant. Come on, you got to admit it is funny?'

'Actually he's a bit late,' she said and made a face.

'Mmm?'

'Well, you know I had an appointment with Doctor Somen today?'

'Yeah?'

'Well, it seems I'd better stop smoking.'

44

Yuri held a bottle of Tusker in one hand and tongs in the other as he turned over the silver-foil-wrapped salmon and herb steaks on the barbecue. He raised his arm again in a toast. 'To procreation,' he said and tipped the bottle sharply.

Sally sat on the balcony wall and smiled at him. It was strange to see her without a cigarette or a beer in her hand. Instead she sipped fresh fruit juice and fiddled with a handful of frankincense, flicking occasional pieces on to the barbecue where they crackled and burnt and spat at Yuri's bare knees. 'Shit! You crazy pregnant woman. If I get hold of you,' and he shook the tongs at her, then bent to rub his singed skin. 'Shit.'

'Sorry, Yuri, man,' she said in a pretty good South African accent. 'It was an accident, yah?' and she laughed as he lunged a great pantomime-baddy lunge towards her. 'Come on Welsh boy, defend your woman,' she said, skipping to one side as I walked out onto the balcony carrying bowls of guacamole, salad and sun-dried tomatoes.

I nodded at them and mumbled, 'Carry on. You're big enough to take care of yourself.'

'Pretty extraordinary, yah?' said Anya as I sat next to her on a low sofa. She had just got back from Somalia and was writing a story on the floods around Kismayo. She looked tired, but smiled and patted my knee. 'Takes a while to get used to it, I bet?' She looked up at Yuri, and I wondered about their nomadic lives. She smiled, but perhaps with a touch of sadness that she was not the one that was pregnant. 'So what happens now?' she asked.

'Well, we've handed in our notice at Greenfields and are already applying for jobs back home. Hope to leave here in June and get settled somewhere by the summer, before she starts getting too chubby. If she gets too large while we are out here, well, I'll leave her behind. I can't abide fat chicks.' I looked up at Sally and beckoned to her. She smiled and came over to sit on my lap.

'Where are you going to go?' asked Yuri.

'We'll see where the dice settle. It might be good to go to my family's home, back to Wales. My parents would love to fuss over a grandchild.' I shook my head grinning, 'Jesus, I can't believe I'm talking like this. I can't believe this has happened. In my interview for the Greenfields job, they said I'd have a life-changing experience out here, but I didn't expect it to be quite like this.'

'No regrets?' Sally whispered, and I shook my head and kissed her. 'Say it.'

'No regrets.'

'Staying teaching?' asked Yuri. 'You hate teaching.'

'Yeah, I do, but I think it will be that way for a while, anyway. Sally can't speak Welsh, so it would be a problem for her to find a teaching job. She's got this crazy idea she'd like to be a farmer's wife, anyway. I guess we'll do our best to get home safely and see what happens next. See how my parents are doing.'

'And let Kenya become a distant memory,' said Anya.

'Safely in the past,' I agreed.

'Shame.'

'Mmmm. But I doubt we'll forget much of it.' Sally said. 'Just the rubbish bits, and in a couple of years we'll look back on our great time out here and wonder why we ever left.'

'Maybe we'll write about it during those long winter evenings,' I said. 'Everyone's got a book inside them, haven't they?'

'Supposed to have,' said Yuri, who nodded and went into the house. 'Read this first. You remember I told you about this book on your first day?' He threw me a dog-eared copy of *My Traitor's Heart* by Rian Malan. 'The best book about modern Africa ever written. You should read this before you even write a single word about this continent.'

I looked at the cover and John Le Carre's recommendation: 'Here is truth-telling at its most exemplary and courageous.'

'Thanks, Yuri. I will certainly do my best.'

'My Dad did his National Service in Belize in the 1950s,' said Sally. 'He used to say he'd write a book about some drunken Mexican general he met then. I don't know what happened, but he swore there was a great story there.'

Yuri laughed. '*My father, the Army and the Drunken Mexican General*? Jeeze woman, what a shocking title for a novel,' he said.

'It's funny,' Sally continued, not rising to the bait. 'If we wrote about all the things we have seen here, and things that have happened to people we know, it would sound like we had a terrible time. But it's not like that. Not really. I'm looking forward to going home of course,' she said and smiled at me, 'but I'm going to miss this place and the people so much.'

'There's a teacher at the Banda School who says he's writing a book,' I said. 'He's going to call it, '*Sir, There's a Snake in the Art Room*,' which takes up the market for comical books about working in Kenyan schools. But if you try to write it any other way, it would probably be too close to the edge of what is acceptable, anyway.'

'You have just got to be honest,' said Anya thoughtfully.

'Ah, you'll never do it, anyway, big guy,' Yuri scoffed. 'Talking is one thing, but you won't have the time to write a book. Change of job, of home, of country. Hell, you are going to be a father, man. What's the matter with you?' and he shook his head contemptuously.

'Well, you write something, mate. Can he write, Anya, or is he just a great goofy lump with a pilot's licence and no imagination?'

'He's alright.' She got up and stood beside him. She rubbed some ash off his cheek with the back of her hand. 'He'll do me fine.' She reached up and kissed him. 'This is good, yah?' she said. 'Our friends have done well.'

She smiled as he put down his beer, and she sank into his embrace. She had told me that in the past she felt swamped by the size of big men. Overwhelmed by their maleness. With Yuri it was different. He was huge, sure, but she always felt his respect for her, and she simply felt safe.

'Very good,' he nodded his agreement.

'Makes you think, no?'

Yuri leant back against the balcony railing, still holding her close. 'We will see,' he said. He unhitched his arms and headed down to the kitchen to bring up some more food. Anya patted his bottom on the way past and followed him.

Sally and I sat quietly on the balcony, listening to the sounds of the city at night. 'It'll be badgers we'll be hearing in the future,' I said. 'Badgers and foxes rather than stray dogs and sirens. You sure you can handle it?'

'I'm looking forward to it,' she said.

I leant against the railings where Yuri had stood and turned over a piece of steak on the barbecue. From downstairs I heard Anya's voice. 'It wouldn't be so bad, would it,' she said, rather than asked.

'Wouldn't be so bad? Damn, woman, a child of ours would be beautiful,' Yuri replied. 'With our genes it would be a wonderful child. How could it not be? But not here. We could not raise a child here.'

'No,' she said softly, and I heard her sigh. 'Not here.'

They were quiet for a moment, and then Yuri said, 'We will leave the dishes for Monica tonight, love. We can bring them all down for her, but leave them for Monica to wash. I don't want to wash up tonight. I want to practise making babies.' I heard Anya giggle, and when they came back upstairs she was blushing.

'You don't have any regrets, do you?' Sally asked me later, as we sat in her car waiting for the *askaris* to open the gate to Yuri and Anya's compound. They took longer than usual, so I got out and banged on the door to their little shelter.

'Sorry, *mzungu*,' said a voice from within a huge coat, and

275

an *askari* I didn't recognise fumbled with the padlock and let us out.

'No regrets,' I said, but I was wondering about the *askari*. Benjamin had let us in with a smile and a leaping wave, and he normally chatted as he let us out again.

'Good,' she said, and weaved round the potholes on the mortuary roundabout and bounced onto Ngong Road. 'Me neither.'

And as Sally and I got home and fell asleep, closely entwined, all hell broke loose at Yuri and Anya's.

45

I never saw Yuri and Anya again. I was out when Anya called
to say goodbye the next morning. She told Sally what had
happened after we had left their house, and Sally told me and
Donald later in the evening while we sat on our doorstep
sipping tea as the sun went down over the national park.

'We were going to leave the dishes for Monica and turn in
for an early night,' Anya said. Yuri went upstairs and poked
the remaining embers on the barbecue, throwing on chicken
bones and labels that Sally had peeled off the beer bottles. 'I
was pushing things around in the kitchen. Not doing much,
more thinking about you two. Yuri had said he was so pleased
for you. He said you were a woman with balls.'

'A woman with balls?' asked Sally, and Anya smiled. Sally
said she looked so tired.

'It is supposed to be a compliment. He said you are a good
woman. A woman with a good heart, but also a woman with

courage. Someone who could be a lover and a friend, but someone who could beat you around the head if you overstepped the line. These are what Yuri looked for in a good companion, and he said many times that Griff had done well.'

Anya heard a knock on the door to the yard from the compound. 'Often the *askaris* came if they needed tea and to ask if we had any food left over after the barbecue,' she said. 'I waved up at Yuri, who was leaning over the edge of the balcony. Then I opened the door and three men in large black overcoats forced their way in, knocking me to my knees.'

'I stood up and backed away up against a kitchen cabinet as the men pulled rifles from beneath their coats, pointing them at me.' The lead man smiled and spoke gently to her. 'He told me to be quiet and do what he said. If I did, nothing would happen. If I didn't, well, and he reminded me what happens to people who make a noise. "What do I have to lose by killing you?" he asked me. "In this country it is the same punishment for murder as it is for armed robbery, if we are caught," and he smiled again. "We will not be caught. Dead *mzungus* cannot point their white fingers."'

Anya felt her knees buckle, and she bore her nails into the palms of her hands. She told them there was a stereo with one speaker blown and not much money in the house, but that she would give them what there was. 'I will get it,' she had said, and pointed towards the lounge room.

Two of the men followed her through the door while the third opened the fridge and took out three Fanta Orange drinks. He cracked the lids off on the worktop, chipping the enamel, and handed one to each of his colleagues. '*Asanta sana*,' they said. 'Manners maketh man,' one said to Anya and winked at her. 'So said Father Dominic when I was a child.'

He took a swig from the bottle, rinsed the sweet liquid around his mouth and spat a great orange discharge onto the floor. He told Anya to take the covers off the pillows on the sofa and to put all the trinkets on the sideboard into it. 'And the music disc things,' he said, as he bent to unplug the stereo system.

He motioned to the other men to go upstairs, telling Anya he knew she was a good girl and would behave.

'Upstairs, Yuri had got out his Beretta and knelt on one knee in the doorway to the bedroom,' Anya said. 'He had the pistol in his hands held behind his back. "I am here," he said loudly, as he heard them climbing the stairs. "I am here. It is OK."'

'I saw them dither on the landing halfway up the stairs. They looked at each other and then back at him. Apparently before they had beaten up our *askari*, Benjamin, he had told them I was a single woman living alone. He knew Yuri would be here, and that he had a gun to defend us. We had more chance of defending ourselves than anyone else in our compound. One of them shouted down to the leader, who was stuffing the stereo into a cushion cover, "Simeon! *Njoo. Haraka, haraka!*"'

'*Anasemaje!*' Simeon had cursed. '*Vipi* Martin?' Anya had watched him put the cushion cover and stereo down on the sofa and hurry to the stairs, then she turned quickly and let herself out into the garden, sliding the glass door closed behind her. She crept into the shrubbery and bent down with her head in her hands. 'Oh God,' she said. 'Oh God.'

Seeing the big, unexpected *mzungu* kneeling at the top of the stairs, Simeon cursed and lifted the rifle to his shoulder. Seeing this, the others began to fire, peppering the floor and walls around Yuri.

Yuri fired four shots from his pistol before he was hit, the bullet shattering his leading foot, and he slumped sideways into the bedroom and out of sight.

The shooting stopped and two men fled down the stairs and away, as dogs barked and lights came on around the compound. Yuri looked down at his foot and cursed. 'Shit man, no cricket for a while,' and then he laughed. What a thing to think of at this time, and then he passed out.

Through the window, Anya watched two men run away and the third one fall backwards. She watched him grab his stomach, and his gun slipped out of his grasp. She opened the glass door and stepped back into the lounge room. 'Yuri?' she had called. The fallen man on the stairs lifted his head and groaned '*Msaada*, mama. *Msaada*.' He tried to reach out to her as she approached, but his pain was too much, and he held his stomach groaning again.

Anya shuffled past him as she heard her neighbours shouting outside her door. At the top of the stairs she saw Yuri's bloody leg, and she screamed. 'God, oh God no,' and she ran to him, collapsing by his side.

'Hey, honey,' Yuri mumbled, swinging in and out of consciousness. 'Time to go home, yah?' He nodded and licked his lips. 'Time to go home.'

'When the police came, they shot the man who was bleeding on the stairs,' Sally said. 'They claimed he would only get off on appeal, but Anya said she was sure they recognised each other, and that the bleeding man was better off dead than being able to name names in a court.' The intruders had carried the same kind of guns the Kenyan police use, and when a trail leads high, you can't afford to take risks.

The neighbours had found Benjamin in a battered and

bleeding heap behind his shed. 'I know them,' he said as he was patched up and taken by taxi to Kenyatta Hospital. In the morning, when Anya went to see him, he would tell her nothing. 'I do not know them,' was all he would say, 'I do not know their faces,' and he could not look her in the eye. An hour later he discharged himself and disappeared up-country. Better to vanish than to be a witness.

Yuri spent the night in Nairobi Hospital, and then AMREF flew him down to South Africa.

Anya called by Greenfields looking for me on her own way to the airport, but I was out, so she told Sally. I didn't get the chance to say goodbye, and never heard from them again.

'Your friends were very foolish,' said Donald, shaking his head once Sally had finished speaking. 'They are very lucky to be alive.' Sally said nothing, just stared out into the distance, wincing at the lights of the cars screaming along outside the compound wall.

She crossed her arms and leant back against the door jam. She looked at me, and I tried to smile. 'Bloody hell,' she said. 'I could do with a cigarette.'

I put my hand on her thigh and squeezed her knee. 'Thank God they survived,' and then she started to cry. I put my arm round her and pulled her close.

'If they had come earlier, we would have been there,' she whispered almost under her breath. 'If I had been drinking, we might have stayed the night.' She pulled away and stood up. 'But you are right; thank God they survived. And it's OK. Nobody died.' She walked into our room and lay down on the bed. 'Nobody white, anyway,' her tone was acid. 'Nobody that matters, eh?'

'Tomorrow you talk to Mr Rivers,' said Donald, pulling

himself to his feet. He rested his hand on my shoulder, and I patted it. Then he turned and walked down the concrete steps to the compound yard. I heard his bare feet shuffling in the dirt as he walked to his room, a quiet greeting to the *askari*, and the jingle of his keys as he unlocked the door.

Over the compound wall the policemen sat on a bench on the corner of Ngong Road. I saw the red embers of a cigarette, as the men took a drag and passed it back and forth. They had been there for three days now. I should feel safer with the police nearby.

Was it really my time to go home? My mind was blank.

When I went to ask Mr Rivers for his advice the next afternoon, I found him sitting with Sally on the bench in the school front hall. He had his arm round her, and she was crying. She lifted her head from his chest when she saw me, wiped her eyes and smiled wearily.

Mr Rivers sighed, straightened his corduroy trousers and stood up. 'Well, well,' he said. 'It's a fine mess you have got my niece into, isn't it?' He looked me squarely in the eye. 'I have called David Brown at the High Commission, who has managed to find you two seats home on tomorrow night's KLM flight. Caught him just before he went off to Mombasa on the cricket tour.' I looked at Sally who smiled hopefully. 'He called in a favour on your behalf, young man. You see you repay David and me by being on the flight.'

'But the school,' I said. 'We can't just leave you in the lurch?'

'Well, I am still the headmaster here,' he said, 'and I have just sacked the both of you. No more arguments, especially not if you want to keep the excellent references I have planned for you. I am off to Nakuru for a weekend's golf. David assures me everything is in hand. I will see you at Christmas when I come back to the UK.' He kissed Sally's cheek and shook my hand. We stood on the steps outside the school and watched him as he strode purposefully to his car. 'The best of luck to you both,' he called. And then he was gone.

The next morning Sally went out early to buy some soapstone souvenirs from Rikesh Patel's father's shop in town. Her spirits were high, and she bounced around our room like Tigger, telling me to get packed early and to collect together the things I didn't want to take home so we could give them to the *askaris* for their families. 'I'm going to give the car to Donald,' she said, as she bounded out of the door and away.

I sat out on the steps in the sun wearing only my shorts, drinking tea and watching two young boys fighting in the street outside the gate. At first I thought it was a serious fight, but then realised they were only playing. 'Onyango, son of Suji Expat Bamba' laughed at them as he shaved the head of one policeman and chatted with the other, who leant against a battered Peugeot police car, smoking a cigarette. One of the boys found a stick in the shape of a rifle and held it to his shoulder and shouted 'bang' at his mate, who fell down in the dust giggling.

Donald crossed the compound and called up to me. 'Would you like anything from the Yaya Centre?' he asked, and I waved back '*Hapana* Donald. *Asante sana*.' He waved back and smiled. He cried last night when I told him we were leaving, but he said he was glad. 'I will never forget you,' he said. 'I feel blessed to have met you both for many reasons. Watching you playing basketball, your prayer in Reverend Mironko's church, the cricket. I will miss you so very much, my friends.'

'One day you will come and see us,' Sally told him, but we all knew he never would. Even if he could save up the cost of a flight to the UK, he would only use it to pay for another Aids orphan to go to school.

I watched the *askari* open the gate and saw Donald cross the road and pass Onyango. He said something to the boy with the 'gun' and reached down to take it off him. 'Even replica guns are illegal in Kenya,' I imagined him telling the boy, and the moment he took the piece of wood, the cigarette-smoking policeman called out to him, walked over and arrested him. Donald dropped the 'gun', held up his hands in surprise, and the policeman hit him in the belly. He dropped to his knees with a grunt and called out my name.

By the time I had pulled on my shirt and trousers and ran down the stairs, cursing as the *askari* fumbled with the lock, and tore out across the road, the police had lifted Donald into their car and were turning round the corner onto Ngong Road. I stood in the dirt bewildered. 'Where are they going?' I asked Onyango, but he just smiled a battered tooth smile.

'You want hair cut, *mzungu*?' he said, as if nothing had happened. He pointed to the sign behind him. 'I am expert barber.'

46

When a white man goes to Africa he often arrives with big plans. He wants to make a difference, to do his bit for the developing world and its people, so that there is at least one thing he can look back on with a degree of pride. When he lies on his deathbed as an old man he can know that, despite everything else he may have done, at least he had value then.

He arrives with innocent eyes, knowing for a fact that all men are equal and should be treated the same. That a good deed will generate another in return, and that a hand offered in friendship will be reciprocated. He knows what he has read is biased when it is critical of his poverty-stricken brothers, but truthful when it glorifies their efforts in adversity, and he knows he will have an uncanny affinity with the poor because, after all, hasn't he always felt strangely out of place in his safe, middle-class home in the West?

For a time he manages to ignore the potholed roads and

piles of putrid garbage. He smiles at the street-boys and stoned beggars and gives them a little loose change. This is not wrong, he tells himself, despite the sneaking suspicion they will spend it on glue and not the warm and wholesome food he intends. But his heart is true, so it's worth the few shillings and hassle.

He will probably get dysentery and salmonella and spend countless hours on the toilet cursing the damn place, but he will love it more as a result. He will drink his Diralite and sip his flat Coca-Cola to replenish the lost salts and sugars, and when he recovers he will go back to buying corn from the guy with the barbecue on the corner, and he will smile as the vendor turns the cob with his dirty fingers and fans it with a ratty piece of cardboard picked up from the dump behind him. This is the real African experience. An upset stomach is a passing thing, and it takes time to get used to the local germs. An African would get ill too as he adjusted to life in the UK.

He will purchase food from the *duka* on the roadside like an African. He will visit the poorest housing areas on the weekend, sharing *ugali* and sickly sweet tea in someone's tiny tin home. He will smile when he is patted on the back and called '*mtw wa watu*' – 'man of the people' – by his host, and he will be delighted when he is told they truly value him as a '*rafiki*' – 'friend' – and that they hardly notice the colour of the skin he is wearing, for he understands them, and they him.

He might show how African he can be by sharing *nyama choma* on a Friday night, sipping warm Tusker beside the smoky barbecue with the village elders. He will chew *miraa* with the youngsters as he wanders with them in the bush wearing just a *kanga* around his waist, and he may even consider a bareback ride with some bedraggled woman he met in a tavern on the wrong side of River Road.

But at some point during this game, Africa will grab him by the throat and offer him a choice that will define him for the rest of his life. It will lay bare his posing and posturing and may point him out as a phoney and make it all too clear that he is just another *mzungu* passing through. A prince playing a pauper for kicks.

Perhaps something dramatic will happen, or maybe he will simply wake up one day with a strange feeling, and he will decide he has had enough of the game, and he will make the call, book the flight and use the return strip of his ticket and fly home at the shortest notice, leaving Africa to the Africans and to the next hopeful white man with fresh and innocent eyes, and not his now cynical ones.

And in his soul he will know he has let Africa down. Just as the West has been doing for decades.

In my turn I let Donald down. I got on the plane that evening and sat dry-eyed with the mother of my unborn child beside me, watching the lights of the city disappear behind us.

I watched *Mr Bean* on the small jumpy KLM movie screen, as Donald sat in a small cell in the Kilimani Road police station. I passed Sally an orange juice and drank the complimentary Australian beer, and we shared a small bag of nuts. We held hands under the blue airline blanket, and I kissed her sleeping head as the sky lightened over the wing tips.

But what should I have done? The answer is always the same, and it is always what I did not do.

I should have stayed. I should have got Sally on the plane and gone back to help my friend. But as I walked back to Greenfields along Argwings Kodhek Road, past the body of a swollen dog, bloated in the heat on the side of the road, I watched Sally climb off a crowded *matatu* with bags in each hand, and saw her swamped by a group of glazed-eyed urchins and I wanted to get out. To go as quickly as I could, to hell with the lot of them.

'Donald told me to say goodbye to you,' I lied later, as Sally and I loaded our bags into a taxi. 'He was too emotional to be here himself.'

'That's so sweet,' she said and kissed me. 'He was such a good friend to us.' She waved a cheery farewell to the *askari* as we pulled out of the compound and out onto Ngong Road.

And all the time I saw Donald in my mind's eye, clearly as I see him now as I stare into this computer screen.

It took me three hours arguing and two thousand shillings *chai* money to persuade Sergeant Josphat Mboya to let me see Donald, and then only for a moment through the cell door held ajar.

'How are you Donald?' I asked.

'Can't grumble,' he whispered with a bad Yorkshire accent, and he tried to smile. He looked up with bruised face and cut cheeks. His shirt was ripped, and one of his shoes was missing. 'You will miss your plane,' he said.

'We will get you out first,' I told him, but he shook his head.

'This will take a long time,' he said calmly. He was resigned to his fate. 'Your place is with your wife and child. She will be your wife, yes?'

'I must do something?' I said as the policeman pushed me backwards and began to close the door.

'Tell Mr Rivers,' Donald said, 'and go well.'

'The list of charges is long.' Sergeant Josphat Mboya grinned when I asked what would happen to Donald. 'We have been watching his movements for some time. He was involved with anti-nationalistic activities during the election. He is a bad man.' The policeman shook his head and nodded. 'Very bad.' He opened his notebook and looked down at the immaculate writing on the tatty paper. 'The charges go on. Possession of a replica gun is as serious as having a real gun in this country.' He flipped over the pages scornfully.

'Yeah, but you were there,' I protested. 'You know it wasn't his. It wasn't a gun. It was just a stick, and you know he took it from a child.'

'You will help him, *mzungu*?' Sergeant Mboya smiled and shook his head. 'I hear he has many *mzungu* friends. I am from Sololo in the north. I have many friends from there.' He looked at me defiantly, and I knew who he was talking about, and Father Marcus Abdi's threat came back to haunt me.

Acknowledgements

I would like to say *asante sana* to many people for the support and friendship they gave me during my time in Kenya particularly Peter, Elvis, Baba, Lolo, Pamba, Jimmy, George and all the NPCA coaches, the Waters family, Kongoni Cricket Club, Steve Turner and his family, Georgina and the VSO volunteers who enjoyed our flat, Anita, Heather and Jennifer, Sheri, Emma and Rhian, Steve and Lynne, Mark and Polly, Raphael and Inez, Rod and Dee, Mrs Chandrasekhar and Tansy.

Special thanks to Maji, Tom and Suka – the best bosses I could have asked for – and to Scotty for his friendship, shared pizzas, and for keeping me out of trouble.

Thanks to Richard Davies who suggested I write this story and who agreed to publish it once I had done so, and to my editor, Norman Schwenk, for his immense patience and for tidying it up no end. Many thanks also to lloyd robson, Lucy Llewellyn, Dom Williams, Gill Griffiths, Marc Jennings at Parthian whose time, expertise and fine toothcombing made this story the one that it is today.

Many thanks to my wife, Vic, and my brother, Noggin, who offered boundless encouragement, and had the patience to read through the early drafts, and to my Ma and Pa for my home and love of reading.